Edgar Fawcett

The Confessions of Claud

A Romance

Edgar Fawcett

The Confessions of Claud
A Romance

ISBN/EAN: 9783744665124

Printed in Europe, USA, Canada, Australia, Japan

Cover: Foto ©Andreas Hilbeck / pixelio.de

More available books at **www.hansebooks.com**

THE

CONFESSIONS OF CLAUD

A ROMANCE

BY

EDGAR FAWCETT

AUTHOR OF "AN AMBITIOUS WOMAN," "TINKLING CYMBALS," "A GENTLEMAN
OF LEISURE," "SOCIAL SILHOUETTES," "THE HOUSE
AT HIGH BRIDGE," ETC.

BOSTON

TICKNOR AND COMPANY

1887

ELECTROTYPED AND PRINTED
BY RAND AVERY COMPANY,
BOSTON.

TO MY FRIEND,

JULIAN HAWTHORNE,

IN THE HOPE THAT ONE WHO HAS ALREADY GIVEN TO
THE WORLD SO MUCH OF BRILLIANT IMAGINATION
AND UNIQUE FANCY,
MAY FIND AMID THE GLOOM AND TRAGEDY OF
THIS TALE
A SLENDER PARDON FOR ITS EXISTENCE
AND A FAINT EXCUSE FOR ITS
DEDICATION.

THE CONFESSIONS OF CLAUD

THE CONFESSIONS OF CLAUD.

I.

MORE than thirty years ago, in a part of New-York which was then open field and is now densely-populated city, I, Otho Claud, first saw the light. My home was a square, prim cottage, guiltless of a single ornament. From its rear doorway, across rolling acres clad in the short verdure which is a sure token of barren or neglected soil, you could see the waters of the Hudson, sparkling and spacious. Our house stood in a solitude; hundreds of yards lay between ourselves and the nearest neighbor. To the northward rose masses of that abundant native rock whose bulky and rigid recurrences form so continual a feature of Manhattan Island, and whose stolid challenge against the expanding metropolis has met tardy but certain defiance.

Often on winter nights I have watched that rocky mass from the window of my little bedchamber, looming black and jagged against the

brilliant stars. Child as I was, I soon realized
it to be overhung with the doom of destruction.
Slowly, like a devouring monster, I knew that
the city crept every year closer to where we
dwelt. So many of us look for romance only
in the age of a great town — in its hoary cathe-
drals, its scholastic universities, its feudal towers.
But the youth of a city, stretching its big, strong
limbs like an awakening giant, carelessly and even
lazily levelling a forest, quenching a stream or
crushing a hill, has in this gradual birth of might
and prowess a sombre romance quite its own.

I think that my early childhood must have
shaped some thought like this. Each new year
brought the sure advance closer. And it was the
steadfast, pitiless march of a foe. Dull booms
from blasting-works began to reach us through
the more temperate seasons. Every spring we
heard them a little more clearly. I knew what
they meant; I had learned; I was now eight
years old. We held our home by no legal right:
we were mere squatters upon an unguarded territory, valueless when first found, but now gaining
with speed in worth and note. Soon we must
fare to other quarters. The fiat of dismissal
might reach us to-morrow; it might be delayed
for many morrows yet.

In my childish way I had grown to hate the
enlarging city. It seemed to me like a dark and
monstrous threat. I traced the shadow of it in

my parents' faces. It made me fear my father more, as it made me love my mother more. He was a German, she a Frenchwoman. Their marriage had been a hasty and stolen one, and their voyage to America almost a flight. My mother had been the petted daughter of a wealthy Breton bourgeois. Leopold Clauss had come to his farm in the capacity of a serving-man. He milked the cows, stalled the sheep, tossed the hay. My mother, naturally delicate, had been most gently reared. Of keen intelligence, she had richly profited by the tutorship of an old erudite priest, whom her father held in devout esteem. She was good, beautiful, obedient; there had been some talk of giving her to the church. For her to look with tenderness upon a farm-servant like Leopold Clauss would have been deemed something abominable. But one night she fled with him. She loved him, and she fled with him.

In a foreign land, beset with ills of want and toil, facing a wholly new and often bitter mode of existence, she remained his clinging, uncomplaining wife. Nothing could alienate her affection. I have seen many good women since I first recognized her goodness, but no feminine nature has ever touched mine with just the same chaste and sweet force.

Memory yields to me her image now, with tints that seem to live, with lines that hold a vital grace. She had great, dark, shining eyes, that appeared equally to express a controlled melancholy and a profound patience. Her black hair, of a charming wave and gloss, was so plenteous that it seemed to overburden the slim support of her frail white throat. Especially when she drooped under fatigue I would observe this effect; it was then that the fragility of her body made her resemble some plant whose crest of bloom too heavily weights the stem. Her brow had a sort of holy arch, and the curving lashes cast a faint little shade upon her pale cheek. She was devotedly fond of me. And I, if I had been more like her, should probably have cared for her less. As it was, she inspired in me something like wonder. She seemed as secure above all the baser gusts of passion as the white top of an alp is above ordinary tempest. I used to ask myself, after I grew older, what she had given me, if she had given me any thing. It is true that she had dropped some sort of leaven into my nature. I will not only grant this; I will assert more. By heredity I had received from her a distinct set of good impulses, and by education she had nurtured these into firm if not hardy growth. The heritage from my father had been of darker and sterner stuff. I was not to know in full, until a still later day, of the evil flaws which he had transmitted to me.

He was a man of great physical beauty. From my earliest recollection he had cultivated a vegetable-garden lying near our plain abode, and I

had often admiringly watched the supple movements of his commanding frame, the fine play of
his massive yet just limbs, the careless gold curls
gleaming from the rough hat which surmounted a
face of chiselled symmetry. It was this beauty
that had won my mother's headstrong and impolitic passion; perhaps it was this beauty that
now kept her unfailingly constant. He had a
light-blue eye, as cold as steel, as expressionless as
ice. I always shrank from that eye of his; I had
seen it glitter cruelly, and I had soon in a vague
yet secure way determined that a coarse brain lay
behind it, a hard heart below. He ignored me for
six good days in the week, and would accept me
as a fact, so to speak, on the seventh. But it was
not as a pleasant fact; it was, on the contrary, as
a mouth to feed, a form to clothe. I was always
in dread lest he should strike me; I had seen our
neighbors strike their children and send them
screaming or limping into the squalid huts that
were their dreary homes. But though sometimes
harsh of order and epithet, my father always re-
frained from dealing me a blow. He did not hate
me; he did not in any sense cherish me. He was
simply indifferent to my needs, aims, hopes, joys
or ills. He completely lacked the paternal instinct; he had begotten me, and there was an end.
Most Germans tenderly love their children. I do
not know that I should call him brutal for not
loving me, since there are many brutes that will

face death for their offspring. And moreover, there was a distinct reason that such a strange man as he should regard me precisely as he did. That reason was the lavish affection of my mother.

I think that if I had been anyone except her son — and her son by his own fatherhood — he would never have forgiven her for the enduring worship she paid me. It would have seemed to him intolerable that another than himself could so engross her thought, her life. He was often rude in speech to her; he would show her by act and phrase the fret and hurt of his struggles against need; he would upbraid and reproach and satirize her; but beneath all his curt or even savage deportment slept for her an immense and fervent fondness. I have seen his cold eye melt as it met hers; I have seen his big, shapely frame tremble as he took her own slight one in his embrace. Here he was indeed brutal, for he loved as a brute may love, and he compassed the object of his idolatry with a rampart of suspicious hates. This incessant and alert jealousy was an experience that had for me no real beginning; its stormy horizon dipped into the haze of infancy; I could never remember any time when my father had not had a grudge against somebody or something because of too much regard for his wife. The bounds of madness are hard to draw; human nature forever stalks abroad with greeds and prejudices that if colored a trifle more vividly would tempt the cell and the chain. I believe that my father, in this one headlong and insensate trait of his, was irresponsibly mad; and the pages which I now mean to write shall most pitiably have missed their purport if I do not win some few converts to my sombre theory. I have known him to kill a poor outcast dog because my mother had not only given it shelter and succor but an occasional caress as well. I have known him to fling a pot of mignonette from the sill of her bedroom window because she watered and tended it too zealously. He sent adrift more than one serving-girl because the scant wages they got from his own light earnings left them still eager and active to fulfil their loved mistress's least command. It was like grudging a lily the odor she gave to air, and yet he bore grudges just as wild and vain as this. Moods of rage, it is true, roused them, but their betrayal was volcanic only because the soil itself held malign heat. For days and weeks he would be tractable enough in his demeanor toward his wife. Then the flame would leap, the bolt would fall. For all men who looked on her with a gaze of more than careless heed (and it was so hard for anyone to look on that pale, lovable, starry-eyed face indifferently!) he would hoard severe rancor. My mother had no friends of either sex. Our lonely dwelling-place forbade intercourse and companionship among her equals, and the men and women whom she sometimes met were of a low and common type.   But she was forced, in my father's presence, to regard no man except with studied coldness.   The insult of his vigilance must have pierced her.   I marvel, now, that it did not alienate her love.   But that seemed imperishable.   As I flash a new light upon her acceptance of this outrageous treatment, I find myself seeing it only in the hues of martyrdom.   It was nothing less violent, and yet she endured it with ideal meekness.

If any excuse of a sane sort can be accredited to my father's action, it might deserve the name of morbid irritation, exasperation, disappointment. He had expected full forgiveness, in time, from his rich French father-in-law.   He had written more than once to the Breton farm-house after reaching America with his stolen bride; he had made my mother write as well.   Their letters had been repentant, respectful, self-accusing, even supplicatory.   But the result had all been one.   No answer had ever reached them.   The French father-in-law remained obdurately silent.   Perhaps this silence preyed upon my father's mind.   Insanity, like every other mortal ailment, has its chief goading spur.   We say of a man: "This or that caused his illness;" or of a madman: "Such an event unseated his reason."   I am sure that my father took grievously to heart his kinsman's persistent disdain.   It ate into his self-love, which was large, and stung his pride, which was overweening. He saw his place in the new world, whither he had immigrated, to be a small and mean place. His vegetable-gardening brought him little profit; his lack of funds for use in that sort of investment which first plants, then waits and then reaps, was one long ban against financial exploit. His austere nature precluded with him all gainful intimacies and friendships. He could never have smoked a pipe with a man in his parlor and strike a compact for mutual advancement through the social tobacco-fumes. He would always have been thinking of my mother in the next chamber, and wondering if any aid proffered him were not the fruit of a seed which her fair face had sown.

I know that I describe the self-torment of an exceptionally gloomy soul. But such chronicling will have its dark autobiographical uses hereafter, and for this reason I must not and shall not spare a single black line. He who has set himself to paint with shadow should not shrink through fear of too grim a picture. The pathos of our situation, just as my ninth year crept toward a tenth, was indeed woful. A winter of unwonted rigor had yielded to a spring of chill rains. Warning had reached us that in a month we must go. Already I had seen, more than once, groups of men on the huge mass of rock near our home. One of these would point here and there; he seemed to tell the others of plans and schemes for future action. I used to watch him in dumb fear.

I was like the dweller in some conquered town, marking the movement of the foe. Once he pointed straight at the panes of my own little casement. It was almost as if I had seen him aim an arrow there; I sprang back and hid my face. Once again the same man pointed to my father in his garden. Work had been quite futile that day. The rain had fallen in sheets for hours, and now under a blurred sun the ground lay sodden and viscous. My father's head was drooped; he stared at the limp green lines of some vernal growth that the rain had spoiled if not killed. I could see a scowl on his face. He was at war with all the world, which cared no more about his being at war with it than a cyclone cares for a wherry. He had not moral strength enough to put his own weakness in some sort of defensive state. The blood of Teuton peasants ran in his veins; he came of a race which had been led instead of leading, been driven instead of driving. I think an old inherited torpor bound him, in his present straits, and put sullen passivity in the place of brisk self-help. But the pity of his position was the same. They were going to blast the great rock, and to crush and raze his fireside under the tumbling fragments.

I saw that my mother was suffering much. But a restless flicker in her dark eyes, or a furtive tremor of her delicate lips, alone told me what pain she really felt. She had never let me work at my father's side out of doors. I was never very strong in my boyhood, and she had used every care to make me robust. She gave me such continual care, indeed, that if I had been a rosebush instead of an only son, my father would long ago have flung me out of the window. And now I plainly perceived that she dreaded absolute privation chiefly on my account. There lay her worst grief and fear. I put my arms about her neck one morning. I searched her pale face, so beautiful and yet so. sad. There are some faces that seem to be touched by the shadow of vague future calamity. My mother had such a face. When this tragic hint is blent with beauty the bearer of both has a perilous gift, like that of Mary Stuart, who wrecked souls with a smile.

"You are breaking your heart," I said to her in French. We always spoke together in French.

"Do not say that, Otho!" she protested, surprised and trembling.

"But it is true," I went on. "And it is because of me — oh, you need not hide; I can guess if I do not see!"

"What do you see, my son?"

"That you are very unhappy."

She pressed her lips to mine. "Why do you say that it is because of you, Otho?" she asked.

"You think that I am weak," I said. "You think that if sharp poverty comes on us I will not have enough to eat. You do not fear for yourself.

You do not fear for papa. You are always tormenting yourself about *me*."

She clasped me closer before I had ended, and for a moment her head fell upon my shoulder. I believed that she wept; but presently she lifted her head, and the composure of her voice almost startled me.

"No, Otho. I tell you no! I do not think you weak. You have grown to be a great boy; you are strong. If anything happens " . . .

" If anything happens," I broke in, "you may trust me to work ! "

She kissed me and put me away from her. That night my father came in later than usual. It was never his custom to drink. But as I lay in my bed and failed to sleep, I heard his voice sound thick and unfamiliar while he addressed my mother.

"So you are still up?" I heard him say.

" Yes, Leopold."

" Why did you stay up ? "

" I waited for you."

There came a low, bitter laugh. " Has the boy gone nicely to sleep ? eh ? "

" Yes, Leopold. Why do you ask ? "

" Oh, you pet him so!" My father spoke in German, which I understood perfectly. " You should not have hugged him so close. What will become of him now? He cannot do anything but starve. We have all three got to starve. It is coming to that."

I heard a long, soft sigh. I knew that my mother gave it. That was the end of my pardonable eavesdropping. But I lay awake for a long time, thinking how she lay awake also. I hated my own boyish weakness while I let the thick dark of the room meet and weigh upon my open lids. I wanted so much to be strong, and fight the vast city that was thrusting us toward ruin. We must go. But where? Would men come and thrust us out of doors? Must we be beggars, like those I had seen often? Must we stake our daily chance of life on a stray bit of bread? Shame thrilled me as I thought of my feeble thews and childish limbs. I yearned to help my mother, yet even while I so yearned a desire came upon me to steal toward her and be comforted.

The next day it rained again through half the morning. My father went away. My mother set me my lesson, just as usual, but I could not study it; my thoughts were elsewhere. Twice, thrice, she chid me and even spoke of punishment if I should leave my task unlearned. I shut myself in my room a little later, and strove to fix attention on the two or three books which meant work. But presently I heard voices, and went downstairs into our little parlor.

My mother did not notice me as I softly pushed the door aside. A man was sitting quite near her, but she stood. There was a pink flush in her cheeks, and I knew quickly that she was not her accustomed gentle self. The man was he whom I had once seen point to the window of my little bedchamber. He wore clothes that were neat and smart; his face was feminine of outline, and he had a pair of cloudy auburn whiskers. He was smiling, and in an eager, vivid way. "You know that I don't want to do what I must do, Mrs. Clauss," I heard him say. "But the thing cannot be helped."

"My husband is not at home," my mother replied. She seemed to speak as if she forced each word. "When he comes I will tell him just what you have said. But I must ask you to go now, for he may return at any minute, and " . . .

The man rose. He drew near my mother. He put forth a hand, and his smile had a gleam of bold familiarity. "I've heard hard things of your husband," he said, "but I think very nice things of you. No one could see you and not do so. I'm a plain and rather blunt fellow. I hope you'll look on me, whatever happens, as your friend."

He did not speak at all like a plain or blunt fellow. If I had been older I must have caught from his mien and accent the undertone of flattery in both. My mother did not take his hand. She glanced nervously toward the doorway, discovered that I had entered, and beckoned me to her side. She put her arms about my neck, a little later, and held me thus while she answered her visitor.

"I cannot accept your friendship, Monsieur, though I do not doubt it to be kindly meant. There are certain reasons which I—I will not explain. It is best. And I must now beg of you to go, yet not in the least spirit of rudeness or ill-feeling" . . .

Her voice faltered here; she seemed wretchedly embarrassed and perplexed. The stranger gave a light, saucy laugh. "You're in mortal fear of that husband of yours," he exclaimed. "I have heard about him. He is a jealous tyrant. He frowns and scolds if you look at a man besides himself. It's abominable for such a lovely creature as you are to be bound to such a master. They say that he is half crazy. That handsome boy should have a start in the world when he gets a little older. His face is like a picture—and so is your own. You shouldn't throw by a real chance of help. I could see that you and the boy were safely cared for, and not dragged down into the slums and gutters. Your husband hasn't a friend; nobody will give him a bit of help; he's turned everybody against him by his bad, surly nature. If you don't listen to me now you will be sorry afterward. The house must go, and you with it. I can put you both, for a little while, where he can't find you, and perhaps get you decent means of support. As I said, you had better listen to me, and "—

"I shall not listen to you!" broke in my

mother. She drew me away with her as she spoke. When we had reached the threshold of the door, she added, in a voice full of frightened pleading:

"Oh, I pray of you to go! I will stay with my husband always! I wish never to leave him. No matter how he treats me — no matter what people say of him. I shall accept no help that he does not give me. And it shall be the same with my little boy here. Go, now, Monsieur, if you have any pity in your heart!"

She had receded into the hall, still closely clasping me. He followed, a moment later, and stood watching us, with one hand on the knob of the outer door, as though it were his intent very soon to depart. I thought his face had altered to a much graver look; and his tones were quite serious as he said:

"I have a great deal of pity in my heart, and I think it a shame that you and the child should suffer as you will. But, of course, you make it impossible for me to give you aid. The house must be vacated in two days. The owners of this property have sent me their positive orders. . . . Good morning."

He passed out of the house, and I was glad for my mother's sake that he had gone. I dare say that she had inspired a distinct sentiment in him; but very possibly he had meant to give this only an honorable expression. Still, though it is easy enough to feel compassion for one we love, unselfish compassion is another affair. So many of us stop short at that.

My father re-appeared about an hour afterward. The instant I saw his face I knew that something had happened. He threw himself into a chair, without a glance toward my mother. She quietly drew near him, however. "Leopold," she said, in her smooth, sedate voice, "it will be best, will it not, for us to begin packing together all the things we wish to take? Everything here is our own, you know, and when we leave" —

"Who told you we were to leave so soon?" he interrupted, turning upon her most suddenly. The sharpness of his voice made me start and tingle, as though I had felt the prick of a knife. His light-blue eyes gave a sort of livid flash as they met her own dark ones. But he still held his wrath in, whatever its cause.

"Who . . who told me?" she repeated, stammeringly.

"Yes," he pursued. "*I* did not say that we were to leave just yet. Someone else has told you. Who was it? Was it the man they sent here days ago to prowl about and give directions? You know the man I mean. Has he been here to-day?"

"Yes," responded my mother, "he has been here to-day."

My father rose. I saw his nostril quiver. "And many times before," he said, under his breath. "Many times when I did not suspect. Answer me, Gilberte, is this not true?"

"It is not true," said my mother. Her mild eyes never flinched as she fixed them upon his.

My father snatched one of her hands and held it by the wrist, scanning her face in its pure, spiritual candor uplifted to his own. I felt my heart stand still with terror, then. It was almost certain to me that he hurt her by his tense, ruffianly grasp, although she made not the least sign of pain.

"You deny that he has been here many times?" he cried. "And yet, but a few minutes ago, an impish young child of those people on the rocks below us, danced before me as I came homeward, and yelled jibes about . . about my being jealous, and . . and about the gentleman with the yellow whiskers visiting my wife."

He still held her hand as he thus spoke, but he had put the free hand toward his throat, pressing down his collar as though he breathed ill and this made him hoarse of speech. My mother still looked him straight in the eyes. "That is no fault of mine, Leopold," she said. "You have forced people into jesting at your continual jealousy." She addressed him in German, as she nearly always did, and the less dulcet language, never quite glib upon her lips, gave to her words an unwonted dignity. "I cannot help it if your strange distrust of me has made us both the sport of our neighbors."

He released her hand. He threw back his fine head, and laughed with shrill force. Then he fumbled for a moment almost wildly at an inner pocket, soon drawing forth a paper, which he thrust toward her.

"You say truly," he shouted, "that we are the sport of our neighbors. But who has made us so? Is it I or is it you? Read that! Read what I found stuck among my garden-tools here at this very door! Oh, I will grant you that the writing is very rude — that some clod has done it — that it bears no name. Yes, I will grant you this. But why should it throw blame upon you for letting that man into this house in all kinds of secret ways, if you have been quite without the fault it lays to your door?"

My mother took the paper and read it while he peered at her drooped visage. Then, after a little while, she crushed it in one hand and threw it away. She was looking at him as if each dark, liquid eye held a separate soul by itself, as she said : "Leopold, it is a lie. I swear to you on my honor as your wife that it is a lie! Some malicious trick has been played upon you by those whom you have made your enemies. My husband, you do believe me — you must believe me !"

"And if I say that I do *not* believe you!" he cried, threateningly, while he drew nearer to her.

She closed her eyes for a second or two. Then,

as she unclosed them, her slender figure seemed to rise and dilate with a womanly grandeur.

"If you do not believe me," she murmured, "then all must end between us. I have borne much from you — I have loved you — I have clung to you — but I will not endure *this!*"

It was her first absolute defiance. It seemed to appall and rout him at first. Then his face grew black in its reckless rage, and he lifted one clinched hand.

"I do not believe you!" came his husky answer. The next instant he called her a terrible name — a name whose meaning I did not then know — and struck her. It was a blow of the same vile strength as the gross charge that shot from his lips. She fell beneath it. There was a cry, but the cry was mine as I sprang toward her. . . .

Everything seemed to dance and whirl about me for many seconds. Then I knew that I was kneeling beside her, and that her still, white face gave no sign of life, with the heavy glossy hair framing it. We were alone. He had gone. I cried passionately, in my childish French:

"*Maman! maman! es tu morte? C'est moi, c'est ton Otho! Dis-moi, maman, es tu morte? Il est parti, ce cruel papa! Réveilles-toi et réponds!*"

But she did not speak or move while my arms clasped her in frantic affright and grief.

II.

THE blow had stunned her, and no more. I rained kisses upon her face as I saw consciousness return to it. I forgot the outrage from which she had suffered, in my delight that she was still alive. She was at first very weak and shaken. Even after she had gained a lounge and sunk upon it, speech was for quite a while nearly impossible. Then by degrees both calm and strength returned to her. She made me kneel at her side and hold her hand while she said: "Otho, my son, you must never speak a word of what you saw pass. Mamma and you must go away together, now. We must go without . . papa. He must not know when we leave, and we shall leave *him* forever."

"I am glad," I said. "I want never to see him again. He struck you. It was a great sin, because you are so good. I shall never forget it."

She leaned her lips to mine and kissed them. "Be sure that you never *do* forget it," she murmured, with an emphasis that I did not then dream of understanding. (How I was fated to understand hereafter!)

"Shall we go soon, mamma?" I questioned.

She did not answer for a little time; she seemed to reflect. "We will go, my dear," she presently told me, "as soon as there is any chance of our going unwatched. Otho, you are a clever boy — clever beyond your age. You are still not ten years old and yet you can quite grasp my meaning, I am sure. Your father will come back; he will come back to repent, to beg my pardon, to kneel before me and call himself all kinds of bitter names. But that must not be, Otho. It is not because my heart is hardened against him; it is not because I do not already forgive him what he has done. It is because I fear, for his own sake, *what he may do hereafter.* That is why we must go together, and very secretly. I have a little money saved; it is but a few dollars, and yet it can help us till we find Martha."

"Martha!" I exclaimed, not without a sudden joy. "Martha, who lived with us when I was a very little boy, mamma, and who was always so good to me, and . . and whom papa sent away, one day, because?" —

"Yes, Martha," my mother interrupted. "It is the same Martha, my dear. She has married since. She wrote to me not long ago, and asked me to come and see her in her present home. The address was in her letter, but I have lost it. Still, I remember the address — or nearly. It is in the lower part of the Bowery."

"The Bowery?" I repeated. "That is very far away, is it not?"

"No: we will find it. It is eastward from here. I — I have seen so little of the city that I have lived so near for many years! But we will find it, as I tell you. . . And now, Otho, you must aid me to . . to avoid papa." My mother rose from the lounge at this point. She seemed wholly her composed self again. "Listen, my child," she went on, standing over me and fixing upon my upturned face those lovely dark eyes whose least change I knew so well. "When we go it must be night. If it were not night he . . he might trace us. Others might see us or follow us and tell which course we had taken. What we wish to do is to escape, and night is always best for that. There are many rugged spots in the country hereabouts. If we could once get free of this house and hide somewhere, Otho — no matter where, so that we hide unseen till night has come! You have rambled in these parts far more than I. Do you remember any place? Try to think, my son."

I needed to think only a moment. "The great rock," I said. I pointed northward to it as I spoke. Its rough density, seen clear under a sky that drifted clouds of the storm had left blue and limpid as amethyst, gleamed opaque yet keen to us through a near uncurtained window. I knew that rock so well! Why should I not know if any lair or fastness of the sort now needed were quarried by chance in its crude flanks? I did know of such a covert, and I told my knowledge promptly, with a florid childish pride.

My mother listened. She gave a slow nod as she heard. She bade me steal to the outer door and watch with caution for any sign of my father's approach. While I thus kept vigil she was to make all swift use of time in preparing our flight.

How strange and novel a flight it was! This woman still loved the man who had so foully soiled her love. And yet she would have put an ocean, a continent, between herself and him, because fearful lest her presence in his life might urge him toward crime. Other women fly from men they hate: she fled from one whom all the powers of darkness, dismally allied, could neither estrange nor repel. It was for his sake alone that she left him; she would have borne tenfold worse blows than that he had dealt her; she would have hungered with him, starved with him, begged for him; no smile in all the world would have been so dear to her as his harshest frown; to serve him and be spurned by him was pleasure compared with never to find him at her side. And yet, in horror of what harm he might wreak upon himself through the madness with which she saw him cursed, she had resolved to divide her life from his perpetually. Child as I was then, I felt the sublimity of her abandonment.

Man that I afterward grew, I confirmed and revered it.

While crouched half in ambush on the small porch of our dwelling, I soon became sure that the intended exit would pass unespied. The hour was now verging toward late afternoon. Eastward the spent storm lay in one long, low bank of spongy drab. Across the glittering river spring had touched a tract of woodland with vapory green, so ethereal of tint that it seemed like only the airy soul of a color. Cumbrous wharves and gaunt warehouses had not yet made Jersey City their undisputed prey; being still a village, or very like one, she had a few sylvan chances with the turning year. Our side of the river held a more suburban rank, for piles of lumber and bales of merchandise lay frequent along its uncouth landing-places, in that commercial scorn of all riparian grace and charm which has dwelt with New-York at every stage of her growth. But the stretches of moist and twinkling green farther inland were as yet a choice spoil that waited seizure. With the prongs of rock to pierce their turfy sward and make intervals of tender undulation, they were rich in pastoral effect; and one or two nibbling goats (those placid prowlers about so many of our city environs) lent their shaggy shapes to deepen the forlorn sort of picturesqueness. Below a fall in the land rose rocks on which many wretched paupers had reared pitiful huts. Our

home was almost of palatial comfort beside these.
Some of them were shapeless blendings of ancient
boards, as if nailed together in random desperation
of refuge by their outcast tenants. Others had a
more decent contour, with a space of creditable
courtyard. But all were huddled and massed in
woful disarray. Perched on successive acclivities,
they stared at the passer beneath them as though
they were the last miserable haunts of those whom
the near city had denied all honest shelter. Later,
when foreign immigration flooded the island, they
became still more numerous; but even then their
squalid and grizzly fellowships were hard to miss.
The scum and riffraff of humanity clung there.
The stone that underlay their zigzag walls and
precarious roofs could brace both against overthrow when blasts drove. Their inmates were
used to the nip of frost and the chill of rain.
Like new Noahs they had fled hither to these bare
heights from the deluge of civilization beyond.
And alas, each Noah had borne with him his
family, as in the tale of old! You saw mothers
there, suckling young infants in the sun on clear
days. You saw frowzy unkempt children descend
the wooden stairs that led below. Some of these
poor waifs had spoken to me and sought my company during past rambles. But I always gave
them cold response; it was my parents' charge, and
I was glad enough to heed it, for often I had heard
drunken yells from those grimy dens aloft, and

once the news had reached us of a sickening murder done at night there by a man wild with drink. From these bad and drear quarters had come, I am certain, all our present ill. The boy who had shrieked his false, evil message to my father was one of their lawless tribe. They had set him to deal that sting, as they had set some one else in their sorry group who could wield a pen to write that malignant letter which my father had found. They hated us because we shrank from them; they hated my father because he was almost one of them and yet scorned their rabble. On Sundays they would meet us in a certain grimy wooden church, where the service was droned by an old asthmatic priest, the attendance was meagre, and the benches ascetically hard. Here their scrutiny would be torture to my father, and they soon got to understand why. His jealousy became a source of great secret glee to them. Perhaps their amusement might have transpired more openly if it had not been for my father's big frame and bold, cool eye. As it was, they giggled, whispered, and slanted meaning looks. They no doubt regarded us as a grotesque threefold joke. They knew we were "squatters," like themselves, on territory for which we never paid a dime. Our reserve would possibly have hurt them more if they had not found in its armor what they deemed so comic a crevice. I marvel now that their mockery took no other form than it did — the child's elfin jibe and the ribaldry of that nameless letter. Perhaps a residue of respectful dread vetoed all such treatment until they learned that we were to be driven away while their own exalted colony remained for a little longer unmolested. But then our last shred of superiority had been torn from us; misfortune, that most merciless of levellers, had made our cottage in the vale quite mentionable beside their shanties on the steep.

For some reason the great rock close to our dwelling had not yet known the invader's foot or heard his hammer ring. As I now looked about me, in wary quest of an observer, all was lonely and silent. If you listened closely you could hear a vague hum, which always came by day from the adjacent city, and which was its way of living and breathing. Nearly all gigantic things breathe audibly.

My mother soon called to me from the inner hall. I went to her at once. She looked relieved when I bade her be certain that the coast was clear. She was clad in shawl and bonnet; she had a little bundle, which held a few trinkets and souvenirs of her past life in France, but apart from this she bore nothing that could prove a clog or burden. Her hand shook a little as she clasped mine with it and went out of the house at my side. We were about to face so vast a change; no wonder that she felt distrustful of what might befall us both. And yet the impulse that drove her on was like the goad of fate itself. She dared not pause. Her conscience spoke to her with the voice of her love. "You must go," it said, and she obeyed.

A few steps brought us to our proposed hiding-place. It was a damp, dark, grewsome cavity under one corner of the great rock. It was just the spot for a roaming child like myself to chance upon and prize. Its hollow gloom was touched with the mystery that all children love. I had stolen into it timidly; I had rushed from it in dire fear; I had returned to it with morbid entice-ment, and I had finally accepted its existence with a sad critical disdain, since its prosaic inte-rior had at last convinced me that it was incapable of producing a bear, a ghost, or even a mere bat. I had long ago become familiarly and contempt-uously intimate with it. The other children of the neighborhood, being mostly of Irish parentage, and hence packed with superstition, would enter it rarely and then but for brief and scared so-journs. I knew that the risk of my mother and myself being now disturbed was in every way slight. We passed inside for perhaps twenty yards, and then paused. The dusk was at first very obscure, but in a little while it seemed to lessen, and we saw the dark, jagged walls and the tawny soil with tolerable clearness. All this time my mother had held my hand. We had crouched down together. Suddenly I felt her clasp tighten. Where daylight gleamed at the mouth of the cavern, I saw a human shape. It had just appeared there, and it moved with a staggering pace and a drooped head. The next minute, however, its head was raised. I plainly discerned my father's face.

But then all fear of immediate detection fled from me. The face, bathed in that outer light, was full of a lurid and fierce pain, which had evidently no concern with our discovery. While I gazed from the shadowy ambush my mother and I had reached, I saw him knot both hands together and stare down at the ground. The gesture, the attitude, was one of mental misery.

Abruptly, a second time, he raised his head. Turning full toward the cavern, he gave every sign of entering it. His look was directed straight toward our hold of refuge. The pressure of my mother's hand grew still more.tense. My own heart stood still. I believed that he had indeed seen us, and was about to confront us.

But I was wrong. He had doubtless been somewhere near us as we slipped into the retreat. But he had not seen us glide past its threshold, and as his eyes swept the obscurity in which we hid, they gave no trace of detective intent. But they gave trace of a desperate, remorseful turmoil. The thought of having injured her whom he loved with such an ill-ordered and tyrannic passion, was stinging him into keenest repentance.

He was telling himself that, after all, she might have been wholly guiltless. The force of his dreadful jealousy was yielding to that of reason, of rational reflection. His lucid interval had come, as it comes with nearly all madmen.

He moved away. I breathed again. I heard my mother give a low, quivering gasp. I turned and kissed her in the dark. Her cheek, as I did so, was cold as ice.

But my father had gone. He had known nothing of our partial escape. Would it be a complete one? I felt new fears of this as I waited and whispered with her, longing for twilight to come, for evening to deepen, for night to lend us its black aid.

And night at length did so, although its advent, in all my brief life, had never yet seemed as loitering as now. We finally emerged from the cavern, still hand in hand. We must descend the hill and pass the rocks where the huts clustered. There was no other course. Westward lay dim slopes which might trip our feet into the very Hudson itself. Eastward were the raw, inchoate plans of streets and avenues that are now paved and populous, but were then treacherous with untold pitfalls. We must pass cityward by a single road, and that skirted the hovel-crowned heights which we were fain to shun.

But with hand still grasping hand, we took this compulsory route. As we left the cavern we seemed

to gain air that was almost bright. No breeze
moved, and a yellow mist alone told of the sunken
sun. Stars had begun to beam in the cloudless
heaven; the prongs of rock rose spectral on every
side; we saw the home that we had deserted;
a light shone from several of its lower windows.

"He must be there," my mother whispered.
A stifled sob was in her voice.

"If he is there," I said, "it is better. Then
he will not see us and cannot follow us."

She did not answer me, but I heard her sigh.
I think her love was tugging at her heart in that
moment. She wanted to go back to him. She
wanted to give him another chance — to get his
kisses of penitence, and return her own of pardon.
But her step did not once falter. She was flying
from him because she loved him. And her love
nerved and steadied her as she hurried onward
at my side. No one met us while we descended
the hill. The rocks soon loomed on either hand.
Lights glowed from their flat summits. We heard
a loud laugh or two, and again we heard a harsh,
ireful oath. Life there was at its usual nocturnal
ferment. A few of the men were jovially drunk,
a few of them savagely so. And now a thin
scream told us that some child had been struck
and hurt. As a boiling liquid will throw scum to
its top, so the rush and strife of this augmenting
city had cast these poor lawless and mutinous
folk toward its barren outskirts.

We hastened along. In a little while we had gained a region where flag-stones met our tread, though somewhat brokenly, and street-lamps, with wide interspaces, began to gleam upon our sight. We had reached the town itself, and were presently well past its limits. To strike westward into the Bowery was now an easy feat. I should say that we came upon it by the approach of Bond or Great Jones Street. It was then much as it is now in point of ugliness, but its shops were fewer and its private dwellings more numerous. We had arrived at Canal Street before my mother, always keeping note of the numbers over the door-ways, told me that she was nearly sure Martha lived close at hand. The precise number had escaped her, but it was certainly not far off. She stopped before a gigantic black-bearded Jew, who stood at the entrance of a little tobacco-shop, and asked him if Mrs. O'Hara dwelt near by. We were evidently in luck. The Jew took a pipe from his hirsute lips and pointed next door.

"O'Hara," he said, with an urbane smile that put little creases in his cheeks. "I s'pose you meen de untertaker's, ride dare."

"Ride dare," was a little two-storied abode. In its large lower window loomed a huge, solemn coffin.

"Martha *can't* live here!" I said, as we paused at the narrow glass-door quite close to the rigid, angular box which no child of my then age can see without a thrill of sombre association. I recalled the brawny, buxom, merry Martha of earlier days. She always had a laugh and a jest on her ample, ruddy mouth. It seemed impossible to connect her vigorous, mirthful life with any custody of death and the dead.

"Yes," my mother answered. "I remember, now, that Martha wrote me she had married an undertaker. This must be the place, Otho. At least we had best inquire here. It would be almost strange if we had not found her now, though I shall feel thankful indeed if we have had the good fortune to find her so soon."

We had found her. Martha herself responded to our summons. She threw up both her hands as she recognized us, in jovial amazement. She was not a bit changed. Her sepulchral surroundings had not left her touched by a trace of their shadow. She drew us into a back room, and made us welcome with a splendid cordiality. She possessed the sunny Irish nature in its fullest exuberance. She was more genially alive than any man or woman I have since met. She hugged me in her stout arms and made me sit on her strong knee while my mother told her all that had passed. She had hated my father honestly and frankly even before he had turned her simple devotion to his wife into a reason for driving her from his house, and she blamed him now with all the ardor of which her explosive brogue was capable.

"Shure, ma'am," she cried, "I knew it wud come to this afore you'd finished wid 'im. Shure, the loikes o' you an' the loikes o' him is as diff'rent as a rose frum a cabbage. If I'd been there when he sthruck yer, ma'am, he'd a felt the weight o' this hand, bad luck to 'im! An' the dear little Otho's come along wid ye! Well, God bless ye both! Ye'll have bed and board here wid me fur manny a day, so ye will. Th' ould man, as I call 'im, 'll be back soon. He'll be glad when he finds ye here, fur he knows well, ma'am, how I've been pinin' to see ye both, so I have! An' the bishness is payin' furst rate jusht at present. We washn't doin' very much till about a month ago, but now there's a shtroke o' fortune come to us, so there is, an' the vicinity's got koind o' unhealthy, so's we can live an' save a little as well. It's three good funerals, ma'am, that's fallen from Heaven upon us this very week, an' we're promished another to-morrer, fur the pawnbroker's eldest gurl, across the block, ain't expected this very minnit!" . . .

Martha's husband soon appeared. He was a gaunt, bony man, with a great, drooping black mustache, and a glassy yet benevolent eye. Martha rarely permitted him to finish a sentence. She browbeat him at every turn, mocked him, criticised him, bewailed him, objected to him. And yet he bore all her effrontery not merely with resignation, but seeming pleasure. He accepted her sarcasms, her sudden assaults, her biting personalities, without a disapproving murmur. But I soon saw that Martha's eye always had a sly twinkle in it, and I soon grew sure that he saw the twinkle too, and loved her for it, as he loved her for every other trait or mood, whatever she was and whatever any chance might make her become.

I got to be very fond of him. During the next few days he was always trying to tell my mother how glad he felt at welcoming his wife's old mistress. He would begin somewhat in this fashion, with his haggard, sallow face drawn into painful lines of premeditated suavity :

" Well, ma'am, it's loike seein' the face of an old frind, beggin' your pardon, ma'am, to meet the lady that Martha's tole me about so often, an' praished as wan o' the shweetist ladies that ever " —

"Be off wid ye, now!" Martha would roughly break in, at perhaps this point in the poor fellow's gingerly gallantry of phrase. "Shure, d'ye think Mrs. Clorz 'll put up wid yer blarney as I did when I married the loikes o' yer? It's her that'll see through ye, sur, as if it was glass an' not brass that ye're made of. S'posin' I shud tell ye, ma'am " (and here Martha would set a hand on each hip and face my mother, after frowning with an awful momentary gloom sideways upon her lord) — "s'posin' I shud tell ye some o' the foine compleements of another koind, ma'am, that he's been payin' ye behoind yer back, an' w'at a double-faced rashcal he can be when he chooses ! "

O'Hara would shake his head meekly at such dark innuendoes as these, and it was not long before my mother would chide Martha with a reproving smile when she let her coltish wit kick up its heels after this mettlesome manner. My mother and I were not slow to recognize into what good hands we had fallen. They were four hands in all, and two were plump and soft, two big and horny. I think I got to love O'Hara's big and horny ones a little the best, as time elapsed, though I still preserved my old allegiance to Martha. The great, grim, sweet-natured Irishman loved me in return, I am sure. He would often stroke my hair and whisper in my ear, " Plaise God to send me, some day, as purty a boy as you, mee little man!" And I might have been some rare bit of porcelain for the way in which he treasured and guarded me. I have spoken of his hard, large hands, and of my love for them. This is literal truth, for I would often nestle my own within one of their coarse palms and follow at O'Hara's side while he led me into the loud, plebeian street near by, and thence into calmer but more wretched haunts. We saw many strange sights together. He seemed convinced of my untarnishable purity ; I was like a pearl to him that one could drop in mud but lift again and unsoil by a careless brush. Like many of his race, he drank, but unlike most he never drank to rash excess. I have stood at his side in dingy liquor-stores while he called for his

" mixt ale " or his " drop o' hot Irish," but though glowering faces might be near me and bloodshot eyes peering at me, I never felt a qualm of dread. A tough biceps was not far from those solid fingers that my own frail ones could seize at an instant's notice.

Spring had meanwhile slipped into summer; summer had ripened to autumn; winter had come again. I had seen with pleasure that we were no longer dependent for bread upon the O'Haras. My mother, by nature as well as early training, was a deft needlewoman. Martha, with fingers all thumbs, revered her skill, and told tales of it among the neighbors, in which eulogy not seldom borrowed the wings of fancy. Most fame owes its loudness to one special trumpet; my mother was soon approached with offers in the way of dressmaking, which Martha, sedate as any grand chamberlain, at first haughtily rejected, then promised to consider. The end of it all was that she threw just a fabulous enough atmosphere about her favorite's powers to raise prospective profits a good many dollars. Heaven knows what arts of lying were needed to accomplish this result. But Martha knew. My mother made gowns, finally, for the resident customers who sought her, and made them so well that they spread her praise abroad. This brought us an income; shaping apparel for all sorts of feminine figures at a lower price than could elsewhere be secured, soon became her frequent task. But other work claimed her diligence. She sewed shrouds for the dead as well as frocks for the living.

Shrouds in those days were used far more commonly than now. I shrank, at first, from seeing her ply this uncanny office. There was, to my young thought, a kind of daring in it — a rash alliance with that cold enemy who waits for us all. Besides, it seemed to deepen the melancholy of her mien, as if she were always wearing a thin film of black over her sad face. I knew that her life now held but a sole spark of cheer or hope. That was myself. Without me to guard and prize, it is doubtful if she would have cared about life at all. I was sure that she always thought a great deal of my father. But she never even mentioned his name to me. She wanted me to forget him if I could. She wanted to forget him herself, but could not. She had wrapped the past in silence, but she failed to clothe it with oblivion likewise. She yearned to hear from him or of him, and yet she equally desired neither event. For his sake she would have been terrified if she had learned that he had searched the city in quest of her, though for her own sake she would have secretly rejoiced at such knowledge. It was a strange blending of resignation and discontent. Perhaps the two feelings did not blend, after all, and there was a gulf between them which I somehow spanned. She might have sought him and found him again, spurred by her undying love, if it had not been for me. But to do this would have been to place me under his influence, apart from giving him fresh incentive for his frightful jealousies. She had looked her fate calmly in the eyes, and had decided. She plied her needle, smiled often, never went out of doors, and tried to make me believe she was happy. One day I put my arm about her neck and kissed her, watching what she sewed. It was a yielding white stuff, and she was fixing broad plaits in it. It was another shroud. Mike O'Hara and his Martha had been thriving of late, and we throve with them.

"Mamma," I said, "why do you never go out? Sometimes the days are very pleasant. And after I have done with my lessons in the mornings you let *me* go out. Why do you never go yourself?"

She looked at me intently for a moment. I put my arms still closer about her neck. I kissed her again. "Mamma," I whispered, "tell me. Are you afraid of *him?*"

She drooped her gaze. She made a feint of continuing to stitch at the white plaits. "You know, Otho," she faltered, soon. "You must know."

I did. But almost cruelly I persisted, strengthening my caress. "You *are* afraid he will find us, mamma. That is why you never go out. But you let *me* go for long walks with Michael."

She slowly nodded. "Yes. I let you go with

Michael. He is very strong. He will take care of you. And you need the air every day, and the exercise. Michael understands."

I put my lips close to her ear. "Michael is strong," I whispered, "but *he* is stronger. If he should see me what could Michael or anyone do against him? He would tear me away; he would make me tell him where *you* are ; he "—

But I paused here, for she had dropped her work and had clasped me round the body with eager arms.

It was like a revelation. She was in a sudden tremor of excitement. " Oh, my son, my Otho," she exclaimed, "I let you go, but I suffer when you are away from me !" She had drawn my head down to her bosom; she was kissing my cheeks, and patting my hair with little rapid motions of one hand. "If—if he should find you and take you from me, I—I should go mad or die —I do not know which."

And then she fell to sobbing excitedly on my shoulder. I was silent for quite a little while. At length I said, very solemnly and meaningly:

"I shall never go out again, mamma, unless we go together. If he meets us he must meet us both. Remember what I tell you. Michael and Martha may know why, or not, just as you please. But I will never go out again unless I go with you. If anything *should* happen we must be together. If he is waiting and watching for us, let him find us side by side. Do you understand me, mamma?"

Still clasping me, she lifted her dark eyes to mine. They swam in tears. She could scarcely utter the words that now brokenly left her lips.

"Yes, Otho. It — shall — be as you will. I *do* understand. When — we — go, we will go together!"

How fateful those words of hers sound to me, echoing through the departed years! And for what a mournful reason have they found a lodging-place in my memory, ignorant as I then was of the disaster they foreshadowed!

III.

THROUGH weeks I firmly kept my resolve. It was sometimes hard to keep, for I loved my walks with Michael, and had grown used to entering houses with him where the black sign of death met us at thresholds, and where loss would not seldom wear as much snivelling hypocrisy as real regret. Michael, too, was very keen-witted, in his way; he had a swift knowledge of his clients; he was born for his dreary calling. There was nothing unctuous or mock-sober about his approaches. He saw through shams and dealt with them by a shrewd and summary diplomacy. I remember that we once entered together a narrow little room in a German tenement-house not far away from the Bowery. We were received by a woman nearly as tall as Michael himself, who wore not a vestige of mourning, and carried an ornate gold ear-ring in either prominent ear. Her gray hair was drawn tightly backward from each temple; she was the most Dutch-looking old woman, with her big, tallowy visage, and her hirsute wart, and her small rheumy eyes, that I ever recollected having seen. She received us in a frayed wrapper and a pair of carpet slippers. She put her head a little on one side as she said :

" Vell, Mr. O'Wara, he's gone." (" He " was the late Mr. Schmitt, a grocer with whom Martha had formerly dealt.) " He pass avay chuss lige a shild. I guess 'bout an hour ago. I vas vaitin' fur you ever since. I *thord* you mide be arount."

Mike nodded, and scratched one bluish cheek. He had on his best professional expression — something between a leer and a scowl. I had become perfectly familiar with it, and knew its wholly commercial nature ; he put it on and off at a moment's notice, like the white cotton gloves then in his pocket. " Yes, ma'am," he now said with great sobriety. " I haird lash' night as Mr. Smith was putty low, an — well, well, I'm sorry, ma'am, an' I guess there's manny another that'll even be sorrier nor me ! "

" He vas a goot man," said Mrs. Schmitt. She did not appear to be sorry. " He alvays gif your vife goot measure, ain't it, Mr. O'Wara ? " she suddenly asked.

"Oh, shure, ma'am, yes, indeed ! " declared Mike, thoroughly thrown off his guard.

Mrs. Schmitt put her head a good deal more on one side, and a sickly smile crept out at the corners of her lips. " I thord you say so, Mr. O'Wara. . . Mr. Rosenbaum vas in shuss before you come, an' ve vas a talkin' 'boud de casked."

To talk about the casket with Mr. Rosenbaum

was, of course, a serious matter for Michael. Rosenbaum was a rival undertaker, an oily little Jew with a sliding scale of prices; he could be "beaten down" unmercifully, as he usually was and expected to be. Michael, on the other hand, had a set of inflexible prices for all his dismal wares and services, and held the haggling Rosenbaum in grand contempt. Still, business was business, and Rosenbaum was a German and must not be roughly spoken of here, if the present "job" was to be secured. So Michael scratched his cheek again, and cleared his throat, and said:

"Well, ma'am, an' did ye come to anny turrums wid . . the other gintleman?" He disliked to pronounce the odious name, but it must have cost him a pang to call Rosenbaum a gentleman.

"Vell," said Mrs. Schmitt, with a cough as dry as the rustle of a dead maize-stalk. "I guess I ord to teal vit Rosenbaum, Mr. O'Wara. I ord do 'cause he's a coundryman o' mine if fur no odder reason. . . Still, sphsosin' you'd lemme haf de casked sheaper . . say a toller or so sheaper, vy, I mide go to you. I do' vand no ice nor noddin', you unnershtand, akcep' de casked. It's cole vedder, an' I god bode de vinders up, an' a liddle salpeeder alvays on his face, an' he'll keep firsd rate till de funerrel. So now, how mush you sharge fur shuss de casked an' vat has to be done de day of de funerrel, an' vun carridch besites de hairss? I do efryting clss myself. Vat you sharge?"

Michael promptly told her, and received a little falsetto scream of dismay. Rosenbaum would do it nearly six dollars cheaper. It at once became evident to Michael that Mrs. Schmitt had beaten Rosenbaum down just as far as she could possibly make him go, and was now using the last desperate offer of the Jew as a means of forcing his rival into a still lower offer. Young as I was, I felt this raw greed, shown at such a time, flush my cheek. Michael drew me out of the room very soon afterward. There was a look on his face wholly unprofessional and sincere. And just before he left her he told Mrs. Schmitt that if she had been a very poor woman she might have had some excuse to stand there and barter about her husband's burial-fee, but that being a woman of thrift and means, it was disgraceful in her. I forget his precise words, but they were very trenchant. He left the house at once after speaking them, and in the sort of low rumble that his lips made during the next few minutes I am afraid that I detected a good deal of hard profanity.

Still, his disgust was quite pardonable. It would have made a good many men, worlds more lettered than he, swear just as roundly. "Shure if he hadn't left her the shtore an' the bizness," he presently said, becoming coherent and perhaps a trifle apologetic to myself as well, "I — I wudn't moind a bit. But it's a heap o' money he's left her, so he has, ·bad luck to her fur as stingy and misserruble a wan as ever walked ! "

The sadness of such glimpses as this into human life would often stay with me and haunt me. I was just at the age when we begin to think and muse, if we are dowered with fair intelligence, what sort of a planet fate has cast us upon. But Michael was not always so obdurate and unyielding to his customers. I remember going with him up several stairs to an attic in Hester street. The room which we entered contained the corpse which we had come to bury. It was sheeted, and the inevitable Romanist candles burned at its head and feet. A Mr. Lynch had died, and his relict, Mrs. Lynch, greeted us amid a family group of no less than seven children. The eldest of them were girls, who stared upon us blankly, and all of them had bare feet, gear torn and dirty, and tangled hair. There was a print of Our Lady of Seven Sorrows over the mantel. I could not help thinking, as I counted the frowzy children scattered about the room, that Mrs. Lynch was a lady with seven sorrows, too. The little girls were plaintively noisy and the little boys harshly so. One was a baby, and it had been left quite naked on the floor near a basin of water which it wished to paddle in and could not, having fallen over on its back. I recollect going to it amid the clatter, and pitifully raising it up. While I did so I heard Michael's deep voice say :

"Well, Mrs. Lynch, I'll do the besht I can fur ye, an' no man can do more, d'ye undershtand, nur that, ma'am."

Mrs. Lynch was very stout. Her bosom was simply exorbitant, and over the insecure cotton stuff which clothed it towered a very coarse, red-cheeked moon of a face. She listened while Mike explained his charges.

"An' it's you, Mike O'Hara, that talks to me loike this!" she cried, in withering reproach and anger. "It's you, is it, that knew mee family in Dundalk! Shure, w'at was your father compared to mee own annyhow? He was a farmer, so he was, an' not loike yours, begorra, that moight 'a wurked under 'im, so ye moight! An' I sent fur ye to bury my Jerry daicent, so I did, an' not to come here wid your big prices!"

"I ain't haird about no big prices yet," said Michael, in very docile tones, scratching his cheek.

"Oh, ye ain't!" cried Mrs. Lynch, in hot satire. "Very well! Ye may lave mee apartments, Mr. O'Hara. I knew ye well in th' ould country, an' ye can't impose upon me here. So that's all there is about it. If Jerry's to be buried in Calvary he'll be buried there daicent, ye moind, but he'd rise an' shtand roight up here among the seven child'en he's left me, so he wud, if he haird w'at ye're after ashkin' to put 'im reshpectable in his grave!" . .

"Why did you let her have a coffin at such a

low price, Mike?" I said to my companion, after we had regained the street and heard no more either of Mrs. Lynch's yells or those of her children. "Is it because she's Irish, like yourself?"

No, it was not because Mrs. Lynch was Irish. It was because Mike, who knew the pinch and stab of poverty so well, had pitied the loud, aggressive widow as she did not deserve to be pitied. That was all. . . . And these episodes happened every day with us. I have narrated two salient ones, but we witnessed others, just as comic, just as pathetic.

Mike was so fond of having me for a companion that I could not understand why he now accepted so resignedly the change of my indoor life. But he did accept it without a word of objection, and I naturally supposed that my mother had talked with him in private.

I began to fail in health, however, and chiefly, no doubt, from my sudden cessation of all exercise. Languid fits overcame me, and sometimes my food for days would be almost that of a bird. Afterward strong, I as yet gave no sign of my father's vigor; the physical part of me seemed mostly of maternal origin; I had my mother's large dark eyes, her sensitive outline of face, her slenderness of shape, though I promised to be tall, which she was not. I had not my mother's hair, however, for my own locks were sunny, and indeed almost as if threaded with gold. In those days I never thought of my being handsome or not. No one told me that I possessed beauty, except possibly Martha, in her most beaming moods, and even if I had become wholly assured of this fact I do not think that it would have concerned me in any serious way.

And yet I am compelled here to record (without the least impulse of vanity, but simply as a chronicler who sets down the black and white of what he states) that I was then, at the age of eleven years, a notably beautiful boy. This heritage never left me; it was my birthright, and as that it remained. In after years it became a great aid to me, as the succeeding pages of my story will show. But I think the endowment was at its best in my childhood, and perhaps because my complete ignorance of it lent it the element of unconsciousness. More than once, during my rambles beside Michael, I remembered saying to him with a touch of puzzlement in my tones: "Michael, why do people look at me so hard? It seems, sometimes, as if they knew who I am, or had known me before, and wanted to speak to me."

Michael would laugh in a low, chuckling style that did not at all disarray the sombre repose of his haggard face. But I never understood. My beauty came to me as my disposition came, from wholly explainable sources. My parents, in their different types, had been of striking personal gifts.

I had inherited a combination of these. Until later there was no one to tell me the worth or even the meaning of such a legacy.

I still kept the vow made to my mother about not leaving the house unless she went with me. I often saw her eyes dwell worriedly upon my face; doubtless my loss of health made me very pale. But she did not ask me to break my resolve. She comprehended that no amount of asking would make me do so. She saw that my determination sprang a great deal more from love than from fear. But at last she yielded. I did not want her to yield, but the concession came, nevertheless. I was contented enough to bide indoors. Since our talk together about my father, there *had* grown within me something like a terror of going out at all. If *he* were really waiting to confront us, why not remain in retreat and obscurity until the lapse of time brought with it safety of emergence?

One day my mother said to me: "Otho, you are not well, my son. You need the air. Will you not go with Michael, as you used to do?"

I looked at her. I shook my head as I did so. "No," I replied. She understood me, and for the time held her peace. Two days later she said to me: "Otho, the weather is very fine this morning. You have studied hard, of late. You have got so far in your lessons that, as you see, I am unable to follow you, or to teach you more.

There is a public school only a little distance from here. I want you to go there with Michael and present yourself as a scholar."

"No, mamma," I answered, calmly and stolidly.

She put her hand on my arm. "Otho," she said, "will you go with *me?*"

"Yes," I at once answered. "But you must promise to walk to and from the school with me, every morning and afternoon."

"No . . I cannot."

"Then I will not go to the school," I said.

"Otho, you are wilful and disobedient."

"I can't help it, mamma."

"But your health is not what it was."

"Yes — I know. You want me to walk abroad. I will do so, with you."

My mother heaved a low sigh. I was not wilful or disobedient in other ways, and I am sure that she gave me full credit for being neither.

"Very well," she presently said, rising, "we will take a little stroll together this morning."

I sprang toward her and threw my arms about her neck. "Mamma!" I exclaimed. "You hate to go!"

"Yes, Otho."

I drew backward. I was very stubborn in my intent; nothing could shake me. "Then you need not go," I said.

"But you force me," she responded gently.

I bit my lip. The tears had rushed to my eyes.

"Oh, mamma," I cried, "you know why I will not go without you!" . . .

A little later we left the house, side by side. We did not go to the school. It was pleasant to be abroad once more. The sun was shining; there had been a winter thaw; great drops came from the awnings of stores; enough melted snow remained in the streets to let a few sleighs pass with their merry jingles. I grew gay and garrulous before we had taken a hundred paces. It felt so pleasant to breathe the free, open air!

That afternoon I returned home with at least the semblance of an appetite. Martha watched me at supper and rapturously praised me for my renewed powers of consumption. Michael watched me, too, but he said nothing. I had my long talks with both husband and wife, just as of old, but they never presumed a word regarding my self-immurement. Of course they both had learned its cause from my mother. The next day she went out with me again. I soon grew better. My strength returned; I ate; I ceased to take tired naps at midday; my laugh rang louder and blither through the house — this little house in the Bowery, dedicated to the sale of coffins, the making of shrouds, the appurtenance and concomitance of death.

My mother was still sad. Our walks did not gladden her, though they gave new life and strength to me. For this reason she made them a daily occurrence. We always kept within the close neighborhood of the Bowery; it somehow seemed to be safer there, though the Bowery was then almost the chief New-York thoroughfare.

One evening, in my twelfth year, a most memorable event took place. We were about to seat ourselves at supper. Michael, as usual, brought in the evening paper. He always handed it to my mother. She would sometimes spend a half-hour with its contents while Martha busied herself preparing our meal.

But on the especial evening to which I refer my mother suddenly dropped the paper, three or four minutes after it had been handed to her, and uttered a sharp, bitter cry as she did so.

We all hurried to her side. For some time she was quite speechless. She could tell us nothing; she could only stare at us with glazed eyes. But at length she pointed downward at the journal which she had been reading. I ran my gaze along its columns. On a sudden a very familiar name arrested it. That was the name of my father, Leopold Clauss.

Yes, there it was, in large type, glaring at me. And what words accompanied it? Heavens! had I lost my senses? Had my mother's agitation alarmed me out of my reason? No, the printed lines were too clear for that. It must be true. I looked up at my mother. Her face was very white, but no whiter, I fancy, than my own. If ever two human creatures exchanged a glance of silent terror we did so then. But it was not a selfish terror. I knew that her heart could not feel a selfish thrill if it had tried; and with me the thought of her dire peril had leaped horrifyingly uppermost. Martha, seeing the pallor and distress of our faces, broke into a frightened wail. The next minute Michael had taken me in his strong arms, with a tenderness exquisite for so rough a creature.

"Whist, Mashter Otho," he said. "Luk at me an' tell me w'at it is ye seen in the paper . . Mashter Otho!" (for I could not heed him, I could not keep my eyes off my mother's hueless face), "Mashter Otho, I say! It's Mike that's ashkin' ye, dear little wan! Luk at me an' tell me!"

But here my mother found a voice, though it was quite weak and husky. "There — there is something in the paper about my husband," she said. "He has attempted a murder."

"A murthur!" echoed Martha, with a little scream. Poor Martha dropped into a chair and covered her face. Then, in her misery at my mother's misery, the ruling passion asserted itself, and she began to assail her husband with reproaches.

"W'y didn't ye have more common sense, man, than to let Missus Clorz see the paper at all until you'd skhimmed it over yerself? That's jusht you, Mike O'Hara, through the wurld! Anny other man wud " . . .

But my mother stopped this absurd torrent of rebuke by a wave of the hand. She was fast growing herself again. She pointed once more to the paper. "Read, Michael," she said. "And be silent, Martha. How can you blame your good husband? What will you not blame him for, soon? . . Read, Michael — I cannot, yet."

Michael presently did read. He made a grotesque herald of the sinister tidings which my mother and I now waited to hear in full. Some of his pronunciations might have hinted striking novelties to an eccentric verbalist. He floundered, he stumbled, he treated certain words as if they were hurdles, and indeed a few of them wholly upset him. But the terrible truth stealing upon us through this medium of the quaint and the ludicrous, perhaps took a new irony and sting. What he read, put into other language, was this:

My father, on the previous evening, just at dusk, had suddenly attacked a lady named Dorian, as she was leaving the stoop of her residence in Lafayette Place, and about to enter a carriage. His appearance at the time was excited and dishevelled; he looked like a man under mental aberration, though he bore no signs of being intoxicated. Mrs. Dorian — well-known as the widow of a wealthy New-York merchant — was of course quite unprepared for the attack, and uttered a cry as Clauss drew a small, sharp knife upon her. In another minute he would have inflicted a wound, had not a passer-by of powerful frame and quick courage (his name was of course given, but it has long ago escaped my memory) dashed up to the would-be murderer and seized his wrist with both hands. Instead, however, of a struggle ensuing between the two men, Clauss had abruptly dropped his knife and showed great docility. For, as the lady rushed back toward her dwelling, he had seen her face in a new light, and discovered that she was not the person whom he had at first believed her. He attempted no flight, and police-aid being near at hand, he was at once taken into custody. On arrest, he refused to give his name, but merely muttered, in a gloomy way and with a strong foreign accent, that he had mistaken the lady for his wife, who had deserted him, and that he was sorry for having been misled by a strange resemblance. He also declared that it had been for several months his intention to kill his wife if he ever met her, and that he had constantly gone armed for this purpose. He had been committed promptly for breach of peace, and had afterward still refused to give his name. His person having been searched, however, several letters were found upon it addressed to Leopold Clauss. He had subsequently admitted this name to be his own. The prisoner's general appearance and his great physical vigor were here described. Several bystanders, at the time of this singular occurrence, had expressed the opinion that he was insane. But although in a state of severe mental turmoil, his sanity was hardly to be doubted. In any case he was certainly an individual to be placed under restraint. The address on his letters had been that of an inferior boarding-house in a street near the lower portion of the Bowery. Inquiries concerning him had been made here, and although his sober habits were admitted by his landlady, she stated that he was much in her debt and that his morose and odd behavior had for some time made her anxious to be rid of him. She knew, however, nothing of his antecedents. A report had become current that Mrs. Dorian, the lady whom he had so curiously attacked under the conviction that she was another person, had recently changed affright for interest, and was very desirous of investigating the whole remarkable case. Mrs. Dorian was confident of never having seen Clauss before. She was a French lady, who had lived in New-York since her marriage, about twelve years ago, to the late Mr. Charles A. Dorian, formerly a prosperous importer of foreign silks. It was rumored that Mrs. Dorian, both through curiosity and a certain misplaced pity, had resolved to visit Clauss in his confinement and hold an interview with him. And there the newspaper article ended.

I shall never forget that night. My room adjoined my mother's, and I sat beside her bed till dawn, holding her hand. I knew well enough that neither Michael nor Martha slept in any but the most fitful way, for I could constantly hear their voices across the hall. Still, they did not disturb us. They left us alone with our grief and our fear.

If I had not been so sure that my mother still loved this wretched man I should perhaps have suffered less than I did. But I was certain that such indestructible love all the time gave a fresh pang to her agony. My counsel, as we remained there, side by side, was of one sort. We must fly from the city. Never mind if they sent my father to prison for weeks or for months. Let us leave New-York. Let us go where he could never find us. Some day they would set him free again, and then he would watch and wait, just as he must have done before.

But my mother shook her head. She did not at first explain to me her reason for doing so. Perhaps she could not yet explain. Her brain was still throbbing and whirling; her nerves were still tingling. Late that night, however, she said to me, lying there at my side in the stillness and shadow of the room:

"No, Otho. It cannot be. I will not take help from Michael and Martha, and that is what we should have to do if we went elsewhere. They are themselves poor enough, as you know. I have

gained a little place for myself here; it lets you
and me live; it is not much, perhaps, but it does
that.   We have a home, Otho — a *coin du feu.*
Michael and Martha are far more like servants to
us both than I wish them to be.   I should like
to live with them always; I love them, and so do
you.   And then it is so pleasant for me to remember, Otho, that if anything should befall me, they
would be near you, almost ready to die for you.
I never saw anything like the love you have inspired in them.   I wonder if it will always be thus
with you — if you will always win hearts as easily
as that.   If you do you will be one of God's most
rarely gifted creatures, since there is nothing so
precious as to have the power of making ourselves
beloved at will — though, alas! there is deadly
danger in the gift, too! . . But we will speak of
that hereafter, *mon chéri;* we will speak now of
going away.   It would be folly.   The more that I
think of it the more I feel it.   It would be to
change welfare for poverty, solvency for debt,
peace for struggle.   Besides, in a large city there
is, after all, the least risk of his finding us.   Here
one escapes in the crowd, as it might be said.
And then, Otho . . there is always my trust in
the *bon Dieu.*   I am not a good Catholic, as you
know; there was never anything of the *dévote*
about me; but I have faith in God's goodness, and
I do not believe He thinks me sinful enough to
let your father . . Well, my son, you understand

what I would say. It is almost terrible. It will
haunt me for weeks. I feel as if some part of me
had been dipped in blood, and I could not rub off
the stain. But he is your father — never forget
that, Otho!"

"And you love him still, mamma," I said to her,
under my breath. "Even though he has tried to
kill another woman, thinking she was you, you
still love him!"

I saw her breast quiver and her lips tighten as
she lay there at my side. "Otho," she said, "it
has been dreadful for you to remain up like this.
To-morrow you will be ill. Go at once to bed,
my son. Do as mamma bids."

"You love him still," I persisted, with no
questioning in my tones, but rather a sad accusation there.

She did not answer me. It was true. A sudden passionate feeling swept through me. I had
never known it before, and I did not recognize it
then. But it was jealousy, pure and simple. It
was jealousy of this love which no outrage could
weaken, no villany lessen. I clenched my hands
as I slipped out of the room. A little later I lay
in my own bed, beset by a lurid mood which I
strove to control without avail. There seemed to
me a cause for burning resentment in my mother's
unalterable affection. I felt as if the fresh insight
I had gained into that ideal wifely constancy were
a wrong, a jeer and a slur to my own filial love.

But the mood at length died away in a troubled sleep, and the sleep was followed by a dolorous awakening of headache and fever. A severe illness ensued, and I lay for a fortnight prostrated by one of those fits of nervous exhaustion which to a boy of my frail health might easily have meant death. Need I tell, at this stage of these confessions, whose care and devotion helped me to live? But she was not my only nurse. Four other eyes watched me besides her two dark, patient ones. I remember waking from a sleep full of delirious dreams, on a certain afternoon (I have a fancy that it somehow must have been afternoon), and crying out wild words in French — words like these: "*C'est papa! Prends garde, maman! Il veut te tuer! Il a un couteau — un grand couteau! Dépêches-toi!*"

And then an arm of iron, except that it was gentle as any girl's, slid under my hot form, and I was drawn so closely to a broad, hard breast that one or two of the bristles of Mike's beard grazed my cheek. And I was not startled, though I expected my mother; she had always been near me hitherto when I had had these unhappy seizures. But Michael did just as well, that day. The tears rush to my eyes now as I think of how that man had grown to worship me. I never gave him half nor a third of the love he gave to me. I never gave it to Martha, who would (I verily believe so!) have laid down her life to preserve mine.

I never gave it — yes, let me write the plain words where I wish all to be plain and unsparing — I never gave it to the mother whose passion for me was an absolute sanctity. I have never really known what it is to love — except once. I have been capable of a great fondness in more than a single case. But it seems to have been my fate, my doom, that others should care for me better than I cared for them. I did not realize all this till long afterward. I thought that I loved my mother just as well as she loved me, but I now see, looking back through the solemn vista of experience, just how wrong I was! . . What has it always been? Has it been my beauty, which grew as I grew and stared me in the face like a challenge to vanity? Has it been a trick of smile, an unconscious mode of speech, an inherent mannerism of charm? I cannot say. I only know that I could win without choosing or caring to win, when the years made me older, and that then, in my boyhood, a sense of this power had begun to dawn upon me. God knows that there is no vainglory in these words I now write! Sooner or later they must have been written in the pages whose record means the laying bare of a life, the exposition of a soul! . . . .

My illness lasted a fortnight, as I have stated. But with all these grim facilities at its hand, as one might say, death did not claim me, there in Michael's abode of undertaking. If I had died I suppose they would have called it cerebral congestion. I wonder how poor Mike and Martha, in that event, would have told their friends with what malady I had passed away. Ah, no! they would neither of them, good souls, have been able to pronounce the big Latinity of the words. Their tears would have choked them even more than their ignorance!

My convalescence was rapid, considering my dire peril. But it is thus in nearly all functional disturbances of the brain. Less than another fortnight left me comparatively well, though still weak and nervous.

I soon questioned my mother about the event which had so sharply preceded my ailment. Where was my father now? What had happened since I last heard of him? What tidings had the newspapers given us?

My father had been sent to prison. It was not to be a long incarceration. His assault might have been a crime, but the law judged from results, not intentions. An effort had been made to find the wife, because of whom he had planned his vile deed, but without success.

I shuddered as I heard this last meaning detail.

IV.

WHEN I was strong enough to leave the house I went out hand in hand with Michael, as formerly. I had forgotten — or I chose to forget — the vow made to my mother in former days. But my walks with dear old Mike were much briefer now than they had once been. Sometimes I would have to return with my arm hanging wearily on his, though each day made me stronger.

My mother had meanwhile greatly altered. She had not, like myself, fallen prostrate under the shock of that hideous news, but it had laid upon her, none the less, a few signal traces. She had grown thinner, and the liquid darkness of her beautiful eyes held a more wistful gleam. At times it seemed as if the terror had never quite left her face — as if through the rest of her life she would always be expecting, dreading some new calamitous thing. A slight sound would make her start; a sudden current of air would cause her to shiver, or to bend like a blown reed. He whom she still so stubbornly loved was now an image clad in fear, almost in the red garb of crime. And I am sure that this shape never quitted her mental vision — that it was stamped there as indelibly as if it had been a scar on her flesh. She saw my father in all phases of inward agony. She realized what he suffered and why he suffered it. She pitied him and longed to help him. Meanwhile, she could do nothing. Nothing but hide from him! It is not a pleasure to love in that way. I think one might truly call it an anguish.

I had noticed for several days certain signs in my mother's demeanor toward me which seemed to indicate either that she was hiding something from me which it hurt her conscience to hide, or that she was dubious about telling me something which she was by no means convinced that I ought to hear. When we incessantly see and associate with only three or four people it is marvellous how swift is our note of the least change in them.

"Is there something you want to tell me?" I said to my mother, at last.

She started. Then she smiled her melancholy smile. "I knew you were an enchanter, .Otho," she said, "and I forgot that enchanters and wizards are one. Yes," she went on, hesitatingly, "there is something I want to tell you. Otho, it concerns . . your father."

I was not surprised to hear this. Whom else could it concern? "Well," I questioned. "What is it?"

My mother put her arm about my neck and drew me to her bosom. "Otho, that lady, you know — the one he attacked. I want so much to see her — to speak with her. The desire to do both torments me. I might have gone to her alone. But I will not go without you. Will you go with me, Otho?"

"Why do you wish to see her, mamma?" I asked. I put this question mechanically. I knew why, quite well.

"It is hard to answer you," she said, hesitatingly. "My chief reason is" . . .

"The love you still feel for him," I broke in. But I did not speak reproachfully. I was recalling her recent devotion through my illness. "It is wrong," I continued softly, "you know it is wrong. It is giving a clew."

"A clew?" she said. "How? He is in prison now. Why should she tell him anything? I have heard about her; she is well known; she is a lady of prominence here. She gives large sums to St. Stephen's Church, not far away. There could be no possible danger."

"Very well," I said, after a pause, "I will go with you."

She kissed me twice or thrice, almost passionately. "We will go to-day," she said.

We went that afternoon. I disapproved the plan, but my heart was so full of gratitude, just then, that to refuse her what I knew her whole soul was set upon doing seemed almost sacrilegious.

We easily found Mrs. Dorian's house. It was smart-looking, with polished window-panes and fresh-painted trellises on stoop and balcony. Lafayette Place was then a quarter of distinction; even now its breadth has more dignity than that of most New-York streets, and then the comparatively even heights of its buildings missed that ugly irregularity which we notice with regret in Fifth or Madison Avenues. A maid-servant, tidily garbed, admitted us. We were shown without delay into such a drawing-room as few of the wealthy magnates now possess. Its doors were of heavy, panelled mahogany that shone like glass. Its furniture was of hair-cloth, and its mirrors rose from the rather sombrely carpeted floor to the plain white ceiling, with no frames except a slim, beaded verge of gilt. It would strike me to-day, no doubt, as very bare and dull; but years had to elapse before Queen Anne structures would rise in the region of Central Park, modish with tiled mantels and effective wainscots, and I then thought it all quite elegant and imposing. My mother had spoken a few words to the servant which were both too low and too quick for my hearing. I suppose they were simply a brief expression of her strong desire to see Mrs. Dorian.

And very soon Mrs. Dorian appeared. The instant she did so I detected her striking resemblance to my mother. She was a trifle taller, however, and carried herself with a much more assertive air. And yet if you regarded her with any degree of scrutiny you discovered that this likeness was altogether superficial. The eyes were brighter, but smaller; the cut of the features bore no real similarity; yet the general contour of both face and figure, as also the prevalent tints of coloring, were oddly in accord with those which had made her the object of so dire a mistake.

The moment that Mrs. Dorian began to speak I found myself forgetting that any resemblance whatever existed. Her voice was high, and with a ring in it like that of a sweet bell. In speaking she threw back her head a little, and disposed herself with what is called an air. But she revealed no touch of arrogance. It was not an unpleasant transformation. It put a gulf of difference between my mother and herself, but it developed the sense of a fresh and new personality.

"You said that you wanted to see me about some important matter," she began, using English that promptly betrayed a slight foreign accent. She remained standing while she thus spoke, and of course addressed my mother, who had risen on her entrance. She was attired in flowing silks of more than one shade, that were somewhat odd in make but extremely tasteful.

"I did wish very much to see you," answered my mother, in tones that made clear her keen excitement. " And for this reason I must lose no time in telling you just who I am. I "—

But here Mrs. Dorian went quickly nearer to her, giving a sharp exclamation. Her eyes had widened with evident astonishment. " You — you are the image of myself!" she broke forth. "Good Heavens! perhaps you are *she!* Perhaps — yes, you must be *his* wife! "

My mother smiled. There was a pained relief in the smile; she had been spared a disclosure deplored though sought. " I am the wife of Leopold Clauss," she said, using her own language as if unconsciously. And the next instant she dropped into a chair, weak and unstrung.

Mrs. Dorian at once took a seat at her side. She peered with eager scrutiny into my mother's face. Her next words were also in French, and so fleet that they seemed to leap from her lips.

" You are she, then! I have thought of you so often! That terrible affair had, after all, such a romantic touch! And I love all things that are quaint and extraordinary. Our resemblance is both. I am very glad you came to me. Of course you dreaded to come. . . It is wonderful how we look alike. I have always doubted it until now. And yet we are so different — I perceive this in a moment; it is easy to perceive. . . Ah, that dreadful matter was such a shock to me! I was ill for days because of it. My friends said I was foolish to do what I did. My friends are always saying that I am foolish to do what I do. By 'friends' I mean the people who carp and rail at one for nothing. I have no friends. I have only one friend, that is; I mean myself, and she is also quite often my enemy. But do you know what I did? I went to see your husband. I visited him in his cell."

"You saw him?" faltered my mother.

"Yes. I felt like someone in a novel by Balzac. It was so delightful to feel like someone in a novel by Balzac. I mean the great Frenchman — our countryman — who wrote those superb tales that seem to be alive while you read them; the printed lines are to me like little veins with real blood running red through each of them."

"I do not understand," my mother murmured. She did not know of Balzac, or at best he was a mere name to her.

Mrs. Dorian gave a light, soft laugh that had no jar in it; pity alone seemed to dwell there. "I know, I know, my poor woman," she said, laying a hand on my mother's arm. "You do not understand, and you want to hear of your husband, who in turn wanted to kill you. You need not tell me that you still care for him. I knew it some minutes ago. I think, truly, that I have known it for months. He is a monster of jealousy; he is also a madman; but he is a wonderfully fascinating monster and madman. He has the shape and face of an old Norse god. He re-

ceived me with a scowl, but it was such a magnificent scowl. There was a strong light; it was
midday, you know. He saw plainly enough that
I was not you. I did not go into the cell alone,'
of course. But if I had gone alone there would
have been no danger. He simply did not wish
me there, and that was all. He would tell me
nothing; he sat staring at the floor, and he answered all my questions in monosyllables. I could
get no satisfaction from him — none whatever.
He would not speak of you; he would not even
speak of himself. He grumbled a sort of apology
to me for having wanted to murder me. It was
immensely interesting; it was what I should call
a thrilling experience ; and one gets so few thrilling experiences in a huge overgrown village like
this New-York, where I am forced to live for
horrid commercial reasons that concern my poor
dead husband's business. But in spite of his
surly treatment I went away from him with a
kind of glow. I had been brought face to face
with raw, naked human nature. And I insisted
on forming my own conclusions, though people
laughed at me in their superior wisdom. I insisted that his jealousy — which was like something fresh from the Middle Ages, with all the
coarse, bloodthirsty color of that period — had for
its object some true, kind little woman who had
loved him and never wronged him. And now I
have only to look at you and feel certain I was

right.   You see, I am constantly judging, concluding, from impulse and instinct.   Anyone who does that is always held to be more or less insane.   I am not at all insane, and I did it in this instance, and am convinced that I formed a correct opinion. You do care for him still, though he has treated you infamously.   I can understand it; I have only to look at you well in order to understand it.   I have seen him, and it is all clear to me.   Englishwomen, American women, are often clever, but they have neither the depth nor breadth of a clever Frenchwoman.   We do not merely see through things; we possess imagination, which is an enormous help to reason."

Mrs. Dorian and my mother spoke on together for a good hour.   Or perhaps .I should state that only Mrs. Dorian spoke, for the pauses were rare in her buoyant, rattling monologue.   During these she would listen, but my mother had, after all, little to communicate.   She had come but for one purpose, and this had failed.   She had hoped to find out more concerning my father, his present frame of mind, his health, even his baleful grudge against herself.   But Mrs. Dorian could tell her nothing, except that he had looked very handsome and treated her with great sullenness.   Two women were never more mentally unlike than my mother and this lady.   One was all gravity and stability, the other all volatile flightiness.   Mrs. Dorian was a kind of intellectual Proteus, in fact

— as I remember years afterward calling her. To meet her every day for a month was to discover that she had received at least thirty distinct sets of impressions. She afterward would often make me think of her as of a person who has come into our planet on an exploring expedition — who has been given just so much time to look about and no more, and who is determined to do as much observing, thinking and feeling as may be possible within the allotted sojourn. But though a weather-vane of change in many ways, this woman had much fixity of principle, of conduct, of moral ideal. She enjoyed life, on the other hand, because she got a great deal out of it; what made her not enjoy it thoroughly was because she could not get as much out of it as she wanted to get. Her receptivity was greater than the resources of her environment. She adored Paris, where she had been born, and undoubtedly its brilliance and its activity would at all times have made her most fitting world. She had read everything, and was constantly having some new literary idol, whom she would soon desert for one still newer. With the exception of Balzac (whose multiformity and versatility seemed in letters a semblance of what she herself was in life) she was always forgetting the worship of to-day for that of to-morrow. The great French novelist, romancer and poet held a secure niche in her memory, her affection. Others came and went; he staid.

It was natural enough that one of such a temperament as this should confuse and weary my simple-minded mother. But Mrs. Dorian interested me sharply, young as I then was, though of course there was much of what she said that I failed wholly to understand. Indeed, the words which I have already put into her mouth must not be taken as literal or authentic. They are both only so far as my childish memory may be trusted, and a failure to catch the sense of more than one brisk sentence as it then left her, has compelled its omission from among those which maturer powers help me to recall.

Her notice of myself was like a sudden discovery. Her eyes lighted upon me as if by chance, and a little cry followed. She hurried toward me and drew me back to where she had been seated. "And this is your child!" she exclaimed to my mother. "How beautiful he is! He is you, and yet he is his father as well. Those great dark eyes, with the curving lashes, are yours, and certain delicate lines of the face, too. But the blond hair, and the nose, the mouth — these his handsome father gave him. Oh, what an enchanting boy!" Here she kissed my cheek many times; there was a perfume like lavender about the soft silks of her attire that made it a pleasure to be near them. "How stupid of me not to have noticed him before! I love children, always; they are dwellers in a world that we may never enter, no matter how closely we clasp them to our hearts. But when they are so lovely as this boy of yours their world seems like a garden in some other star. . . But I must not flatter you, *mon petit.* Your beauty will be so much the sweeter while you do not think about it." . . . And now Mrs. Dorian drew out a tiny watch from her belt; I remember how it caught my eye at once; it was oddly enamelled, and quaint, like everything she wore. "Bah!" she exclaimed. "I have to meet some dreadful commercial creatures in ten minutes; I fear my carriage has already arrived. When shall I be freed from the necessity of talking about what I do not at all comprehend with persons who try to make me suppose that they do not perceive my own stupidity and *ennui?* That is it — I am stupid because I am so *ennuyée.* You see, my dear Madame Clauss, my husband died and left me a great responsibility. Everyone knows the house of Dorian & Company, importers of silks. But the 'Company' is a mere sham. Now that my husband is gone, I represent him, solely and absolutely. At first I wanted to stop the business. My friends shrieked at me with disgust: 'What! stop a superb business like that! Choke up a channel through which precious wealth flows to the nation! It would be unpardonable.' Then I wanted to sell the whole enormous affair, patronage, connections, name, everything, as one would sell a horse or a threshing-machine. Again my friends shrieked at me, after every offer which I received: 'What! sell so splendid a business for a mere song like that!' *Ma foi!* I could do nothing for weeks except wonder what I ought to do. Meanwhile my friends shrieked: 'Get some man whom you can trust, and place the whole affair under his control at a handsome salary.' But this made me weep with vexation one minute and laugh with amusement the next. Some man whom I could trust, indeed! I have always made it a point to trust everybody whom I know nothing at all against. It is to me so dreadful for one not to do that! And as for selecting any particular person in whom to repose my faith, that seemed none the less venturesome and experimental. But in a little while I woke to the fact that I had been trusting, ever since I was a widow, an old confidential clerk of my husband's, a creature as juiceless as a hickory-nut, all wrinkles and rheumatism and discretion. His name was Gredge, and after a long interview with him I resolved upon the perpetration of a tremendous deception, a huge hypocrisy. Gredge was my tempter, and I yielded. The world to-day believes that I carry on, with consummate cleverness, the great business of Dorian & Co. But Gredge is at once my mask of guile and my staff of support. If he should die, the mask would fall, and the staff would crack. I should be exposed as a lamentable fraud. As it is, I have only to look wise, to glance over accounts in the presence of other semi-superiors, and to cough with dignity. It is astonishing with what dignity I have learned how to cough. I have somehow got an idea that it is this cough, and nothing else, which saves me from having my reputation ignominiously shattered as a woman of great mercantile shrewdness. I think that I learned the cough from Gredge; he has one a good deal like it. He alone possesses the secret of my gross incapacity. But he is an accomplice not to be corrupted. I glance over accounts which seem to me a chaos of figures. I nod; I cough; I make believe that I am adding them up and confirming the result. *En effet*, I detest figures, and the multiplication-table has always been to me an enigma. I have a conviction that Œdipus asked the Sphinx how much was nine-times-nine or eleven-times-eleven, and that for this reason she cast herself into the sea. . . But if Gredge should die!—that thought perpetually torments me. Gredge is meanwhile a hundred years old, or a hundred and fifty — I never can just remember which. But he is not immortal. Even a Gredge must one day perish. And then I shall have nobody in whom I can repose the least faith as a protective accomplice. . . . But now I must say adieu, for my persecutors are awaiting me in an august body. You must come to me again — you and your charming boy. And if you are ever in need, be sure that

I will help you. That is all. I will not say more on that subject. I might wound you, and I see that you are easily wounded. I wish only to show that I do not bear a shadow of malice for — well, you know what. When you go home and think me over you will wonder at my having received you thus. You will say to yourself that nobody else in the whole world would have done it. And that is what I shall like. I always like to be thought different from anyone else in the whole world!" . . . .

When we left Mrs. Dorian's house and were once more in the street, I began to speak of her with praise, enthusiasm. But my mother did not share my mood.

" She is a strange person, Otho," was her slow, meditative comment. " I do not know that I like her, for all that she seems so kind and good."

" Oh, I am sure that she is both!" I answered, warmly. " I am sure that she meant all she said!"

" There was a great deal that she did not mean," my mother returned. " Or, at least I could not help thinking so. Still, this may be because I have never known persons of her class. Very often she seemed to speak as if she did not expect you to believe her. True, this was only when she spoke of herself — not when she offered us help, or anything like that. I am not certain that she is not good and kind. So many ladies would have shrunk from us after . . after what has happened. Perhaps they would have ordered their servants to make us go away at once. They would have been alarmed at our very presence. . . But I know so little of ladies like herself. I have never seen any of them before. I may be quite wrong in my judgment. I . . I went, as you must have guessed, to hear something about your papa. And she could tell me so little. I did not dream of any help from her. I wish she had not spoken of giving me any help. If I were in great want she would be the last person living to whom I should apply."

"You went," I returned, with blunt frankness, "because you thought she could tell you a great deal about papa. And now you are disappointed. I think she is very nice; I like her. Whether she meant it all or no, mamma, I was somehow pleased with everything she said. There was a great deal she said which I did not understand, for I am not old enough. But I remember much of it, and if I ever meet her again, when I grow older, I shall be able to make much of it clear. I shall have learned more then; I shall have studied and learned."

"You know all that I can teach you already, Otho," said my mother, as we walked along. "He is in prison now. He will be there for two years. That is his time — two years. When you are stronger, will you go to school?"

"Yes," I said. I was thinking of Mrs. Dorian.

She had fascinated me; I wanted to learn more, so that I could find a path into knowledge and education like hers. "Yes," I went on, "I will go to school, as you wished before I was ill. But this lady, mamma? Shall we visit her again?"

"No," said my mother, decisively.

And we did not. In a month or so I went to the school formerly proposed. It was a large brick building, filled with shabby and plebeian scholars. These were all boys, and the teachers, except in a few of the senior classes, were all women. The classes were designated by letters of the alphabet, *A* meaning the highest grade of attainment for any pupil, and final entrance into what was then the Free Academy and is now the College of New-York. (The word "free" had to perish; it bore quite too offensive a sound for certain republican ears.) I went for two years to this "ward school," as they termed it, and I cannot say that they were happy years, or morally improving ones. In the first place, the three teachers under whose successive tutelage a rather rapid promotion placed me, were women of much inherent vulgarity and, as naturally followed, of ill-governed tempers. But it would almost have required an aureoled saint, on the other hand, to deal unruffled with some of the imps and elves who trooped every morning into those plain, dull, cheerless rooms, and sat upon their tiers of gaunt wooden benches. My three teachers were all very

unsaintly women indeed. But I pitied them all.
Their tasks were hateful to them on account of
the excessive badness and mischief with which
they were forever confronted. They had all three
dropped into the habit of being incessantly cross,
because stern measures were so often required of
them. They could not say the simplest thing to
their scholars (myself alone excepted) without
giving a sour frown, a biting curtness, a tang of
sarcasm, to the remark. If either of them had
once addressed us in a tone of real kindliness we
would have felt something very like consternation.
Overworked, often forced to master on the previous nights many of the lessons which they heard
us recite during the day, ill-fed, compelled to
brave the worst weathers in garments not always
of the most resistant sort, it is far from strange
that these women were incessantly out of health.
One was always putting her hand to her head as
if a twinge of pain stabbed it ; another had a
hacking cough ; a third seemed at times nearly
choked by a catarrhal trouble. And whenever
their maladies were most acute the boys were
sure to be most contumacious. Every morning at
nine o'clock, and every afternoon at the hour of
dismissal, (three o'clock, I believe) we had to
assemble in an immense dreary room over whose
doorways were written mottoes from Scripture,
such as " Deliver us from evil," or " A wise son
maketh a glad father." This coming together was

like a gathering of the clans. We would march
in single file from our respective class-rooms to
the sound of a jingling piano lamely played by
one of the teachers. Then the Bible (which Irish
priestcraft has since endeavored to abolish from
our public schools) was read to us for about ten
minutes by the principal, Mr. Barlowe. Mr. Barlowe was a handsome man, with a tall, muscular
figure, a metallic kind of eye, and a large glossy
black beard. As I look back upon him he seems
to me the incarnation of relentless cruelty. If
the public schools yet retain their Bible, they
have, however, sent adrift something decidedly
more worthy of exorcism. I mean corporal punishment. It is terrible to recollect the torture
that Mr. Barlowe inflicted with his slim, biting
rattan. Every afternoon he would appear to us,
like an executioner among a throng of shivering
criminals. Miss Budd or Miss Jenks or Miss
Moriarty (those were the names of my three
teachers) would hand him the fatal list of his
victims. Unless the latter had committed some
special offence, these ladies would use only the one
significant word " disorderly." Then the con-
demned ones were forced to rise, and then a hideous
castigation would begin. Mr. Barlowe would make
his lithe switch descend upon their hands, which
they were forced to put forward and to open. I
have a conviction that the agony of those helpless,
cowering urchins gave Mr. Barlowe a sharp pleas-

ure. Some of the boys used to put resin on their hands to prevent the pain of the blows. The boys were bad enough, but Mr. Barlowe, in his handsome, insolent pride of office, was worse than they. No stroke of his vile rattan ever wrought the least good, and yet he exerted it, day after day, like the hard-grained tyrant that he was. I have learned, in succeeding years, that Mr. Barlowe has gained a name and almost a fame as a public school principal. But now that decency has wrested from him his rattan, I cannot imagine what sceptre he uses, since his former rule was so thoroughly wrong and base.

I used to tell Michael, after school-hours, of how he punished the refractory boys. Mike's grim face would cloud as he heard my tales. "Shure, an' if he ever goes fur you, Otho," Mike would say, "jusht tell me, an' it'll be putty closhe quarters betune oi an' him."

But Mr. Barlowe never "went for" me. I gave good recitations, as a rule, and obeyed commands. Still, I secretly despised the discipline which made fear of personal hurt a reason for proper conduct. I soon grew to think Mr. Barlowe's system revolting, as so many right-minded people afterward held it.

Once he wanted to strike me, and was prevented. Usually obedient and tractable, I had been, on a certain day, peevish and wilful. At the end of the names which the teacher gave him, mine was clearly though rather faintly uttered. I rose when I heard my name. As I did so I clenched my hands behind my back till the nails almost bit into the flesh. A sudden swift look from my teacher warned me to reseat myself. But I did not heed the look. I stood and waited.

Seven or eight boys were mercilessly flogged. It came my turn. I still stood. Mr. Barlowe advanced toward me. He started as he saw my face, and turned toward my teacher. And then she too perceived that I was standing. She waved both hands and hurried to Mr. Barlowe's side. "No, no," she said.

I saw them whisper together. I heard them, also. I caught the words "best boy I have" — "a little unruly to-day — never mind for once" as they left my teacher's lips. But I still stood firm. "Why not?" I heard Mr. Barlowe say, as he shot a look at me from under his fine arched eyebrows. And then, with the rattan still fresh from previous torture, he drew near to me.

I clenched my hands still closer. I thought of what Mike had said, and of what he could do. I longed to have him there then, but he was not there, and I must fight alone.

I meant to fight, as Mr. Barlowe said to me "Hold out your hand, sir." I did not hold out my hand. And just then the teacher rushed forward and grasped Mr. Barlowe's stout arm. "No, no," she expostulated, "not that! I did not mean that for *him!*"

Mr. Barlowe here motioned for me to sit. I seated myself. If he had struck me that day it would have been a day for him to remember.

But very soon afterward the teacher took me aside and begged me to forgive having mentioned my name among those doomed for punishment. I heard her in silence. She was penitent, as I readily saw, but I could not forgive her just yet.

Meanwhile something — let it be called a spell, a witchery, whatever he who now reads may choose to call it — had put me apart from all the other pupils. My intelligence was such that I could easily master every task assigned me, and in each branch of study I always held the highest rank. My teachers petted, humored, and would have caressed me if I had permitted them. My classmates, without a single exception, paid me a deference which resembled homage. I often treated them haughtily, and selected from them my favorites at the prompting of caprice. Some of them were sadly uncouth, and of unbridled license in speech. But none of them ever presumed to address me except in decently courteous phrases. It was remarkable how I managed to win everybody over without indeed managing at all. I do not boast; I chronicle. Boys of from twelve to fifteen years, when they are boys reared in homes of poverty, ignorance, and even of sin as

well, are too often the grossest animal products.
I saw not a few of this sort, and in nearly all
cases I gave them a wide berth. But my avoidance aroused no spleen, no rancor. They seemed
to take for granted that I not only bore myself as
one above them but that I was justly and right-
fully one above them. They were all somehow
on my side; they appeared to be in a manner
proud of me. I moved among them like a little
prince. Many of them would have waited on me
as servants on a master if I had made a sign that
such was my wish. I never tried to account for
it all; I never, in those days, gave it a thought;
I had not the slightest sense of triumph. It had
become a matter-of-course with me that everybody should like me. If any of them had shown
me the least insolence or disrespect I would have
resented it with heat. But none of them ever
did. In most boyish sports I took pleasure, and
acquitted myself with skill. But in these I chose
only certain associates, and always found my exclusive tendencies treated with respect. Whenever I descended during recess into the ugly
flagged courtyard where the boys romped and
shouted, I had a small throng of picked companions ready at once to gather about me. There
is no doubt that I inspired in these a good deal of
genuine affection. But I gave them very little
in return. They were playmates of the hour,
nothing more. I had the unconscious art or trick,

or whatever it was, of attracting whom I chose to attract. My mother had been perfectly right. I was born to win people by a smile, a glance, a sentence.

And in this way two years glided along. During that time I never once alluded to my father while at home. But I counted the months as they lapsed onward. My mother often went with me into the streets, now. But at length she ceased to leave the house. I knew why. It was then early spring. I said to her, one day:

" You remain indoors because he is out of prison. Or at least you know that his term has passed."

She started, and I saw her lips tremble. "Yes, Otho," she said.

"But you cannot live like this, mamma. You cannot shut yourself up always. After a while it may make you ill. After a while it may even kill you."

She lifted her large dark eyes to mine. "If it were not for you," she answered, "I should be very willing to die. If it were not for you, Otho, that would be far better than" . . .

She paused. I understood. The air of the room seemed to turn chill, as if the breath from a vault had swept through it.

We had had two years of peace, and now the old trouble and fear had come back to us. The menace and the shadow were once again over my mother's mind and heart!

V.

In these days I asked myself if I could do nothing to lessen her dread and uncertainty. I wanted to take some secret step, and leave her unaware that I had done so until it resulted in some sort of assured success. With this view I consulted Michael, my unswerving friend and ally. Could no means be hit upon of tracing my father's present whereabouts? He had undoubtedly left prison. Might we not succeed in learning if he were still in New York and if he still cherished those murderous designs against his wife? It was possible that immurement and the recollection of his horrid mistake had tamed and calmed him. Perhaps no thought of seeking my mother's life now fed brain and heart with its fiery poison. In that case how precious would such news be to us! What a load it would lift from the meek, sorrowful woman whose girlish love had become mockery, disaster and shame!

"You nod your head very knowingly indeed," I said to Michael one day, "and you scratch it with a great show of wisdom. But you have not yet told me if you can possibly get this knowledge that I so crave. And yet it seems to me that there must be a way!"

Here Mike redeemed himself from my rather hasty charge of dulness by recommending an application to the police. The truth, he said, could be got at in this way better than in any other. It was not improbable that my father's movements after he left prison had been closely watched. Michael had several intimate friends on the police-force. He would sound one or two of them regarding the best method of going to work, since of course it was highly desirable that great caution should be used. We must contrive to remain hidden while we secured our knowledge of him.

"And if we learn, Mike," I said, after approving this plan, "that my father still nurses the same wicked purpose, then it will be our duty to lodge some kind of public complaint against him. Mamma cannot be made a captive for years. I am no longer a child, and my health is so much better than what it was that I am almost robust and hearty. I feel that I have a duty to perform, a responsibility to discharge. If any thing should happen now, after the way in which we were warned, it would be still more horrible for us, because we should hold ourselves to blame. As it is, Michael, let us learn the facts if we can, and act accordingly. And do not mention even to Martha what you propose doing."

Michael, devoted soul, went to work in great

secrecy. His friends on the police-force were no doubt excellent aids. From day to day he told me nothing, and I asked him no questions. But meanwhile he was urging his stealthy work with much tact and skill. He knew just what I wanted him to do and how I wanted him to do it. An occasional word, and no more, would apprise me that he still strove and persevered. I read his faithful spirit so clearly! He had all that is best and finest in his often-abused race, without its marked powers of intellect which, when best and finest, are so frequently erratic and wilful. His was the sweet Irish nature that can love with such · inexhaustible warmth, and serve where it loves with such steadfast devotion. Brilliancy has been the peril of his people. They fail as great leaders, but in all qualities of allegiance and fidelity no land has eclipsed them.

Life had for many months flowed smoothly in our obscure little home, whither death so constantly brought us its gloom and its plaint that we had grown to regard both as commonplace, like the sure shade wrought naturally by the sunbeam. I could not fail to see that my mother took great pride in me, that she watched my least act with fond vigilance, that she rejoiced at my intellectual promise, that her old instinct of protection had begun to wear the hue of dependence and reliance.

"You are a dear boy, Otho," she tenderly said to me on a certain evening when I bade her good-night before I went to rest in my small room adjoining her own. " I hope you will always be as much of a comfort to me as you are now. And I hope everything will always go as smoothly with you as it does now, *chéri.*"

" As smoothly, mamma ? " I questioned.

" Yes, Otho. I would not flatter you for the world, since that might give you a false estimate of your own talents, and make you prone to flaunt and parade them unduly. But though you possess talents quite beyond the common, I think your good sense is sound enough to recognize the folly of idle pride in their possession. And yet these, like the beauty and the charm of which I am so glad to see you not boastful, render your daily course thus far a rarely easy one. Where other boys of your age toil and strain for eminence, you win it with scarcely an effort. I have so often watched you at your lessons ; there are some of them that your understanding and your memory seize with a strange speed. You are full of gifts. The ills and hurts that beset most lads have never touched you at all. I know your career at school — you have told me what it has been. Everybody succumbs to you — as I do, as poor Michael and Martha do. It often seems to me as if you were born to be indulged. But, Otho, you silently accept too much and give too little in return. Be careful, my son — be careful ! You do not love as you are loved. . . . I hate to speak of this to you now, because you are still so young. But some day you will love. Some day you will give a great love, and want it repaid in full, and question yourself constantly as to whether it is repaid in full. And if it is not, my boy — or if you should think it is not, then " . . .

My mother's voice faltered here. I threw my arms about her neck and put my lips to hers. "Oh, mamma," I said, "why do you worry yourself with thoughts like these? It must come of your making those sad, white shrouds — *ce métier funèbre!* I shall never love as you say. I shall never love any one as I love you. And if I should ever marry, you will see my wife and judge of this, for you will live many, many years — you are still so young!"

"Many, many years?" she repeated, in a strangely musing tone.

"Yes — surely yes. Why not? And you must not say that I give no love back, mamma! It is cruel!"

"You do not give the love that is given you, Otho."

"You judge me unfairly, mamma."

"No. . . I know you so well."

"Do you think I do not care for you as you care for me?" . . I kissed her as I spoke.

With her lips close to mine she answered: "No. I must say it. My heart tells me — my mother's heart. You accept; you are grateful; but though you sometimes embrace me and caress me like this, there is a coldness. . . I cannot explain . . . but it is there.   Oh, Otho, it is there!"

Her last word ended in a kind of sob.   She had not clasped me with her arms till then, but then she did so, tightly and abruptly.

I forced myself from their hold, however.   She had angered me, and perhaps a pang of conscience fed this new mood.   Between compunction and accusative wrath the gulf is seldom a broad one.

"I see!" came my bitter cry.   "You wish to say that I have no power to love except as he, my father, loved!   You wish to warn me against a fault which you have no right to dread because you have never yet had reason to charge me with it!   Is this fair?   Is it not unmerciful?"

"Otho!   What are you saying?"

But my words sped on.   "You tell me that you have loved me so well!   Admit that you have! But is your love for me now, at this moment, what it is for the man — my father, if you please — the man who wished to kill you?"

"Otho.   Do not speak like that."

I caught her unwilling hand.   "Answer my question!"   I demanded, with kindling eyes. "Which of us do you love the better at this moment?   Of which do you think the more?   Who holds your heart the more? Who fills your thought the more?"

My speech must now have been fierce.   But

she felt the poignance of its appeal; she perceived how it clutched the bare fact, and presented this, and demanded a clear response.

She withdrew her hand from mine with force, and then waved both hands confusedly before her drooped face.

"Answer me!" I exclaimed. "You do love him more than you love me! It is true! Answer me! If you do not, I shall know that this man from whom you are forced to hide, whose very existence is a threat to you, holds more of your heart than I can ever gain!"

I stood near her, with burning look, with quivering nostrils, with a sudden dreadful rage racking and thrilling me.

She lifted her eyes to my face. She sprang to her feet an instant afterward. Her expression was one of terror, and that alone.

"Otho!" she cried, wildly. "*I see your father in you now! His curse has descended upon you!*"

Her tones were so shrill and keen that they brought Martha from a neighboring room, in high alarm. But before Martha entered, my mother had sank back into her chair, fainting.

My rage (shall I say my spasm of hot jealousy?) had died as I saw the pallor and the backward stagger that told me what it had wrought. I, myself, unnerved and trembling, let Martha do what she could toward resuscitation. But when those dark, eloquent eyes met mine once more, I felt that if I should grovel at my mother's feet for pardon she would be justified in withholding it.

And yet how readily she gave it! A bitter headache succeeded her partial swoon, and when I left her bed-chamber it was long past midnight. But for three or four hours I lay sleepless, dumbly horrified at the passionate outburst of which I had been guilty.

What did it mean? Did it mean that my father had indeed stamped me with the woful brand of his own madness? This was the second time within my experience that such a paroxysm had caught me like a whirlwind. Was my will strong enough to stand guard against any third assault?

My will was certainly strong, and I vowed that night a most solemn and meaning vow to crush down and control a passion which must need stouter bonds every time that I let it slip leash. A belief in the power and permanence of my resotion brought with it a more placid mood. But not alone through the next day did a dull, slug-gish trouble brood in my breast; for many days afterward I seemed to see the glad spring sun through a dusky mist. I had realized that though I fought against these surges of wild feeling never so strenuously, the source whence they rose, like a stagnant and noisome pool, must hide itself in my nature. That source was jealousy. And strangely enough, when I now sought to analyze the only jealousy my life had thus far known, I found myself justifying and excusing it. My mind would hurry along in impetuous and fervid argument. Was it fair, I would ask myself, that I should be held in my mother's affection lower than he was held who had wrecked her life? Ought I not to expect, to demand, more than she gave my father? Was it not injustice, insult, that she should accord me an inferior place? Had I not been right in resenting what was truly a goad for revolt? Would not many another have felt my mortification, my grief?

But the fallacy of this reasoning might easily have struck me, and nothing except the bigotry and egotism of my own master-fault now obscured it. For if some strange current of attraction still turned my mother's poor misused heart toward him whom it would have been far better to loathe, she had none the less restrained all active indulgence of desire, bravely and firmly. True, she had done so on my father's account; but it had been also on my account. Her patient sacrifice should have shamed my selfishness!

It was not long before I told her of my stanch determination, and besought her pardon for what had passed. It was given with a close, eager embrace, but I knew that henceforth a fresh dread was to haunt her brain and tinge its thoughts.

"I will show you, mamma," I said, "that I am not half so much like him as you fear."

"You made me fear that you were like him in

that one thing at least, Otho," she answered. "But even if you had inherited all that is sinful in him, with strength of purpose and a little true courage you can remake your own character."

This subject of heredity had just begun to fascinate me. But as yet I had scarcely given a thought to the marvellous phenomena of the will. The perception of how we seem to be so absolutely free and yet are shaped and moulded by the agencies of our environment; the recognition of how an immense sequence of mental conditions, from our birth to the actual present instant, precedes, like one long law of iron necessity, our existent state; the admission that any least or greatest act, from the mere lifting of a hand to the slaying of a fellow-creature, inflexibly follows a thousand previous acts, whether trivial or grave; —all this I had yet to ponder, to investigate, to accept. But just now I was not too young to feel awed and startled by the thought that parentage could fix traits and tendencies in its offspring as inseparable as a finger or an eyebrow. It was horrible for me to meditate upon the way in which all disease, whether of mind or body, so often comes to us like a dark, hated dower, like a debt which we have not contracted yet must pay in full. I recoiled before the hopeless fact of woe and sin being entailed and transmitted by sire to son. The misery of the world — and I had not seen so little of it that I was unable to estimate its malign weight and scope — was lit for me, in all its ravage and solemnity, by a new and searching ray. It was like seeing a lurid sun cast dying light upon some wreck where waves broke wildly and shrieks rang out unheard into the deaf storm. I would sleep ill because of the remembrance that I had been born of a father who had perhaps made the taint of his own worst vice bite into the tissues of my being as a mordant will bite into wool; and when my wakeful intervals came I would lie in the dark of my own chamber and wonder why to each of us, brought without asking upon this planet where so many of us must fight to live at all, the start should not be equal, untrammelled, exempt from the bonds and snares of ancestry. I did not know, then, that just such futile questionings as these had driven older and finer brains than mine into sombre agonies of doubt, and even into madness as well!

Michael at length drew me aside, one day, with a demeanor that I at once decided to be portentous. He always had for important events a frown of more or less gloom. I knew all his frowns; this one was of the sort which he gave on having negotiated a specially lucrative funeral.

"Shure," he began, "it's somethin' I'm goin' to tell ye that'll be a big surprise. An' furst off I guess ye won't b'lieve I'm tellin' the truth wan bit, so ye won't."

"Oh, you always tell the truth, Mike," I said, with rather rosy exaggeration. " What is it?"

Michael had found my father. One of his policeman-friends had used influence with a certain very keen detective, who had no doubt done the ferreting work gratis, and just as a bloodhound might dispose of a rat or chipmunk in its pursuit of larger prey. Furthermore, Michael had himself seen my father, without the latter suspecting who he was. This was the first time the two men had ever met. I soon judged, from what Michael imparted, that my father was much changed in appearance. I now heard him described as haggard of visage and rather lank of figure. The place of encounter had been a liquor-saloon, whose proprietor was fortunately, as Mike expressed it, " raised home in the same place wid meeself, d'ye mind." My father was in the habit of coming into this place every night, and taking as much bad brandy (he always drank brandy) as the coin or two in his possession would buy. He always drank alone, always seemed moody and uncommunicative, and never showed a sign of intoxication. He was evidently in great poverty; his clothes, if not of the worst, were frayed and shabby. He dwelt not far away in the attic of a tenement-house. It was not known how he secured the little money which fell to him, for he had had no regular occupation since leaving prison. It was supposed, however, that his great strength of frame made him sometimes valuable about the wharves.

All this interested me keenly. And it seemed a vast advantage to have found out so much concerning our arch-foe. I had a sense of relief as I recalled the location of that liquor-shop and its adjacent tenement-house. Both were well removed from our quarter, being near Bowling Green, in the breezy vicinity of the old Battery, not then as now so smart with flagged walks and marine esplanade.

Strangely enough, as days followed this revelation of Michael's, a curiosity began to assail and tempt me. I wanted to have Michael contrive in some way that I should see my father while myself unseen. I knew that if I once made the request of him he would not be content till he had gratified it. The danger might be great or slight, according to circumstance. But it was not because of the danger that I shrank from taxing Michael's devotedness. It was because I doubted my own right to run the least risk of this sort without the knowledge of her for whom my safety and happiness were all that made life other than a ceaseless pain. Still, confidence in Michael reduced that risk tenfold as I reflected upon it. And as for personal fear, I had none whatever. All the timid qualms which beset a child had fled from me now. I had become a youth of not a little cool courage, and enjoyed in imagination things that bore a spice of venture or peril.

My mother had heard nothing of Michael's recent successful search. She need never know of the somewhat bold plan I was then forming. There was not the slightest chance — unless some dire mishap should occur — that she would not remain in continued ignorance of the whole matter. Why should I not confirm any doubt still existent — and I confess there was a lurking one — that no mistake had been made in the precise identity of my father? Besides, I wanted to look upon him once again. It was wholly a curiosity, and I suppose it was clearly morbid as well. He had never loved me, or shown me a shade of tenderness. But I wanted to see what changes remorse, passion, dissipation, perhaps defeated vengeance, had wrought in him.

I finally spoke to Michael. He at first shook his head with decision. Then I spoke more persuasively, and he scratched it in characteristic doubt. There must be a way of my seeing my father, I told him, and yet of my remaining undiscovered. He could surely hit upon a way. "You're so shrewd, Mike," I added, with a touch of flattery, open and yet adroit. "I am sure you could find it, if there *were* any way."

"Anny way?" murmured Mike, gutturally and a little crossly. "Of coorse there ain't."

I felt that I had gained my point. Whenever Michael was the least cross to me it meant that a big fund of indulgence lay behind his grimness

And I was right in this case. On the following Saturday — my holiday from school — he had arranged everything. I was to see my father and yet be securely unseen by him.

Michael explained to me just how the affair would be managed. I listened and gave my approval after I had heard. He must have been on rather intimate terms with Patrick Costello, the proprietor of the liquor-saloon I have before mentioned. My father was in the habit of entering there at about four o'clock every afternoon. An ambush in this place had been provided for both of us. We would be due, so to speak, at a quarter of four. And we kept our engagement punctually to the minute.

The ambush struck me at once as wonderfully secure. Michael and I found ourselves placed in a small apartment at one side of the general entrance. It was a little chamber intended for the bacchanal use of convivial parties, and judging from its pasty, grimy table and its two or three effete chairs, I imagined what riotous cliques must have clinked glasses there. The door of this resort had a key on the inside, which Michael turned. But the upper part of this door was a blind, with slats easily moved, so that one drawing a little backward could command an oblique but fair view of the saloon itself. I knelt on a chair at the side of my towering companion, and our survey was complete. To-day, no doubt, such an ambuscade would scarcely be possible in any similar haunt. Æstheticism — or something comically like it — has made the modern liquor-seller decorate his lair with gaudy stained-glass windows, doors of polished oak or walnut, and a " bar " of prismatic splendor. The trick of rousing a drinker's thirst by tickling his eye had not yet come into vogue. Here everything was plain and even scurvy, as befits dens where workmen pour out into tumblers the earnings that should get their wives decent gear or their children shoes. As I knelt at Michael's side, I saw dark rows of bottles perched along a wall misty with cobwebs; I saw the apparatus for pumping ale from a cellar below, with tarnished faucets and shabby woodwork; I saw a counter whose very edges, worn and sagged, looked as though it had accommodated the shifting elbows of multitudinous drunkards; and lastly I saw Mr. Costello himself, the genius — shall I say the evil genius? — of the dive, with his veiny, sanguine cheeks, his dull, bloodshot eye, his copious fall of dyed mustache, his flabby bulge of stomach. It is possible that Mr. Costello might have known better than to sit the spider of this noxious web, but there is no doubt that he did not look as if he knew better.

Of course it was all an old story to me. Michael and I had seen it all before. But that afternoon it somehow seemed new and unwontedly loathsome, because I realized that the man whom my mother still loved might soon enter its woful domain. But four o'clock came without bringing him. The minutes preceding that hour brought more than one customer to Mr. Patrick Costello. I write of New York as I saw it years ago, but the years have not changed this horrid, alcoholic part of it, and what I record of past time is true of to-day.

I remember that afternoon so well, while Mike and I waited in our hiding-place! A woman staggered in, with a big white pitcher, and a wrinkled face as white as the pitcher itself. "I'll give ye no more," said Mr. Costello, wiping his bar imperturbably. This was in its way moral; it raised Mr. Costello in my opinion; he was not all for sordid gain. A little later two negroes entered. They were at once told to "get along out o' that," with a fierce vehemence, and they departed. The hate of this enslaved race was then rampant with the Irish of New York. Still later a little child appeared, in filthy rags and with bare feet, carrying a jug. The little creature could just lift the jug to the bar's edge. "Where's yer money?" said Mr. Costello, unwilling (and doubtless because of past impositions) to fill the jug without first getting the price of what he would put into it. The frowzy child, standing on her naked tip-toes, lifted a coin. Mr. Costello eyed it suspiciously as soon as his blue-nailed thumb and forefinger had touched it. Then, still with a dubious air, he placed it under the glossy cascade of his dyed mustache. A moment afterward he flung it into the empty jug, returned this to the child, and grumbled out — "Get along wid ye. It's bad. Get along, now." The child, whimpering a little, "got along," just as the proscribed negroes had done.

And at last *he* came. I clutched Mike's brawny shoulder as I saw him enter. I knew him instantly. But he was greatly altered. His face had lost all its cold, stern beauty: there was only the coldness and sternness left. His cheeks were sunken, his hair was streaked with gray, his limpid eyes were dulled; and new harsh lines had crept about lip and nostril. You saw plainly that he had suffered past the common human measure. But there was an acerbity in his face that slew all sympathy. I felt as I looked at him that he was harder and crueller than ever before.

He poured out a tumblerful of tawny fluid from the black bottle that Mr. Costello handed him. It was an uncompromising tumblerful, and he drank it quite raw. I remember that the thought flashed through me, here: "If he drinks often like this it may kill him, and then poor mamma will be free."

Mr. Costello, with an evident motive of detention, now leaned across the bar and said affably to his customer:

"Have sumethin' wid me, sur. W'at'll it be, sur?"

"Brandy," said my father.

Mr. Costello graciously waved a hand toward the bottle which still remained on the counter.

My father drank again. Mr. Costello poured something from a private bottle of his own, among the many which thronged his shelves. "Well, here's luck," he said, drinking. And after drinking he said: "Ye're votin' wid the Dimercrats, I s'pose."

"No," said my father, almost gruffly. "I'm not in politics at all."

This was quite too much for Mr. Costello. I think he temporarily forgot that Michael and I were listening and observing. He leaned toward my father and began a eulogy, in fervid brogue, of the present Democratic nominee for mayor. My father listened, or seemed to listen, with ill-hid annoyance. Mr. Costello individualized one of the curses of New-York political life; his liquor-den was a means of distributing bribes to those who frequented it, for the purpose of making them vote a certain "ticket." Agents of the nominee for mayor, alderman, or whatever the municipal position possibly was, would place certain money in his hands to be discreetly used for electioneering purposes. Mr. Costello had a five-dollar note for my father if he would pledge himself to vote in one special way, and he soon showed that he had. He showed it in this fashion:

"Look here, mee man. You go wid us, d'ye

undershtand, an' it'll be a good job annyhow. I'll see ye on 'lection-day, so I will, an' if you'd want to borrer five dollars or so, d'ye mind, I'll " —

Suddenly Mr. Costello paused. He remembered himself. He became conscious of his unseen auditors. Representing as he did one of those vicious elements which have cast shame upon the greatest city in America for many years, he naturally recoiled before an open display of his own political corruption. He could hold a good many five-dollar bills in that big soiled hand of his. Men had given them to him who would not have precisely rejoiced in having their names made public as the donors. They used the lust for drink as one of their aids to slipping within fat electoral places. They turned democracy into infamy, and they have been doing it for a good many years since the period of which I write.

But my father was a bad subject for all such bribery. He shook his head and moved toward the door. I am sure that he saw the rottenness of this kind of attempted government, and that he shrank from it with merited disgust. I will pay him this one tribute of respect. Black as were his other faults, dishonesty was not among them. . .

When I regained our home I had a guilty feeling as I met my mother's eye. I had seen him, and she did not dream of it. How eagerly she would have questioned me if she had known!

But she did not know, I told myself, and never should. I had seen that in my father which made me believe him capable of any desperate act. What he had tried unsuccessfully to do he might try to do again. His face, his mien, his blasted and shattered personality, had told me this. The prison had not cured him. He still suffered, in his bad, wild way. And he still waited.

The next day was Sunday. It was a day of days with me. The season was latter May, the weather balmy, bland, exquisite. Even that ugly Bowery of ours took a certain grace and glamor. The house-tops, unsightly as they were, could not hide the brilliant blue of the sky. It was a day that tempted one out of doors. "We will go to church together, this morning, if you wish," my mother said to me.

"Very well," I answered. The church was not far away. I recollect that I had a new suit of clothes, that morning, made by my mother's deft hand. I felt proud and happy as I walked at her side to church. The delicious air of the May weather dispelled all the gloom of yesterday's discovery. My mother spoke as we walked along together.

"How pleasant everything is, Otho."

"Yes, mamma. I am so glad you were willing to walk out. I thought you would always be afraid . . nowadays."

She did not speak for several minutes. "The

sweet weather made me come forth and breathe it," she replied. There was a pink flush in her cheeks as she said this; I had never seen her more beautiful. "It is hard to realize that disease can lurk so near us when the air has so much purity."

" Disease, mamma? " I questioned.

"Did you not know, Otho? Smallpox has broken out in our neighborhood. Old Mrs. Joyce, the furniture-man's wife, died of it yesterday. And several other cases have also occurred quite near us. Michael is to bring a doctor to-morrow, and we are to be vaccinated — Martha, Michael, you and I, all of us. You were vaccinated when a little baby, Otho, and I remember what a dreadful arm you had. The doctor said then, laughingly, that you would be safe for the rest of your lifetime."

Just as my mother finished speaking I saw a man coming toward us whose face and form I recognized with a sudden horrible thrill. We were in Chatham Square, almost at the verge of East Broadway. In a moment more we would place our feet upon the curb-stone. I seized my mother's hand while we gained the pavement. I did not dare to point. "Mamma," I said, in my usual French, and with great speed, "there is papa. Be careful. Come."

I wanted her to turn with me. But she halted, and then stood motionless. My father advanced.

"Come — come!" I urged wildly. "He does not see us yet. He"—

But now he had seen us. And as he did so a great recognizing start showed itself in both his frame and face. He abruptly paused. And then, very suddenly and swiftly, he darted forward, straight in our direction.

"Mamma!" I cried. "Do not stand still like this! Hurry away." I dragged at her hand, but she did not move. Was it terror that made her so spellbound? Or was it something far different from terror?

My father was now rushing forward at headlong pace.

VI.

HE reached us a little later. His eyes blazed with wrath; his face was white. He held something in his right hand, which I could not see. He caught my mother's arm with his left hand. He did not speak; he stood for a few seconds breathing so that I could hear him breathe.

"Leopold!" gasped my mother. I think that was all she said; if she spoke another word I cannot recall it. I still clutched her hand. And then, with my flesh like ice, I saw him strike at her with what he held. I saw no flash of a knife. He struck toward her throat, on the left side. The blow meant death; it had severed a great vein; the blood gushed in torrents. My mother tore her fingers from my mad hold. In an instant the sidewalk about us was one crimson pool. She reeled and staggered, but as she did so he kept her with one arm from falling, and then I perceived that he had a slim, keen knife, for he suddenly plunged it several times into his own breast. My mother and he both fell an instant later. . . . I cannot record what I now did. The street swam about me; the noises of the passing

carts grew a fierce thunder. People thronged up
on every side; it seemed to me as if their number
was an untold legion. The tumult, the clamor,
had in it, to my distracted sense, an almost infinite fury. The whole experience was like some
ghastly dream of hell. I strive now calmly to
review it all, and wholly fail to pierce the lurid
fog of my own bewilderment. I only remember
that I was not unconscious. If I had really fainted,
the impression of uproar, of pressing faces and
jostling forms, of excited shrieks and garish publicity would have proved far less distinct. It
seems to me that I sank upon my knees. A hundred questions in a hundred different voices beset
me, but I could neither answer nor understand
one. Not that I failed to realize what had passed.
I realized it, indeed, with so thrilling an acuteness
that all other sense was for the time blurred and
weak. Mine was the very paralysis of horror.
And yet, strangely enough, my thought, so im-
potent in other ways, flashed backward through
certain previous events. This frightful thing
seemed the fulfilment of dire prophecy, the con-
summation to which horrid omens had pointed.
My regret became one terrific enormity; it ceased
merely to fill consciousness; it was consciousness
itself — the air I breathed, the surrounding multitude, the sunshine, the day, the busy city. I
fancy that words of a wild and wailing sort must
have left my lips. The unearthly crime might

have been averted; I had known and dreaded the danger; all four of us had known it and dreaded it; this formulated the anguish of my despair. It need not have happened! In that one sentence might have been condensed the whole dark volume of my suffering. We constantly speak of pain as something wholly separable from ourselves, like a scorpion or insect that clings to us but of which in time we may be rid. In that supreme interval I had no such feeling. Between my torture and myself there lay no boundary. All was one incarnate agony; every pulse of my heart meant a pang; every throb of my brain dealt a blow.

It is marvellous that I lived. If this tensity of mental strain had lasted a few minutes longer I have now no doubt that death would have ended it. But torpors like these, which are a death-in-life, tax and goad each nerve, fibre and organ to fling them off, and it is when we fail in this that we die. My own relief came in a storm of tears. When I began to sob and tremble I was saved. Nature had fought for me and saved me. But until later I did not know at what cost!

Someone tried to raise me, but I struggled and would not stand. My mother's white face, peaceful and with closed eyes, had dawned upon me. I leaned toward it and touched its cheek, still warm in death. Then I drew backward with a horrible cry. My own hand, from contact with my ensanguined garments, had left a blood-red mark. I heard my own shriek. . . I can hear it now. "Take him away!" shouted a voice. "No, no," exclaimed other voices. "Wait for the police — he knows who they all three are — he'll be needed," sounded next from the close-packed bystanders.

Then a pell-mell of questions once more assailed me. I answered some of them as best I could. I had now risen. To left and right of me stretched one great sea of heads. Two or three sturdy men kept the crowd back from the fallen bodies. Plaintive voices rang from many of the women. My father's face was obscured; he lay so that it came in contact with the pavement. I don't know how many times I heard it called and shrieked and moaned and muttered all about me that he had killed her first and then killed himself. Now and again a bit of humor would lend its baleful discord to the din of the mob, and a kind of laughter greeted it, that was like a shudder put into sound. These outbursts were perhaps less barbarous than hysterical; mirth is sometimes a sort of treble note to the deeper bass of sorrow and affright. I cannot believe that there was a single spirit, no matter how hardened, in all this motley congress of gazers, untouched by pity for myself and her.

It seemed an eternity before the police came. Several women had begun not only to murmur fresh queries in my ears but to caress and offer me soothing words. I must have told one of these my address, though I do not recall what responses I made any of them. At length two policemen pushed roughly through the dividing crowd. The sheen of their buttons and their up-lifted clubs made me start and cower; the coming of these men turned a new and merciless glare upon my woe. I heard gruff tones quite near me say something in which I caught the word "am-bulance." . . But even then a singing had crept into my ears that grew louder each instant, and the pavement seemed to drop away from the soles of my feet, while all the dense concourse of men and women began to whirl giddily in vague tur-moil. Then came a blank. . . I had fainted.

I awoke in my chamber at home. Martha was bending over me. I at once recognized her. There was a light in the room as of waning after-noon. She spoke my name softly in her familiar voice. I had no memory of what had happened to my mother, but I was under a vague conviction that I myself had met some sharp injury.

"Where is mamma?" I asked. "Does she know that I am hurt?"

And then Martha seemed to melt away, and Michael took her place at my bedside. Possibly this was all real enough. But after I had watched Michael a few moments, his gaunt form and dear, grim face vanished, and I clearly saw my mother.

She hummed an air, and appeared quite her wonted self. But there was a reddish mark on one of her cheeks, and I reached forth my hand to brush it away. Then her shape receded, and a great drowsiness came upon me. . . .

But after that I had many episodes of wakefulness, which impressed me dimly (for everything was now dim as a dream) that they extended through days, weeks, even months. Some of my visions were appalling; others were tranquil enough and even pleasant. It was all the changeful phantasmagoria of continued delirium. My distempered brain was like a blank wall on whose surface a magic-lantern causes image after image to gleam. The mysterious master of these weird revels plied his task with incessant zeal. I will not describe either the sombre or cheerful phases of my hallucinations; some of them were the fit kindred of frenzy, others wore the spell of calm and ease. I can recollect no special period at which the dawn of sanity showed its first ray. When I became aware of the walls that enclosed me, the bed in which I rested, the details of my apartment, the hands that served me, the tangible and human shapes that came and went, the very taste of the draughts put between my lips, all had somehow acquired an air of previous acquaintance. The change from dementia to reason had doubtless been one of slow and irregular progress. I was afterward told that I would lie for hours with every rational sign in my look, and would not seldom utter sentences that betokened lucid faculties. Then the cloud would wrap me again, as a mist wraps a shore. It had been at first a fiery fever of the brain, but the fever had now passed, and an organic mania was feared. Still, my aberrations became of less frequent recurrence, and hope of my full recovery strengthened in those who watched me.

"You are better, Otho, are you not?" said a voice at my side, very softly, one day. The voice spoke in French, but this did not strike me as at all strange. I had heard it many times before near my bed, lower, and using the same language to a tall, placid female attendant.

"Yes," I said. "Everything is much clearer now. Has it been a long time?"

"Since you were ill? Oh, not so very long. Do you know me, Otho?"

"Oh, yes," I answered. "One day . . . was it yesterday, or many days ago? . . . you came quite close to the bed and I thought you were mamma — or her poor ghost. But then I looked at you again, and I knew. You are Mrs. Dorian."

The lady pressed her lips against my cheeks. "So, then," she faltered, "you remember that your poor mamma" . . .

She paused, and I said: "Yes, yes; I remember. I have seen it all, over and over and over in my dreams. Were they dreams, madame, or were they . . . ?" I did not know just what word to choose, and a soft hand was laid upon my lips, then, while another smoothed my temples.

"They were dreams — ugly dreams, my son. You must think no longer of them; you will get quite well if you have a little more courage, a little more patience. And we have talked enough to-day. To-morrow we will talk again."

Through a good many morrows, before I was able to leave my bed, we did talk. These conversations, at first very brief, were afterward prolonged according as my renewed health would permit. And finally, when I was strong enough to move about the comfortable house in Lafayette Place and even to accompany my protectress in her carriage during long, agreeable drives, the moment came for me to confront another great sorrow. I had asked, for almost the twentieth time, why neither Michael nor Martha ever visited me, and always had been answered in some cleverly deceptive way. But the truth had to transpire at last. Mrs. Dorian told it me as we sat together in her own large, airy room, which overlooked the broad street below. It was latter November, now; it had been early May when the illness fell upon me. I gazed out upon the mellowest of Indian summer days. We had taken a drive into the country, that morning, and had seen the dismantled trees rising round us in so golden and bland an air that we almost wondered new buds did not start from their dark branches. I did not feel at all tired after my drive, though I leaned back in a great easy-chair near one of the windows, more through an old lingering habit of convalescence than because of the least fatigue. The light outside had lost its sunny fervor; this autumn day, all too short, would soon reach its dusky limit. Often, of late, my moods had been melancholy ones; but now there was a tender luxury in the sadness I felt, like the dreamy repose of the exquisite season, pride and charm of our American year. A window at some little distance off was half open; the roll of wheels, louder on this account, brought us their fitful reverberations, full of the stir yet not the jar of life, amid so much drowsy atmospheric peace. Opposite me the high roofs of houses almost merged their outlines in the hazy blue of the sky. No word had passed between Mrs. Dorian and myself for several minutes. I knew that her eyes had been stealing more than once to watch my face, above the embroidery that busied her. But I had grown well used to this covert scrutiny. Bodily weakness had before made me passively accept all her care and vigilance; but now its devotion was a perpetual shield against the keener grief of loneliness than my mother's loss must have dealt. Then, too, the effect of a changeful, ever-recurring resemblance — of a sameness blent with a difference, in attitude, movement, expression — was not without its gracious comforts, for all that it brought constant living and fading souvenirs of the dead.

I broke the silence that had come between us. "You never told me where poor mamma is buried," I said.

"In Woodlawn, Otho. It is a lovely cemetery, not very far away. Some day we might drive out there — or we could go by train."

"You had her buried there?"

"Yes. I bought a little plot of ground. Some day — many years from now, I hope — you may lie there at her side. And perhaps your wife and children, if you marry, also."

"You are so good — so wonderfully good," I murmured. "Often, when I think of it, I ask myself if there are many people in the world with your kind heart. You sought for me there at Michael's house in the Bowery; you had me taken here; you have nursed and tended me ever since, with all the regard that my own mother would have shown — except that she, poor soul, could not have done half what you have done, not having your wealth. . . Still, it cannot last forever, this goodness, madame."

"Last forever?" she said, starting. "Why, Otho, I have been on the verge of telling you, for some days past, what will no doubt surprise you. So, now, you force me to tell it at once. I want to go abroad with you and stay for a long time — stay till your education is finished."

She had thrown aside her work, and had drawn much closer to me. I smiled, and the tears filled my eyes. She bent down and kissed me on the forehead.

"Oh, you have the face of an angel, *mon petit*, do you know it?" And when you smile like that you make this world-worn old heart of mine tremble. You were born to be loved! I believe in Heaven when I am near you, and I believe that Heaven has sent you to me for my own sweet son in my childless old age. I was forty-four my last birthday. When you are grown up I shall be in spectacles and a cap. No; not a cap — I detest them; they are a voluntary surrender to old age, which I shall fight against, tooth and nail, till it crushes me. *Tiens;* we will go abroad next month — to Paris, and afterward to Switzerland."

"Next month?" I said, astonished yet deeply pleased.

"Yes. It will be dreadful to cross in December, I know. I shall be ill the whole way. I always am, unless the ocean is like a mill-pond. But since you last heard me talk of my affairs I have accomplished an immense change. I have consigned the whole business of Dorian & Company to a brother of my late husband — Mr. Steven Dorian. It is what one calls here "selling out." I have received a great sum of money; my brother-in-law has raised it with the aid of other capitalists, though the name of the firm, now representing his own interest and not mine, continues more suitably the same as before. Well, I thank my lucky stars that I am so well rid of future trouble. They say I should have got six millions instead of three. Bah! it is absurd. What can one not do with three millions? One can surely dwell happily abroad for years — and that is what I intend. You see, poor old Gredge expired one fine morning, quite suddenly. Do you recollect how I told your mamma about Gredge? Well, after he had gone, my reputation as a woman of finance hung trembling in the balance. I was very fortunate to escape when I did. And now, at last, I am free. My money has been safely invested by my lawyers, and I can go where I please."

I reflected for a moment after my companion had ceased to speak. And then I answered, slowly shaking my head: "You offer to take me with you, but is it right that I should desert Michael and Martha, who saved mamma and me from starvation, and who love me still very dearly, I am sure, though I have not seen either of them for so long?"

Mrs. Dorian rose with startling haste. My look followed her as she moved about the room. I thought at first that she was in quest of something, and asked myself if it could be a message from one or both of my still-treasured friends. But a little later she again approached me. Her eyes were sparkling, and her lips quivered. She sank into her former seat, and as she searched my face I saw that her own was filled with agitation.

"Otho," she said brokenly, and in tones that scarcely seemed hers, "I — I would not have you here with me now, my son, if — if they were there still.   Yes, that is why you are here!"

"What do you mean?" I cried anxiously. "Have they gone?"

She bowed her head before my eager glance. "Yes, my dear boy, they have gone," she almost whispered.

But in another instant, as though urged by the impulse to employ self-control where weakness would be worse than impolitic, she laid one hand upon my shoulder and looked at me steadily, calmly.

"Otho, I must tell you now, for you are strong enough to hear it, and of course you have the sad right — you of all others — to hear it all. You will never — (oh, try to bear it bravely, my dear boy!) you will never see those kind friends of yours again."

"They are dead," I murmured, as if to myself. She put both arms about my neck, then, and rested her head on my shoulder. I felt my heart go out to her for that simple embrace; it was so like what my dead mother's would have been, if she had been telling me the same sorrowful tidings.

I asked no further questions, but waited in

silence. I knew that she would presently speak. The first force of the shock was over when she did speak. Not a word of what she now said was lost.

"When I found you they were both with you. I had read in the newspapers what happened. Your name did not occur in the accounts, but it was mentioned that you had been taken in an unconscious state to your mother's residence, and this was given. Recalling my own experience in the past, I was made literally ill for several days by what I read. But as soon as it was possible, I went to seek you. Your sweet face had always haunted me ever since you had come to this house, a few months before, with your unhappy mother. I felt as if some hidden power were pushing me toward you; I had seen you in my sleep stretching out your arms to me for help. I did not tell anyone that I went. People would have called it one of my queer freaks; to have a sentiment, to go out of the beaten rut of commonplace, is always to be accused of a queer freak; and my list is already so large in the eyes of my American friends that I do not care to increase it. Well, I found you. You were burning up with fever, and the two watchers at your bedside were half-crazed with what had befallen your mother. I offered to take you here. At first they refused to let you go. Then my arguments prevailed with them. I promised that you should have the best of nursing, the most skilled of doctors, and that they could visit you whenever they wished. I told them, too, of how you and your mother had already sought me, and how I had then offered you both whatever aid I could bestow in the future. Well, as I said, they consented. I had you brought here in my carriage. Florine, the professional nurse whom I had procured, and whom you now know so well, assisted me. That night you lay in my house. Martha came the next day. Then for several days she remained absent. Smallpox had broken out here in the city, and for two months, during the heat of the summer, it raged with much violence. That part of the Bowery where you had lived, and a few other adjacent streets, were the quarters most infested by the horrid scourge. I thought that I understood what Martha's and Michael's absence meant. At last, while you were still very ill, I began to pity them. Florine had no fear of the contagion and was willing to seek them out. I sent her to them with a letter. But . . she could not find them, Otho — she never found them. That row of houses in which you lived had numbered its victims by scores, and many had been taken away by the health authorities, never to return. Your two friends had been among the first whom the disease attacked, and neither of them had recovered. They were buried as those who die that way are nearly always buried, obscurely, and with only an official report of their deaths." . . . .

I lay awake for two or three hours, that night, thinking of my lost friends. There might have been peril to my reason in this news of their double taking-off, but for the persistent recollection of that later friend whom fate had dropped to me from the stars. I have since then asked myself whether Michael and Martha would either of them have consented to the departure that soon followed — whether their love, sharpened and made more fondly clinging by their bereavement, would not have opposed a separation of years. Ah! doubtless they would have seen too clearly that it was best for me to leave them, and in the end have bid me farewell with aching hearts! Well, at least they have been spared that one trial, peace rest them both! I did not care for them as they cared for me. I felt it while I lay awake that night and thought of them. It stung me with self-reproach, for intelligence and imagination made the rugged and homely sweetness of their love very clear to me, and always afterward, equally through the press and clash of events or the drift and strain of mental action, it has remained with me like some bit of moving pastoral verse which we lay between the leaves of a portfolio rich in wiser and more polished lines. . . .

"I feel that you are entirely mine, now," said Mrs. Dorian, as we drove together, on the following day. She used a mingling of the arch and the tender, while she thus spoke, which was always one of her most attractive phases. "Do you know, dear Otho, that I had serious thoughts of adopting a child before I ever saw you? I had hesitated between a girl and a boy, but I had finally decided on the latter. Girls, if clever, rarely grow up to be handsome, and if they are both, then a husband steals them from us before they are twenty. Besides, they are so much less interesting, and they involve so much more anxiety and watchfulness."

"How did you know that I was clever?" I asked.

"Superb!" exclaimed Mrs. Dorian, with a laugh. "You take it for granted not only that I thought so but that you are. Well, I am sure of it already; but you must keep convincing me, all the same."

"Madame," I now said, very seriously, "I have always heard that when a child is adopted by a person like yourself, great care is taken to know whether or not he comes of a race that has been of good repute. Now, in the case of myself, this is not true. There is a stain, a dreadful stain upon my name. And yet you are willing to forget this. But will others forget it? Will not the shame pursue me all through my life? Can I ever wash away the mark of the blood which my father shed? It is no blame of my own, yet will they not always hold it to be one?"

" Otho, what are you saying ? "

" I remember a boy in school whose father had been a thief. I think he had been shot by some one as a burglar. Another boy knew this, and told it to the rest, and they were forever taunting and teasing him."

" Otho," replied my new guardian, most earnestly and gently, " there is truth in what you say. Hundreds of voices would be raised against me if it were known what I have really done. But the shame which you have had no share in, and which indeed would pursue you through life if I had not driven away the shadow of it, makes you dearer and more winning. I shall not deny that your beauty, your French blood, and your natural sweetness of manner have had much to do with my choice and decision. But there is another motive . . perhaps you are too young to understand it . . and yet you seem to understand all that I say. Anyone can perform an act of charity ; but to turn the tide of a human fate by such an act — that is different. That gives me what I call one of my impressions ; and it is an impression that will last, because while I watch your life unfold, leaf by leaf, like a flower, it will divert me with its constant variety."

" I do not think that I understand you now, madame," I said dubiously.

She laughed, but without her usual buoyancy. " Some day you will, and that day is not far off ;

for your mind has a rare quickness, and the malady through which it has passed leaves no apparent trace."

"But I resemble *him*. You said so when mamma and I visited you together."

She turned and scanned my face closely in the carriage. "He was very handsome," she answered.

"But he was a murderer." . . I almost whispered the words.

She took my hand, pressing it. "You are not really like him, Otho. It is only that one can see he was your father after seeing you both. And since your illness you have become much more like your mother — strangely like."

"I am glad of that." And then I added, frankly, "I am glad for two reasons. The first you know. The second is because I must also resemble you."

"What a delicious little turn you give to your compliment!" she softly cried. "Ah, it is easy to tell that you are half a Frenchman!" And now, much more seriously, she went on: "I have conceived a plan, and by means of it I shall throw dust in all eyes. Your name shall henceforth be Otho Claud. You see, I change Clauss to Claud; the change is slight, but it will serve admirably. You are the only son of an old school-friend of mine, who married in Belgium. I have chosen Belgium because one meets so many different nationalities there, and in Paris I am well known.

Just before her death, my friend wrote me, in poverty and widowhood, begging that I would render you some assistance when she herself was no more. I consented; she died in Brussels, and you were sent to me. I went to meet you at the steamer-wharf. The voyage had been a rough one — extremely rough for April — and as your health was very delicate when you started, seasickness developed in you a terrible illness. *Voila!* . . you have now recovered: you are quite well. Meanwhile I have fallen in love with you; I have made you my adopted son. Is not that a charming falsehood?"

Her face was wreathed in smiles as I now watched it. When I knew her better and comprehended more fully her volatile, romantic, Bohemian nature, I could perceive just how and why she exulted in the loving and daring deception that she had used. But as it was, I said gravely:

"No falsehood can be charming, madame — or . so I have been taught."

"And you have been taught rightly!" she exclaimed. "But here is the grand exception which proves the rule. I evade for myself and you all the *scandale publique* that might follow. No one dreams of the truth. Stay — there is that stupid, honest Florine, who was your nurse. She went with me when I took you from your home. But she is already paid and discharged. I paid her twice what was due, by the way, and preached her a little parting sermon against the evil of any idle *bavarderies.* She is perfectly safe, is dull old Florine; it is like burying one's secret in a vault. So, now, you are Otho Claud. My brother-in-law, Mr. Steven Dorian, believes just what I have told him. You and he may meet in a day or two. He has expressed a desire to see you. It can hardly be avoided, since we sail for Europe so soon. He has a son, Foulke Dorian, a boy of about your own age. I have always mildly abominated Master Foulke; I can scarcely tell why, except it be that he is so like his father, who in turn is so like my late husband. Some day I will describe my late husband to you — when you are older, I mean. It would make you laugh then more than it would now." Here my companion heaved a great sigh. "The match was one of those horrid French affairs, forced upon me by my dead papa; it was the only really unkind thing papa ever did. I disagreed with *monsieur mon mari* on every possible subject except one — his remarkable knowledge of silks; and on this point I was comparatively ignorant. We used to average six quarrels a week; Sunday was a day of truce; Mr. Dorian was a person of much piety. Besides, we had to take breath, as it were, for the coming series of skirmishes. . . . But about my brother-in-law, my dear Otho — Monsieur Steven, as I always call him. He may ask you a few questions concerning your former home. He will not do it suspiciously; he suspects nothing.

But you must be guarded, that is all, in your answers."

"How can I answer anything?" I exclaimed. "I know nothing of Brussels, except that it is the capital of Belgium and situated on the River Senne. That I learned at school."

"Admirable, my dear! You don't want to know anything more. I shall be near you — never fear. I will turn all your silences to good account. And perhaps Monsieur Steven will ask you no questions whatever. We shall see."

Before we reached home, that afternoon, I made a direct inquiry concerning my father. It was the first time I had done so; a deep repugnance had thus far sealed my lips. "Do you know where they buried him, madame?" I said.

Mrs. Dorian looked at me with a sudden strong consternation. Her face crimsoned, and then grew pale. "I — I do not know," she presently stammered. "I — I never made any attempt to find out."

Her evident disarray of manner I swiftly explained to myself on the ground of sympathy. This the sole interpretation I could give it, appeared to me a wholly proper one. "I felt sure," was my answer, "that you had not let him lie at mamma's side. There would have been something horrible to me in that. I should have dreamed of him as resting uneasy in his grave because the other dead were so near her in that beautiful cemetery you told me of."

"Oh, Otho, what a strange idea!"

"I cannot even think of him as dead without also thinking of him as still jealous."

"No wonder, my poor boy!"

"And it was so much better," I pursued, "that he should have killed himself when he killed her. There was less disgrace in that. I shall feel the shame less on account of it. He was not one of those murderers who wish merely to destroy others and then escape themselves. Besides" . . I paused, here, and no doubt I showed the shudder that crept through me.

"Besides?" Mrs. Dorian queried.

"There would have been the frightful scaffold, the execution, and all that. For the law would have found no excuse for him, I suppose?"

"Oh, none," said my companion. She spoke much lower than usual. A gloom had fallen upon her which lasted until we had nearly reached home, when she made a gay feint of wearing her accustomed spirits. But I somehow saw through her deception, and began to wonder at it.

The servant who admitted us, that afternoon, told Mrs. Dorian that her brother-in-law and his son were then in the drawing-room, waiting her return. My guardian soon glanced at me. "We had better go in together," she said. And in a lower voice, so that the servant could not hear, she added: "There will be no danger, trust me."

My heart beat a little quicker as I now went

into the drawing-room at Mrs. Dorian's side. A gentleman and boy rose to meet us. Mrs. Dorian presented me.

"This is Otho Claud, of whom I told you, Monsieur Steven," she said to her brother-in-law. Then she made me acquainted with her nephew. "This is Foulke Dorian, Otho, of whom you have heard me speak."

I shook hands silently with both. Mr. Steven Dorian was tall, with a perfectly smooth-shaven face, a nose that described an impressive arch, and a pair of bluish, milky eyes. He was scrupulously neat in his dress; his slim neck was incased in a stock and he wore a fob after the fashion of still earlier days than those. Everything about him expressed precision, accuracy, deliberation. His movements were slow, and awkward enough to suggest a sort of defective physical hingeing. He was lank and ungainly enough to make you think that nature must have set herself some such difficult scheme in his creation as to produce a being without a single actual deformity yet homelier than if he had possessed more than one. His son, Foulke, had a better build, and a touch of boyish grace in pose and gesture; but the lad's face was so freckled that its effect was almost nebulous, like that of a very blurred photographic negative.

Mrs. Dorian and her brother-in-law talked together for some little time, and Foulke Dorian and I sat furtively gazing at each other in shy silence, as boys will so often do. I had begun to hope that Mr. Dorian would offer no comment regarding myself, when he rather abruptly turned his lack-lustre eyes upon my face and said:

"Like America?"

"Yes, sir," I answered, coloring hotly.

"He very seldom speaks of his life in Brussels," said Mrs. Dorian rapidly to her brother-in-law, and in a voice just loud enough for me to catch her words. "That is only natural, I suppose. The poor boy has had so much trouble there."

"Guess he's pretty smart," said Mr. Dorian. His tones were nasal, and as he scrutinized me he had an air of sombre calculation, as if he were deciding upon my suitability for a page or messenger. Nearly all his sentences were somehow elliptical, and he always ignored his personal pronouns when their avoidance was feasible. "Got a good head, and bright eyes. S'pose you'll put him to school on the other side; eh?"

"Oh, of course," said Mrs. Dorian. I thought that I was now rid of further conversational attacks from her brother-in-law, when he again addressed me.

"'Tlantic ocean a pretty big pond to cross, sonny; isn't that so?"

"Yes, sir," I said, my color deepening.

"S'pose you don't want to go over so soon again; eh?"

I thought the rayless eyes were fixed on me with something suspicious in their gleam, unfounded as may have been this fear. I grew so confused that I could have scarcely given a rational reply, when Master Foulke struck in, half-bashfully:

"I ain't 'fraid of the ocean a bit. I wish I was going. I like sailing."

"Do you, Foulke?" said Mrs. Dorian, quite volubly. "Well, your papa ought to take you." She now turned to Foulke's father. "Otho is very willing to cross this time," she went on. "He is in much better health than formerly, you know. I hope it will do him good."

"Sail a week from Saturday?" asked Mr. Dorian, as if he had already learned when our departure would occur.

"Yes," said Mrs. Dorian, and then she named our steamer.

Her brother-in-law looked down, studying the carpet. "Good ship. No better afloat nowadays." He raised his head. In his measured, loitering way he continued: "That German scamp, Clauss, is going to be hanged next Friday. Serves the villain right, too. You ought to think so. S'pose you do; eh?"

I felt a great thrill creep through me. I turned my look upon Mrs. Dorian. She did not respond to it.

"I — I would rather not speak of that," I heard

her say. But her voice sounded far off. I knew that I was growing pale. No one appeared to notice me.

"Been quicker work than usual in New-York this time," proceeded Mr. Dorian, disregarding his relative's last words. "Such an aggravated case of brutality, you see. Wish they'd lynched the ruffian. Can't somehow get over thinking, Louise, that he might be going to swing, next Friday, for you instead of her."

Mrs. Dorian had risen and slipped to my side before the final sentence was ended. She put her arms about me. "You are not well, Otho," she exclaimed. "Our long drive has been too much for you. Come up-stairs, my dear. . . Excuse me, Monsieur Steven," she hurried on, drawing me with her to the nearest doorway, and supporting me under one arm. "I will return presently. I have got to know my pet boy so well; a mere glance at him tells me when his faint turns are coming on."

We passed together into the outer hall. My steps were very feeble as I ascended the stairs, still supported by my companion. At about half way in our assent my lips began to move almost mechanically, and I spoke in a low, terrified whisper:

"He is not dead. He — he lives, and they are to hang him next Friday . . next Friday. They are to hang him for killing *her*."

When we had reached one of the upper chambers I sank, trembling violently, upon a lounge. Mrs. Dorian bent over me now, with a look of keenest anxiety and pain.

VII.

She presently spoke. "Otho, you must not think me to blame for deceiving you! It was far best that you should never know. But for this unfortunate chance you might never have known. I am so bitterly sorry! You have had so much to bear, *pauvre petit!* It is just like that odious Monsieur Steven to spoil everything. Of course he did it innocently enough, but whether he makes himself a nuisance innocently or no, I find that he makes himself one, quite the same."

"You should have told me, madame," I said drearily.

"And caused you more sorrow, my Otho? Ah, do you know that I fairly took joy in my secret! I would have given a great sum to keep the truth from you; at least . . until all was over."

"He did not die, then, after he stabbed himself?"

"No. Ah, if only he had died! His life hung by a thread for several days. Then he began to recover, cursing himself that he still lived, and closely guarded lest he should attempt his life again. His conviction soon followed his trial.

But certain highly merciful people wanted to have him acquitted on the ground of insanity. Your evidence on this point was desired, and for several weeks I knew that you were being searched for. But poor Michael and Martha were no more, and you had been taken away so quietly, just at twilight, from your former home, that your departure was scarcely noticed in the neighborhood. Still, certain people had noticed it, and I think that if the crime had not been so glaring and shocking a one, and if popular wrath had not been so hot against him, they might have postponed the trial until greater effort had resulted in your discovery."

"I should never have testified to his insanity," I said. "That would have been false. Or, if mad, he was still mad in a punishable way."

"Your father, during the trial, was composed, moody and defiant. He pleaded guilty. And when, after speedy conviction, the sentence was pronounced upon him and the judge allowed him to speak, his declarations regarding your mother were full of invective and scorn. He openly exulted in the dark deed he had committed, and also expressed himself most willing, even anxious, to die, now that he had dealt proper punishment to one who had foully deserted him. The judge then asked him if he had no faith in a hereafter, and he replied savagely that he believed this world a hell in which we were made to suffer for sins done elsewhere. Those who have had charge of him since his sentence, Otho, assert that he eagerly awaits death. . . Oh, why should you feel pain or regret for one so wretchedly hardened? Think of yourself henceforward only as *her* son, not as his." . . .

I tried to do so, but the brand of disgrace was nevertheless burned into my heart the same. Those ensuing days, up to the time of the execution, and after it as well, were shadowed with a fearful gloom. When the fatal day itself arrived, Mrs. Dorian watched me in ill-hid perturbation, and I was sure that she had misgivings lest I should succumb to a relapse of my former ailment. But for the stay and help of her presence I might indeed have done so. When all was over she told me of how Leopold Clauss had paid the dismal debt which he owed to his fellow-men, but she permitted no printed account of the execution to reach my hands. He had died with stolid calm, never once flinching as he ascended the scaffold, nor showing a trace of weakness while he met his doom.

During this most mournful and bitter period of my life I was not without a sense of consolation and thanksgiving. The worse woe from which my protectress had snatched me seemed like some direct Heavenly intercession. My knowledge of the world about me was not so limited but that I could more than partially estimate the rarity of. my present position. The caprice of an eccentric foreign lady had completely altered my future.

Thus would have run the general popular comment, deciding that I was one in many thousands. But this conclusion would have been unfair. Mrs. Dorian had countless caprices, and yet the sentiment which I had inspired deserved a graver term. A more conventional woman would have repressed such an emotion as hers. A woman of daintier calibre would have shrunk from my possible inherited faults. A woman of less bold imagination and less vital sympathies would have found in my sombre antecedents a reason for clothing her pity impersonally, and have made it, if regarded at all, a mere benevolent act of alms. But Mrs. Dorian, who loved to gratify her whims, had fearlessly faced the emergency of a much more serious impulse. The shadow of the scaffold bathed me; the stigma of an atrocious crime marked me; I was a human waif which might be swept into that black whirlpool of degradation ever ready for such helpless outcasts. It delighted her to snatch me as a brand from the burning. It delighted her to become my rescue, my salvation, my lucky accident, my star of good omen, my destiny, my personified fate. Her love for me was wholly spontaneous and natural. I had charmed her from the first hour that she had seen me, and the spell of this charm deepened during my weeks of bodily peril, and grew a fascination while recovery slowly buoyed me through convalescence to regained health. I do not know what I did or said to make her so tenderly fond of me. In the after years of our intercourse I have never known. We sometimes hear of crafty adventurers winning with all sorts of clever guile what I had won without an effort. But I am certain that my guardian would have been proof against any such wily siege in one of older years. She had no ready credence for the strategic and plausible, and she was by no means blind to the stolid material vantage which any one who sought her special favor might count upon securing. Her estimate of character was rapid and usually correct. I have sometimes fancied that she gave freer rein to her instincts because of a self-reliant certainty that they could never land her in any awkward swamps or fens. The foot that treads carefully often does so from muscular frailty, and they who walk through life with a lax gait are not always the most easily tripped.

She assured me that she had no cause to fear I had roused the slightest suspicion in Mr. Steven Dorian. "Not that he isn't quite capable of having it about anyone at a moment's notice," she frankly allowed. "He is the sort of person who feeds on distrust of everybody, and I question whether he has ever given a fellow-creature credit for a single unselfish motive. He has been in the silk trade all his life, just as my late husband was. I suppose there is a slippery smoothness about silk that makes the continual handling of it morally hurtful, as if one were always on his guard against oily rogues. He has an idea that I should adopt his boy, Foulke, as my heir, which is purely absurd. What horrid thing have I thus far done in my life that I should be forced to gaze continually upon that firmament of freckles? I should always, in a morbidly nervous way, be trying to count them. Besides, I have blood-relations of my own in France, as far as that goes, and Foulke will probably get a large heritage from his father."

Our steamer sailed so early that none of Mrs. Dorian's friends were at the wharf to bid her farewell. I was glad, for obvious reasons, that neither Mr. Steven Dorian nor his son appeared. I left America with a sad exultation. As her shores receded from my gaze I saw them through tears rather of reproach than regret. What had this land brought me but sorrow and heart-breaking? There lay the dishonor, the infamy of my fatherhood. Why should it not abide there forever, with an ocean between itself and me? A new life was promised me in those unseen eastern lands, of whose art and poetry and precious antiquity I was not altogether ignorant. Far best I should never return!

And these feelings were of long duration. I had thus far seen only what was darkest and most painful in American life; I now saw what was most brilliant and alluring in European. Before placing me at school in Geneva, my friend showed me nearly every country in Europe. We trav-

elled almost *en prince ;* we had our courier, our
servants, our conveniences and luxuries. I drank
deep draughts of peace ; the baneful past lost for
me its raw, flaring tinge ; new association drew a
kindly haze across it, till the retrospective picture
looked as dim as some of those old faded tapestries
in the galleries which we visited. My altered
conditions of living were assumed with slight con-
straint or awkwardness. I had no vulgarities to
live down, either in speech or deportment; my
careful and patient mother had never lost her
own sense of these niceties, and to myself they
came as an unconscious dower. It was strange
with what ease I filled my present place ; it was
like finding a costly garment, quietly putting it
on, and perceiving the fit to be excellent. Sometimes the intense unreality of my fortunes would
confront and impress me; the widening scope of
my own experiences, as I stood before some great
statue in Rome, or watched some masterpiece of
painting in Florence, would bring me a bewildered
thrill. What gulfs of difference lay between our
sumptuous Parisian apartments, whence one could
see that glorious Arc de Triomphe, that mighty
sweep of the Place de la Concorde, and the little
suburban dwelling near the huge black rock, or
the solemn Bowery undertaker's shop, with its
satin-lined coffin in the window and its two or
three tiny upstairs bedrooms !

.   .   .   .

But of all parts of Europe Switzerland became my passion, and ever afterward remained so. Often Mrs. Dorian would leave me for months at a time while I was at school; in nearly all the great capitals she had friends — artists, poets, painters, men of exceptional talent in a hundred ways, whom her vivacious mind and glittering originalities attracted quite as much as the liberal patronage of her purse. At these times, if the season permitted, I would join mountaineering parties and ascend peaks which it horrified her to hear one even speak of attempting. I shall never forget the glow, the vivid delight, the sense of aspiration and achievement which belonged to those expeditions. Switzerland is, to my thinking, the one divine poem of earth. No other land mingles in just the same way sweetness and majesty, grace and grandeur. The irresistible and eternal charm of Switzerland is like that of certain women in whom have lain the secrets of untold allurement; they have been wise, witty, astute, winsomely saintlike or even enticingly the opposite, but they have never lost, with it all, a certain novelty and distinction. Switzerland has every phase of sublimity, but she has never once forgotten to be beautiful as well, and it is this that makes her perpetually interesting.

Mrs. Dorian would give little shrieks when I told her of my Alpine exploits. She pretended to think them desperately foolhardy, but I suspected that she took secret pride in my making them. I was very well aware that she took much open pride in my academic success; this was the sort of mountain-climbing which won her complete sanction. My career at school was brilliant; all tasks were the same to me in point of easy mastery. I would often marvel at the toil which my mates would spend upon their lessons; it was only now and then that some knotty point would puzzle me, and then a little stout effort usually made the path clear. From my Geneva school I passed easily into college at Zürich, whence, four years later on, I was graduated with the highest honors.

How well I remember the kiss of congratulation which Mrs. Dorian gave me when I first met her in Paris after this victory of scholarship had been secured! It was a delicious morning in early summer. I had been travelling all night long, but I felt as fresh and bright as though I had just risen, after an early retirement, from the elegant little bed in that enchanting suite of rooms which my guardian had already prepared for me. The window near which I sat commanded a view of the stately, massive Madeleine; a brisk, thrilling breeze blew along the gay boulevards; Paris, bathed in merry sunshine, promenaded, laughed, chatted, and aired all the captivations of her indolence. It was one of those days when you were only conscious of her as indolent, forgetting the thought, reflection, intellectuality which lie under her graceful filigree, like the solid oak under the delicate carvings which may adorn it.

"How wonderful and fascinating it all is here!" I exclaimed. "You don't know my delight in getting back."

"And you come like a conquering hero, my boy," said Mrs. Dorian blithely. "I don't know how many invitations I have for you already."

"We will accept none of them," I said. "We will do nothing except stroll about the streets during the daytime and visit the theatres at night. I positively burn for the theatres once more. That incomparable Français . . what are they playing there?"

But Mrs. Dorian (herself the centre of an admiring, amused, and wholly loyal clique, which consisted of nearly every known nationality and included not a few men and women of positive genius) was by no means satisfied with my unsocial announcement. She had been boasting of me for months past; the theatres could wait; one could always see them. But Monsieur A—— would soon depart with his portfolio for Scotland, and Madame B——would soon take her unfinished novel to Venice, that certain scenes in the last pages might be written there. And so on, in a tumult of protestation my guardian assured me that anything like personal privacy was at present not to be dreamed of. I dare say I had a much better time in permitting myself to be shown about as a prodigy, since the valiant nature of my exploits existed chiefly in the imagination of Mrs. Dorian, and I received a good deal of genial courtesy without the embarrassing homage that awaits a real hero.

This was my first experience of social life in any capital whatever. Perhaps for this reason — perhaps because of the specially attractive people gathered for a time under my guardian's little banner — it has always seemed to me the most agreeable of like experiences. Talent, in these salons which we visited, showed on every side of us. There was a great deal of wit, raillery, nonsense, and even gossip; but withal there was a great deal of sincerity and purpose. People were in earnest underneath all their lightsome, decorative trifling. In an instant many of them would change their talk from mirth to extreme seriousness. They were nearly all workers in the vineyard, though various were the sizes and flavors of their grapes.

"It is so much pleasanter than going about in the humdrum fashionable sets," Mrs. Dorian would say. "I can go there, if I choose, Otho; it is right that you should know this; I am more or less *dans le monde* here. But I detest it all. The rigors of etiquette stifle me. Besides, one can be Bohemian in Paris with so much more safety. In that dreadful New-York you must know the Amsterdams and the Manhattans or you are socially lost. But I am not quite sure that I am doing right in letting you meet only these clever yet unconventional people. You should occasionally be seen a little elsewhere. I was a De Lille, you know, and they are really Faubourg St. Germain people, the De Lilles. I shall look over my cards of invitation; we must go to a few of the patrician *soirées*, and then dip a little into the American colony."

"I should like very much to dip a little into the American colony," I said.

My old boyish feeling for my native land had wholly vanished. That ineradicable love which so few men have not felt, had put forth new buds and sprays. A great deal in America — viewed from the distance across which I gazed — struck me as lamentably crude and corrupt. To me, as to many European eyes, the young republic did not loom oversea a shape of classic splendor; she appeared almost pitiably to shiver in the nakedness wrought by hands which had seized her robe, to tear it afterward in pieces amid wrangling dispute. The great civil war had ended, and the assassination of Lincoln had turned to dust the first precious fruits of peace. I found myself following with zeal the transatlantic newspapers, and forming opinions regarding the proper policy to be maintained at Washington. Often I would smile over my own fervor. If ever a man should feel expatriated, such a man was I. So little but suffering had ever come to me from the soil of that other clime! So much of balsamic contentment had soothed and healed my wounds here; such treasures of education had fallen to me; such noble resources of art and culture lay close within my reach! And yet to the land of my birth, harsh and hard a foster-mother as she had been, I turned again and again with irrepressible fondness.

The season was hardly favorable for viewing much festal American life in Paris; but it chanced soon afterward that a certain Miss Potts gave a matrimonial dower of six million francs to an Italian prince of meagre purse and interminable pedigree. Miss Potts was a California girl, the daughter of a man who had begun in pauperism and ended as the sole owner of a silver mine. She was a peachy blonde, with the eyes of a fawn and the voice of a peacock. Mrs. Dorian was asked to this wedding, where the guests were a multitude, and she easily procured an invitation for me. I talked a while with the bride after congratulating her as she stood, a blaze of diamonds, at the side of her little prince, who had tawny skin and a short, black, crinkled beard, and whose features were all set close together, like those of a dryad. My reason for talking with Miss Potts (now the Princess Orsini, by the way, since the wedding-rites had been performed) was the simple one of knowing scarcely another person present. She quite astonished me by her civility, though I was becoming used to attention and interest on the part of women. Every now and then she would present somebody to the Prince, or address a remark to him, and always in the most execrable French. Meanwhile, in English not much less phenomenal, I was told what could not fail to amuse and surprise me.

"I guess, Mr. Claud, your ears must have tingled a good deal, lately, haven't they? I'm a married woman, now, and I can say things to a gepman that I couldn't before. I've seen you on the Bois, driving with Mrs. Dorian, ever so many times. I got so that I knew you by sight just as *well!* And now and then Ada Gramercey, or some other girl, would drive out along with me. Well, Mr. Claud, Ada paid you a perfectly elegant compliment, the other day — oh, it's three weeks ago, I guess, by this time. And Ada Gramercey is just the haughtiest *piece* about gepmen that you ever did come across. She's a Gramercey, you know, and her position in New-York is A number one — they move, there, in the very best s'ciety."

"Does this make her haughty to gentlemen?" I asked, for want of some more important remark.

The Princess laughed, and resumed her nasal, piping tones. "Oh, she's just as stuck up as ever she can be to nearly everybody. She kind of took a fancy to me, I guess, on the steamer; we came over together about a year ago. She says I amuse her."

"Princesses are generally amused by others," I ventured.

"Oh, gracious goodness!" cried the dazzling bride. "I don't feel a bit less like Susie Potts than I did an hour ago! Susan Potts Orsini — how does that sound? I'm going to write it out in full — yes, I am! And if he don't like it he can just *lump* it, that's all. . Where was I? Oh, yes. . . Why, Ada Gramercey ain't a bit proud that way. I don't b'lieve she'd 'a married Carlo, and just because they'd have said that she wanted his title. Understand?" (These last few sentences were delivered behind a fan encrusted with precious stones, and bore every suggestion of deep confidence.)

"But you're forgetting all about the compliment which Miss Gramercey paid me," I now said.

"So I am. Well, it was just this: She told me (now don't blush) that she thought you one of the handsomest gepmen she'd ever seen. There!"

A little later I got Mrs. Dorian to point out Miss Ada Gramercey to me. My guardian at once knew the young lady to whom I alluded, and assured me that not to know her was to argue oneself unknown. "The Gramerceys are people of considerable prominence in New-York," she continued. "Ada is the only child of a very agreeable widower, Colonel Gramercey. He is a sort of *vieux soldat*. He fought in the Mexican war with high honor, but he has passed a number of years in Europe. A most delightful old gentle-man. By the way, he is a few yards from us, talking with that lady in lavender satin."

I saw a thin, tall man with a martially graceful air and a white mustache. One glance at him pleased me: he appeared to combine so much amiability and dignity. He was listening to some-thing which his companion said, and his dark eyes twinkled brightly. He was not smiling then, but he seemed to have such a hidden store of benig-nity that it would be an easy matter to win a smile from him at brief notice.

"The dear old Colonel!" said Mrs. Dorian. "He does not see me. I am sure that if he did he would want to come and have a chat. We always quarrel, but we quarrel so picturesquely, so divert-ingly. He declares it shocking that I should detest New-York as I do. But in reality I am sure that he does not think it at all shocking. I always tell him that it is a pity he should have been an American; he would have made such a charming Frenchman."

Very soon after this Colonel Gramercey did see Mrs. Dorian, and as soon as opportunity was afforded him he joined her. She presented me, according to her invariable custom, as "my adopted son," and quite promptly she informed the Colonel that I desired to meet his daughter.

The Colonel seemed flattered to hear this, although I am sure that my existence had been previously unknown to him. He had that grace of faultless manners which are in almost every case the outgrowth of a sweet and lovable nature. He insisted upon taking me at once to his daughter, promising my guardian, with a gallant smile, that he would shortly rejoin her for one of those rare old-time chats which no lapse of years could make him forget.

Miss Gramercey was not far away. Several gentlemen surrounded her as we drew near the little draped alcove in which she stood. Her mien brightened for a moment when we were presented; I plainly saw that she recognized me. But her manner distinctly struck me as being cold and proud. Still, her beauty made an instant impression. She was above the average height of her sex. Her face was delicately chiselled and full of a most sensitive symmetry. The pliant waves of her auburn hair, rippling above a white forehead, just matched in color the rich hazel of her eyes. She had a complexion like the leaf of a tea-rose, and a pair of bewitching dimples that showed themselves by no means readily and never at all consciously. Her demeanor, as she stood with all the lines of her slender and neatly moulded figure in fine relief, was that of a girl who has no fear to be deserted by the usual current of male attention, and who is accustomed to choose her dovotees with no wilful caprice, but rather a calm surety of preference. We had been talking ordinary commonplaces together for some little time before I discovered that she had dismissed, by a process of cool inattention to their remarks, all the other gentlemen who had been grouped in the alcove. She discovered the general departure with a slight start.

" How rude of me ! " she said, in that voice of hers which had for my ears a peculiar cadence, and was like the fall and plash of sylvan water. Her exclamation, I swiftly reasoned, might be full of the flirt's best art. However, it more than half convinced me that she shrank from any voluntary discourtesy, and had a pride well above the exertion of petty tyrannies. Her whole face now broke into the most brilliant smile, and a light danced in her hazel eyes which must have been a will-o'-the-wisp for many a hopeful suitor. " Could you have better proof," she asked, " of how I was absorbed in the idea of meeting you ? "

" It is much better than I deserve," I answered, " but I shall hold it none the less precious because of that."

She laughed. " How prettily that would sound in French ! " she said. " And you have the least touch of a French accent. Are you really French, or an American who has lived for years abroad ? "

" Pray, why do you ask the last question, Miss Gramercey ? " If possible I meant to evade an answer concerning my nationality ; I always tried to escape from that falsehood of my Belgian birth.

"I have seen you driving several times with Mrs.

Dorian," said my companion; "and as a little girl I knew her in New-York, so that I am apt to forget that she is not an American. Then I afterward heard from somebody that you were her adopted son."

"I am. And she adopted me in America, when I was a boy. That is a long time ago."

"And you would like to return?" asked Miss Gramercey.

"Frankly, I would. And you?"

"Oh, I am a very good sort of patriot," she replied. "Europe suits me admirably as a watering-place. I prefer it to Newport, though I confess that this is saying a great deal." And she laughed her clear, flute-like laugh. "Papa and I have been here several times since poor mamma's death, about six years ago. We usually return in the autumn."

"Then you do not envy the Princess Orsini?" I said. "She tells me that she never expects to see her native California again."

Miss Gramercey's pure lip curled a little, though I thought there was more pity than irony in her tones as she responded: "I fear that Susan Potts will sigh for California some day."

"Susan Potts Orsini," I said. "She gave me her new name in full a little while ago. There's an immense geographical sweep in that name. It seems to connect two continents, like the submarine cable."

"So it does," she returned, laughing. "But I only hope it will have equally harmonious results."

"You don't approve of the marriage, then?"

"I approve of very few foreign marriages, Mr. Claud. They are so seldom made with any but the most cold-blooded motives. They are like mere commercial partnerships. I am always sorry to see my countrywomen accepting marriage in that unsacred spirit."

"You believe that the heart should always go where the hand goes?"

"Invariably. Sometimes, of course, there are worldly reasons why it should not, however. These I can appreciate. Then is the time for deliberation, courage, sacrifice, on both sides or one, as the case may be."

"I perceive that you have thought the whole matter out," I said, perhaps less lightly than I had intended to speak. "But when one of these obstacles at which you have hinted should really arrive, are you sure that you would not feel disinclined to accept it as such?"

She shook her head. "No," she answered, with gentle firmness. "I have my little code of matrimonial proprieties, as one might call it. I would as soon marry a man for whom I did not care because he had a great name or a great fortune, as" . . . But here she paused, and the unique smile came again, kindling her mellow eyes and deepening her sweet dimples. "How terribly serious a vein we have struck," she resumed, "and on so short an acquaintance!"

"Pray end your sentence," I said, "or let me end it for you."

"Can you do so?" she inquired, archly lifting her brows.

"I think I can. You were about to add that you would not marry one whom you held as your inferior, in spite of all the claims of sentiment. Am I not right?"

"Yes," she assented.

"Now," I proceeded, "there can be so many kinds of inferiority. "Fortune, for instance"—

"I should except that," she broke in.

"I hope you would also except birth."

"By no means," she asserted, with much quiet positiveness.

"What!" I exclaimed. "You, who are an American, say that?"

"Decidedly I do."

"But there is no such thing as rank in America."

She laughed. "Ah, that shows how little you know it! Social grades and degrees are very marked there."

"You surprise me," I said, and with unconcealed sarcasm. "An American aristocrat — what a strange sound it has! Quite as strange as Susan Potts Orsini."

"I don't at all agree with you," she answered,

flushing a little, and showing more than a shade of pique. "I recognize the old tone, Mr. Claud; I have heard it a good many times in Europe. Because we are a republic, oversea, there is a universal feeling, from London to St. Petersburg, that we should exist as an enormous social monotony— a civilization which allows no difference between yourself and your boot-maker or milliner, and holds a fairly long ancestry of gentlemen and gentlewomen to be a matter of no moment."

"I fear that I must side with the feeling here," I replied. "Ancestry, of whatever sort, should mean nothing in America. In a republic the worth of the individual is alone to be considered. Your boot-maker or milliner may be uncompanionable through a lack of congenial culture, but they should be so for no other conceivable reason. The total absence of hereditary caste is what Europe naturally looks for in a land which gave to all the Old World one mighty and strenuous promise that she would found her very being upon equal civil rights. Here the fulfilment of that promise is expected. How can Europeans fail to be surprised when they witness the descendants of those who defended democracy with their lives, now quietly supporting patrician principles and ideas? More than this, they will be sure to see the ludicrous side of it and pelt it with deserved ridicule."

Miss Gramercey was biting her lip as I ended. "If America—and especially New-York—were what you want it to be," she replied, "I should become a most uncomplaining exile."

She might have continued to speak, if a gentleman with a spasmodic walk and a flaxen head which he carried peeringly forward, had not suddenly joined her and begun to rattle off something in a throaty drawl about having only crossed the channel but a few hours ago, and being so "encharnted" at lighting upon the young lady whom he now addressed.   I was about taking my departure when a second gentleman, also chancing to discover the inmates of the alcove, approached Miss Gramercey and shook hands with her.   He was tall, by no means handsome, but with a marked distinction in carriage and demeanor. Oddly enough, as my eyes swept his face, I recognized something familiar in its expression.   I had, in those days, an excellent memory for faces, and it annoyed me that I should be at fault in recollecting where and when I had met this one.   But later, on learning the actual truth, I was more prone to praise than to blame my powers of remembrance. . . .

"How did you like Miss Gramercey, Otho?" asked my guardian, several hours later that same day.

"Ice is not colder," I said.   "But like ice, she is beautiful."

"I have heard her called cold," said Mrs. Dorian, appearing to muse.   "They tell me she had a great success this season in London, and a still greater one last winter in that horrid New-York." (Mrs. Dorian never spoke of New-York without some prefixed epithet; she treated it as Homer did most of his gods, heroes and cities, though much less flatteringly.) "The Gramerceys have always been people of note over there. Ada's mother was a Southern lady — a Miss Carteret of Virginia, and as good as she was beautiful. I don't see where the daughter gets her pride from — some deceased grandmother, I suppose; she has had a number of them. By the way, Otho, I heard the most surprising thing to-day. Foulke Dorian has been in London, and is devoted to her. They say that he followed her across the ocean, and that she has already refused him three or four times."

"It was he, then!" I exclaimed, giving a great start.

"He? Who?" inquired Mrs. Dorian, surprised at my seeming irrelevancy.

VIII.

"Why, your nephew, Foulke Dorian," I answered. "He came up to speak with Miss Gramercey just before I left her. Yes, there can be no doubt of it."

"Foulke in Paris, and at the wedding to-day?" said Mrs. Dorian incredulously.

"Beyond a doubt. I felt that I had seen his face before, and yet I was nearly certain that our acquaintance had been of the slightest. He is greatly changed, but still there is the lingering look of boyhood about him."

"Ah! I suppose he retains a few hundred memorial freckles."

"I did not perceive one."

"How extraordinary! Has the leopard changed his spots?"

"Not only that, but the leopard has developed into a rather *distingué* young man. He is tall, extremely slender, and most graceful in his movements. He looks like a young English swell, as they term it. I thought his complexion irreproachable, though a trifle too pale. And I am absolutely certain that it was he."

"Foulke should be nice-looking," said Mrs. Dorian. "It is quite in the proper order of things. He is the only child of an enormously rich man. My brother-in-law has succeeded in his business marvellously, and is now the sole proprietor of the house. How odd, if his son is in Paris, that he has not looked me up! I am not devotedly attached to my late husband's family, as you are aware, Otho; but then our poor human nature is so queerly constructed; we are hurt even by the neglect of our aversions." . . .

It was, if I recall rightly, but a few days later that I said to Mrs. Dorian:

"Have you any relatives living in Paris at present?"

She looked at me keenly, and a curious smile flitted across her face. "Strange that you should ask this question when I was about to speak on precisely the point you have brought up. My two married sisters are both dead, Otho — you perhaps remember when I wrote you of each death. But one of them, Mathilde, left an orphan son, Casimir Laprade. Casimir is about two years younger than you. He expected a fortune, but ruinous speculations on his father's part have left him with a very slender income. And now he bears the calamity with calm courage. He is a most charming youth."

"Does he ever visit you?"

"He did," said my guardian, hesitating, "but

.. of late .. well, to be frank with you, Otho, Casimir is proud, yet not after the pattern of Miss Gramercey."

"I do not quite understand you," I said.

"No?" As Mrs. Dorian now spoke she lowered her eyes and fingered a little nervously at the edge of a fan which the warmth of the day had caused her to use. "I—I do not wonder that you fail to understand," she went on. "You have heard nothing as yet."

"What is there to hear? Does any mystery hang about this nephew of yours, madame?"

Mrs. Dorian raised her eyes, meeting my look of sharp inquiry. "Casimir is poor, as I said. He is an artist of striking talent—at least I think so. He is handsome, too—after a very different type from yours, an almost feminine type, in fact—but still handsome. As yet he has obtained no recognition whatever, but he will not employ the least *ruse de guerre* to secure it. He simply offers his pictures to dealers, and has them declined, and eats his heart away with secret chagrin. I have known him only about four months. He came to me nearly four months ago, when I returned to Paris from my long stay in Austria and Italy. I had not talked to him more than five minutes before he had fascinated me. He became one of my impressions—and you know that I am always having impressions. He showed me some of his work, and I went in raptures over it. I suspect that he lives in attic lodgings and spends only four or five francs a day. He has the most poetic face; it is quite Greek, and as if it were cut out of ivory, with a cloud of blond hair, and delicate blue veins in either temple, and the least little gold thread of mustache. I wanted him to meet some of my artist friends, and he fascinated me still more by his almost girlish shyness. I used to make him dine with me. He was such a discovery in the way of a nephew. He wore dark velvet coats, which were infinitely becoming; dark velvet and blond hair are so delightful a combination when one has an ivory face like a young Apollo's. Poor Mathilde, his mother, had been rather stout (Heaven bless her!), with irregular features and a pronounced squint; I never could tell where she got it; there is no record of a De Lille ever having had a squint before. Of course at this time you were still in Zürich."

Here the narrator paused. " You never wrote me of your nephew," I said.

" No." The hesitation had now become a sort of confusion. " I — I would have done so if — if it had not been for a misunderstanding between Casimir and myself. One day, when our acquaintance was still young, I told him of you — of my great delight in your brilliant scholarship — of my resolution to make you my sole heir. This would not have affected him in the least if I had not also uttered a *bétise* — if I had not been unpardonably stupid. I assumed an apologetic tone and declared to him that perhaps the bond of blood between us gave him a prior claim to my bounty, but that circumstances had now so arranged themselves as to make such a claim wholly impracticable. And then, quite suddenly, Casimir interrupted me with a kind of sorrowful anger. He avowed himself unwilling to be the subject of even momentary thoughts like these. He would not for the world have you suspect him of wishing to stand in your light. He had come to me because I was his dead mother's sister, and his long residence in Rome had thus far prevented our meeting. It was best that you should not even learn of his existence. He preferred never to become acquainted with you. The inheritance I had promised to you must pass to you untouched. He desired nothing gratuitously from anyone, living or dead. He desired only what his own honest toil might bring him. . I was dreadfully pained. He had a knot of blue ribbon at his throat, and it was so keenly becoming; and then his large, soft blue eyes took such a sad sparkle while he thus spoke. *Mon Dieu!* how the great Balzac could have described him, with his delicate nature, just like his spiritual face! We still remained friends; we are friends to-day; but he will not accept a *sou* of aid from me, and . . since you have arrived he . . he comes to me no more."

"How pathetically you say that!" I commented, rising, going toward a window, and staring out of it, though I saw nothing. I knew that there was satire in my tones, but I could not repress it. A bitter feeling had crept about my heart. It was the old jealousy at work again. These abrupt tidings hurt and jarred upon me. My guardian's professed admiration and liking of this Casimir Laprade — this unforeseen new-comer who shared what I had so long held in complete entirety — seemed to me like the dealing of an unsolicited wrong.

Mrs. Dorian had meanwhile stolen to my side. But I did not know of her presence there till I felt her hand upon my arm.

"I have made you angry," she said.

I turned upon her reproachfully. "Not angry," I exclaimed, "for I have no right to any anger. You have done so much for me without my possessing the least claim upon your goodness! But still that is all the more reason why this sudden news should wound me deeply." I paused here, not wishing to trust myself with another word, gnawing my lips in the effort to control what I really felt.

"But I never dreamed of wounding you," she faltered, astonished and regretful. "How have I done so?"

"How?" I echoed. "You tell me that this new attachment has filled the place I held! You tell it as kindly as you are able, and yet the truth is clear as day."

Her astonishment had deepened. "Oh, Otho," she exclaimed, "can you possibly be jealous of poor Casimir?—you!"

"No, I am not jealous," I retorted, hating the word and quivering under it as if it had been the cut of a lash. "But you force me to remember who he is and who I am! Ah, yes; you remind me that he is your blood-kindred, besides having won the affection that was mine for years!"

I had receded from her, but she now spread out both arms toward me. A bright smile was on her lips, and her dark eyes (dimmer with age than when mine had first met them) were glistening as at some relished tidings. I had often seen her look like this before, when pleased by one of her many fanciful whims or moods; but to encounter the change then affected me as a slur, almost a sneer.

"You are delightful!" she exclaimed. "Ah, my boy, what a lover you will make, some day! How shocking that I am only a poor old woman, and not some lovely young girl! Still, the impression is very exhilarating. I like it; I positively tingle under it."

"Your pleasantry, madame, is most ill-timed," I said, in freezing tones. The slumbering trait in my strange nature had wakened, like a torpid serpent. Her last reply only stung me as if it were the most cruel raillery. "I had better leave you," I pursued, "without further delay. Let this Casimir Laprade, whose very existence you have concealed from me until now, reign with due honors in my stead. It is not too late for you to bestow on him all the love he merits. I abdicate in his favor from to-day. You have given me an education, and with it I am willing to fight my way alone."

Every word of these rash and ungrateful sentences I firmly meant. But as I walked toward the door of the chamber an alarmed cry broke from Mrs. Dorian. She hurried after me; she almost dragged me toward a couch, and clung about my neck with a clasp that I must have employed roughness to shake off. It was her turn to use reproaches, and she used them in a torrent of tearful utterance. At the same time no impetuous avowal of her fondness was absent. She appealed to my long knowledge of her devotion; she challenged me to recall an act of neglect in all the years we had spent together; she reminded me of how her letters had breathed unaltered tenderness; she accused me of disloyalty in suspecting that a new regard could ever displace the old; she questioned me whether my dead mother herself could have watched more faithfully over my life, or known a sweeter joy at my success.

She ended not merely by convincing me of my folly; I was covered with humiliation as well, and besought her pardon in tones of the most mortified self-abasement. The revulsion had come with me, as it had come in earlier days, bringing shame and remorse. As my own mother had done long ago, she forgave me all too easily.

"I must see your nephew," I at length said to her. "Above all things I now long to see and know him. If he shows aversion toward me I will conquer it. I am determined that we shall be friends."

This was not the sole determination that I had already made; there was another, though as yet I could scarcely have clad it with language.

"You will find that he has no aversion, Otho," declared my guardian. "It is not in his nature. But shall we not go together?"

I shook my head. "No," I answered; "it seems to me better that I should go alone."

She looked at me with a smile breaking over her face. "I understand," she said, nodding. "It is a subtle question; I am excessively fond of all subtle questions, as you know."

She had wholly regained her composure by this time. I very well knew that the episode of my jealousy would soon take a retired place in her memory. It had been one of her "impressions," in which she saw me assume a romantically fiery attitude. Even what followed had not been without its attractive side. As a little bit of drama its residual thrill might even be more permanent;

and then, too, it had stirred her to the depths. She was a woman who was perpetually employing her nervous system as a kind of pictorial agency. There was no experience from which she could not extract some sort of artistic value. I have often thought her prosperity a favor thrown away by fate; she would have so embellished and idealized poverty.

I had little difficulty in finding Casimir Laprade. His studio was not just in an attic, though I should say it came within one stairway of being so; perhaps you must have ascended if you had gone to his bed-chamber, and in that case his aunt had rightly surmised. It was a shabby studio, and yet it bore touches of Oriental color, in a hanging spangled robe or a quaint damascened weapon. Sketches and paintings of many sorts were scattered about the rather grimy walls, and two small windows, draped carelessly in crimson of different shades, as though to hide ugly or dingy cornices, looked down upon a narrow, bustling street of the *Quartier Latin.* The young artist had not suffered from Mrs. Dorian's dainty description of him. The cloud of blond hair, the poetic face, the dark velvet coat, struck me at a glance. His manner, too, as I soon perceived, greatly partook of shyness. When I had presented my card, and he had glanced at it, I saw a slight flush rise in his pale cheek. He appeared abashed and a trifle dismayed, but no embarrassment could make that flexible figure of his, a little below the usual stature, err on the side of awkwardness, or rob his gestures of a native, peculiar grace.

I had already hit, so to speak, upon my proper policy of self-introduction. As I seated myself in the chair politely proffered me, I assumed a mien of somewhat buoyant civility, guarding at the same time against the least phrase that could be construed as patronage.

"Paris, Monsieur Laprade," I said, "is the most distracting temptress to a foreigner, and I, who have the disadvantage of not being one of her citizens, who have known her only now and then by delightful glimpses, must plead the excuse of her many pleasures for having deferred until now this most desired visit."

He looked at me almost wonderingly with his large, dreamy gray eyes. They were eyes in which I seemed to trace the spell of many a lovely though lonely revery.

"I did not hope, Monsieur, for the honor of a visit from you," he answered, with all the courtesy of his race plain amid the diffidence that still thralled him. "I had supposed that you would have many engagements, many diversions."

"None of these," I said, "could have kept me from seeking the acquaintance of one so nearly akin to my beloved guardian, and so high in that amiable lady's esteem." (Ah, what a tongue the French is, and how you can say trippingly in it that which would sound ponderous else where !)

He brightened, at this, and drew his chair a little nearer my own. "My aunt is indeed a most charming woman," he said. "But as for your seeking me, Monsieur, I fear that you will find but little. I have only my drawings and my daubs — many of them crude enough, the *vieux galons* of boyhood. I live almost wholly alone, with my dreams and " . . .

"Your ambitions?" I questioned, as he paused. At this I rose and added: "Pray let me see some of your work. I have already heard your aunt praise it."

He shrugged his shoulders, rising too. "She is a very lenient critic. She had made up her mind beforehand to be pleased with all that I showed her. You will be more severe, Monsieur, and justly so."

I looked him full in the eyes, smiling. I was resolved upon winning his good will. If nothing had occurred to force in me the choice of such an issue, I should still have preferred it. He and his accompaniments, as might be said, had both captivated me. It was all like a pretty page from some French romancer. My imagination seemed to demand of him that his youth, his beauty, his almost feminine sweetness of demeanor, his gentle modesty, his refined solitude, should crown their happy unison by the possession of genius.

"I have seen some good art," I replied, "in

other cities besides this. But I am never severe with originality, wherever found."

He started. "You have heard that what I do is original?"

"I have a presentiment that I shall discover it so."

He became serious and thoughtful; it was plain that I had touched his self-belief as an artist. He pointed toward a picture in oil, half finished, and resting on an easel near at hand. "Tell me if you care for this," he said, moving his eyes more than once while he spoke from the canvas to my face. "I call it The New-Born Soul. You see how shadowy I have made my background; that little white point on the left is our planet, our star, which the spirit of a young girl has just quitted. She is journeying through space. Only a little gleam of the great unknown light has broken upon her; you may mark it in the shining of the hair along one temple. She has not yet realized her own immortality. She is full of wonder, but she is not afraid, and the loves and joys of the earth have not quite left her. . I tried to show this in the tremor of mouth and chin, and in that backward reach of one hand." . .

He spoke hurriedly but with such an unconscious fervor that even these few words told how his art was his life. I remained silent for several minutes, wishing to study the picture well and get lucid reasons for the praise which I was already certain that I should have just cause to pronounce. Then I slowly addressed my companion, weighing every word as I did so.

"You have put into color — and the deepest, the richest color — a bit of exquisite poetry. You have the great gift, you blend the poet with the painter. Your thought is modern; you are a true *enfant du siècle;* but your spirit has lived with the grand dead masters, and in every stroke that your brush has given I note an intolerance of pettiness and finicality. Yes, you have a large, firm, ample style; I have seen little to surpass it in the *salons* of to-day. . . There," I suddenly broke off, laughing; " that is the first elaborate art-criticism that I ever delivered. How would it look if printed in a *feuilleton?*"

He caught my hand an instant later, and so moist a glow filled his gray eyes that I almost expected tears to drop from them. " These are most stimulating words," he said, the quiver of real emotion in his tones. " Ah, Monsieur, believe me, it is not half so much the praise that I love as the sincerity of it!"

He showed me more of his work, after that, and though its merit constantly varied, a uniform sweep and lift of intention — an effort to portray Nature as he felt her and not merely as she was — an intellectual dominance, whether imaginative, visionary or fantastic, had set its stamp on nearly every achievement.

I think we were friends when we parted that day. I knew I had made him anxious to meet me again; the lingering pressure of his hand as he bade me farewell told me so, and the promise which he gave me of an early visit was a still surer sign.

On returning to our apartments, I found my guardian full of eager questions. How had I liked Casimir? Was he abnormally shy? Had he received me with cordiality? Would he come to us and be friendly hereafter? Did I think his talents remarkable? and so on, with an ebullition of vivacious inquiry. My first responses delighted Mrs. Dorian, but her pleasure grew, as her dancing eyes told me, while I said:

"He is a painter of rare gifts. He has what artists sometimes call sneeringly the literary and pictorial quality, but this he nearly always keeps, or tries to keep, subordinate. He is rapidly mastering the important secret of what Art should not do. He has still much to learn, however, as would seem but natural at his age. His moods are exalted, ethereal, mystic, and occasionally even sybilline. He is an enemy of detail, and his handling is broad, vigorous, yet secure. His eyes seem peculiarly open (as I observed in his landscapes) to the power of suggestive analogy between Nature and our own worldly experience. While we talked together he told me that in the rank riots of weeds, the noisome and malarial swamp,

the blighted and incomplete vegetation, the slug-
gish pool, the dried-up water-course and the tract
of barren dreariness, he could trace easy similitude
of the pride, arrogance, tyranny, bigotry, pursuant
misfortune and unexplained destiny of mankind;
and that, on the other hand, purity, high purpose,
the wisdom of self-control, the sweet domestic
pleasures, the rich reward of an unsullied life, are
shown to him in perpetual allegory by the full-
flowing river, the sublime mountain, the rhythms
of tides on their shores, the pastoral tinklings of
brooks through meadows, and the splendors of
sunset over lengths of peaceful country. Sympathies like these are the very life-blood of all great
Art. They err who believe that all the best painters have merely been poets spoiled in the making."

"You enchant me, Otho," said my guardian,
"in ranking Casimir's ability so high. You describe him, too, as only a poet could!"

"A poet! Ah, madame, do not take my gush-
ing little rhapsody for poetry. I shall never either
write or speak any, as long as I live."

"Hush!" she exclaimed, with an irritated toss
of the head. "I treasure those copies of verses
which you sent me from Zürich."

I laughed. "It is so easy to say nothing melo-
diously, in French verse. What I sent you was
only polished commonplace. Trust me, my dear
madame, I have measured my own capacity very
carefully in all directions."

"And in which have you found that it excels?"

"In none. I possess simply a large academic kind of mediocrity."

"Mediocrity! Ah, Otho! *Fi donc!* Everybody thinks you a genius. Wonderful things are expected of you!"

Again I laughed, but there was sadness in the sound. "Wonderful things will never come from me. I am a high table-land; I have not a single peak. My own intellect often surprises me; it is so tantalizingly capable. I am as remote from any superfine accomplishment as I am from any notable stupidity. I made those verses, but I can solve a problem in Euclid quite as well, or construe a page of Thucydides, or even sketch Mont Blanc from Chamouny in aquarelle. I stop nowhere, but I excel nowhere. My muse is a tenth one — a calm, rather erudite dame, an adopted sister of the other nine, and no true daughter of Zeus and Mnemosyne. I can appreciate, investigate, formulate, demonstrate, criticise; but to invent, create, originate, I am wholly powerless. My endowments pause at nothing and yet they pause at everything. I am open to a thousand thoughts, yet I shall never give the world one that is new."

"What melancholy you breathe into your confession!" exclaimed Mrs. Dorian. "You make it quite majestic. Standing by that window, with the late sunlight slanting across your face, you are like Byron in the act of lamentation for no special cause on the face of the earth. Your head, by the way, and the cast of your features, often bear resemblance to his; I think I have mentioned this before."

"You have mentioned many such agreeable matters before, madame," I said — "and fancied their existence."

"Bah!" she cried, smelling her vinaigrette vivaciously. "And you term all this mediocrity! It is certainly something a great deal higher."

I smiled. "It is not Byron. No, and it is not Casimir Laprade."

"Whom you believe possessed of genius?"

"Undoubtedly."

"But of yourself . . have you decided on no profession, occupation?"

"On none, as yet."

My guardian straightened herself in her easy-chair. "Then I must find one for you. I received a letter to-day from my lawyers in America. It was about the property there. Someone must go and look after it. You shall go. Why not? It is yours as well as mine already; some day, when I am no more, it will be wholly yours."

I stood irresolute, for a moment, there by the window. Then I slowly walked toward my guardian, pausing near her chair. "Not wholly mine," I said.

"What do you mean?" she asked, with surprise.

"My will is made."

" You must alter it, madame."

" Otho, what is this ? "

" You must alter it," I said, taking her hand, "in favor of Casimir Laprade. Divide the property equally between him and me, if you please, but at least make us co-heirs. This may not be your duty, since, in spite of his kinship, you are privileged to leave your wealth where you please. But it is my duty to insist upon the division."

She tried to withdraw her hand, yet I forcibly retained it. " Upon my word, you show an extraordinary change of mood," she declared stiffly. " A little while ago " —

" Please do not refer to a little while ago," I interrupted. " That is just what I would like, to have you forget."

" I see. You wish to impose upon yourself a penance."

" Perhaps. And yet this is far from being my only motive. Casimir is your sister's son. But for me you would doubtless have made him your sole heir. I shall never feel mentally at rest until you have accepted my view of his deserts. I throw myself now upon that indulgent goodness which I have so often received from you without seeking it. And if it fails me at this time of request, of need, of entreaty, I shall be sorely disappointed. By acting to your nephew and myself as if we were brothers, you will make the bond closer between yourself and me. Believe, also, that I speak with the most profound sincerity when I add one more clause to my petition. It is this: I would rather you left every franc of your fortune to charitable objects than that you made me its one possessor."

"I will think it over," she said, softening. "There would, of course, be more than enough for two. The money has been piling itself up, there across the water; I cannot have spent quarter of my income for years. . Yes, I will think it over."

I stooped and kissed her forehead. "You will do nothing of the sort," I answered, with a little stroke of calculated boldness; "for you have already consented."

"*Comme tu es hardi, mon cher!*" she retorted, trying not to smile. "And Casimir? If he should refuse to profit by this division?"

"Leave his refusal or consent to me. I will break the news gradually. Trust me."

"You speak as if you and he were to live henceforward in the closest intimacy."

"I should like to make him a member of our little household — with your permission."

She gave her wonted laugh, here, at its merriest. "My permission? Of course you have it. And you will accomplish your plan. . . Ah, I begin to think that is what you always will do, accomplish your plan, whatever it is. Perhaps that is to be your province — always to make everybody do as you desire."

I detected the undercurrent of surrender in these final words, and was not unprepared to have her acquiesce, that very evening, a few hours later, in my proposition of a meeting with her notary on the morrow. Casimir Laprade came to visit us a day or two afterward, but before he came a new will had been drawn, just as I had wished.

The intercourse between my guardian's nephew and myself now rapidly ripened into a warm friendship. It was not till I had induced him to dwell permanently beneath the same roof with us that I ventured upon the subject of his altered prospects. I waited until I was sure of the influence I had gained over him, and then I spoke. Already he had learned almost to hang upon my words: the love I had inspired in him was even more than fraternal. My keen appreciation of his artistic worth had first roused this ardent feeling, but no egotism ultimately held sway there. In my nature he recognized something complementary to his own. Where he was retiring, timid, undecided, even impolitic through a lack of self-reliance, I was assertive, intrepid, equable. All his strength of character seemed to lie in his lovely genius, which I admired still more as I grew familiar with its depths and heights, its glow and shadow. But it grasped his nature and temperament with a weakening hold; it made him unfit to deal with men, and boyishly pliable under the stress of all coarse and rugged contact. So deep and durable was the enthusiasm which it woke in him that I saw with amazement his indifference to womanly charms. His ideal was his mistress, and he served her in devoted transport. The nearest that he ever approached to a sentiment of the heart was his affection for me; that was indeed, in its way, a passion, for it set me upon a pedestal and paid me tender obeisance. I sometimes fancied that he was a being who could love only in this fashion, with the grosser senses quite at rest, and the heart, the brain, the spirit at high pulsation. I cannot call him feminine except in the extreme sensitiveness of his mental mould; for he possessed courage (he had once fought a dangerous duel with swords on receiving an insult from a fellow-student in the Art School, and had severely wounded his adversary); and again, in physical training, nerve, coolness, energy, he by no means missed the full manly share. But for all this, he was of feeble fibre to meet exigencies, to deal with difficulties, to gauge and seize opportunities, to touch and pierce human fallacies. He was not made for the world, though the world was made for him, since he transfigured and re-created hundreds of its harshest traits by the sure magic of his art!

When I told him what my guardian had done for his future, the tidings moved him to tears, unshed though seen. I dreaded his refusal of the boon, however, and while I witnessed his wonder at this intelligence, I hastened to add, before it should really pass:

"The affair was of my own earnest prompting, Casimir, and nothing that I have ever done has given me keener satisfaction. It binds us more closely together, *mon ami*, and instead of a few thousands which I shall not need, it brings me the welcome and cheering comradeship of a brother."

That last word caused him to start; one of the tears that brimmed his eyes now slipped along the dark curve of its lower lash and fell upon his cheek. His chin trembled, and he gnawed his underlip as though to force self-control. But suddenly he threw back that beautiful head of his, and almost sprang toward me. In another second he had seized either of my shoulders and was looking into my face with searching intentness.

"Brother!" he exclaimed. "You do not deceive yourself? You are certain that you already care for me enough to wish our lives joined so closely?"

"Yes," I answered, prepared for the extremely French embrace to which past experience in friendships of school and college had long ago inured me. As it was, I returned the embrace with a fervor truly Gallic. Conscience entered, beyond doubt, into my dealings with Casimir; Mrs. Dorian had hit the truth; I wanted to punish myself for that dark hour of imperious jealousy. But I now felt that the punishment threatened to become a most active agency of comfort and enjoyment, since this fortunately righted nephew had every endearing quality and not a single repelling one.

The consent of Casimir quickly followed that little outburst of sentiment. I went to Mrs. Dorian, proud of my victory, and told her that all was now definitely arranged. If I sailed for America in the following autumn — as at present seemed the inevitable course — Casimir, who thrilled with curiosity to see the New World — would gladly accompany me. "I believe there is little that can ever separate us," I said, "swiftly formed as our mutual attachment has been. The relations between us are like those of an elder toward a younger brother." Here I gave a meaning smile. "It is perhaps needless, madame," I continued, "for me to state which part Casimir plays and which part belongs to me."

"You lead, of course," said Mrs. Dorian, approvingly. "That is but proper. To think that you are now talking of crossing the Atlantic together, you two! How the unexpected does happen in this topsy-turvy world! Well, if you both go to America I suppose it may in a measure reconcile me to going. But I assure you, Otho, I shrink from putting those miles of sea between myself and civilization."

"Such words would stab me to the American soul if I thought them serious," was my reply.

"However, madame, I am glad to hear you speak of going with Casimir and myself. It is all well enough to say that you will give me full power of attorney in dealing with your affairs; but your presence in New-York will be vastly preferable, if not indispensable."

"I will reflect upon your advice," said my guardian, with a rather dramatic shudder. "This means, you know, that I will lose several pounds and forfeit my appetite. Ah, it is so hard to be resigned to certain stern facts! It is so hard to believe that the same wise Providence which gave us Paris was capable of producing America!" . . .

Meanwhile I had gone not a little into the society of my countrypeople, and had made not a few interesting and prized acquaintances. The Princess Orsini had left Paris for Norway with the intention of turning the midnight sun into a honeymoon; but her friend, Miss Gramercey (if the title be not unfair), still remained in town. I met the latter a number of times at various entertainments before she asked me to visit her. When the invitation came I gladly accepted it, for in spite of our differences her society both won and engrossed me. We met on no unequal terms; there was not a millionnaire in the great French capital who lived with more luxury and elegance than myself, though I abhorred the ostentation of extravagance and tempered my splendor with taste. The position of Mrs. Dorian's adopted son and probable inheritor of her wealth was one to provoke much attention among the Americans with whom I was constantly thrown. My guardian had been thought eccentric in New-York, but she had held her select place there, nevertheless, during former years. I soon found myself popular and courted. Besides being a person whom no ambitious mamma could afford conscientiously to overlook, I liked the society of pretty women and agreeable men, even while deliberative criticism pronounced them vapid and unsatisfying. My youth and my long association with studious pursuits made the lighter mood of jest and indolence at least temporarily pleasant. I possessed the art of amusing my compatriots; I had a ready though at times a somewhat caustic wit; I was as gallant, modish, debonair as they desired; and with regard to my good looks I could sometimes ill repress that vanity which pushes forth so facile a crop in the hearts of the young when persistent flattery sows her seed there.

Briefly, even at so unfavorable a Parisian season I had become the fashion. Ada Gramercey had undoubtedly seen this when I began to enrol myself upon her list of permitted admirers, and I was confident that the preference I showed her did not prove the more irksome because of it. Her pride was a continual secret torment to me. If there had not been intellect behind it — if I had not repeatedly caught glimpses of a sweet womanly nature through occasional breaks in its chilling investiture — I might have held the whole manifestation as trivial and paltry. As it was I did not tell myself that I was falling in love with her. I incessantly felt my spirit harassed by the thought: If she knew my real birth, how she might shrink from me! For years no such haunting reflection had troubled my mind. I had accepted my new station in life with a sense that every succeeding autumn cast its fresh relay of obliterating leaves upon the hideous and unhappy past. All had seemed so deeply buried until this young girl, with her proud, soft hazel eye, her erect figure and her elastic step, unconsciously swept away what covered so hated a grave.

Like a death's-head amid all my mirth gleamed this conjecture as to how she would treat me if she were once to meet the actual truth, naked, uncompromising, merciless.

And what was this truth? Again and again I silently reviewed its record. I, Otho Claud, believed to be the child of a beloved Belgian friend of my guardian, whom she had adopted as the heir to her great wealth, was Otho Clauss, the son of a German peasant by a *bourgeoise* French mother, whom my father had foully murdered, afterward paying for the crime in a death of ignominy on the scaffold!

It was in this dreary and pitiable way that a great passion — the first and only one I was ever destined to know — dawned upon my soul! The sins of the parents shall be visited on their children! The inexorable meaning of that dreadful announcement, put by Christians in the mouth of the God they worship, was beginning to warn and taunt me from a new and unforeseen source!

IX.

HE who has read thus far in the pages of these confessions must have understood them but ill if they fail to place before him the solemn truth of Heredity as their stimulus and motive. At the same time I would offer the reminder that I make this record of my life with no wish to employ such truth either as excuse or palliative for the course of action revealed here. I am aware how stern would be the disclaimer of thousands against such a method, and how relentlessly it would be disputed that the victim of any inherited vice or weakness had not, in a case like my own, the stoutest defensive armor against overthrow or surrender. To appear as the champion of a blind fatalism is far from my present aim. However pitilessly science may speak on this point — however exact and clear may be the deductions from certain undeniable data — however psychological proof may demonstrate that moral disease follows the same rigid law as physical, and that both can be transmitted from parent to child with an equal readiness — I am none the less willing to grant the existence, after birth, of vastly potent modifying forces. There are medicines for the soul no less than for the body. The world of philosophy and ethics, as that of surgery and pathology, teems with precious curative discoveries and resources. True, there are many beings who must drag along unhelped the misshapen limb, as there are many who must bear till death the perverse and vicious brain. The aid given to myself was plenteous, cogent. If the weapon is ever put into a man's hand wherewith he may beat out his own future as he will, then just as tough a means of self-amelioration was set within my grasp. I grant this. But the problem of a foreordained destiny must ever remain unsolved — at least with a few intellects, of which mine had now become one. As long, I argued, as human will continues the unravelled mystery that we find it, no adequate answer may be rendered those two sombre questions: How far can we escape becoming what our parents have made us? — how far may education and enlightenment avert from us the doom of sinful heritage?

These reflections hardly concern the present stage of my history, and I do not know why they have crept into this portion of it, unless with some vague relation to the distressing tremors which now disturbed me. It was a period in which one longs for a confidant, and again and again I felt tempted to tell Casimir everything. I would often spend an hour in his studio, watching him paint.   Our affiliation had become complete in all save this one sad, tormenting matter.   Even then he suspected my love for Ada Gramercey, since I had frequently dwelt in conversation upon her personal attractions, or referred with perhaps tell-tale severity to her fault of pride.   But pride on my own part kept my lips firmly sealed.   And oddly enough I had the same reason for preserving silence toward Mrs. Dorian.   She knew my past, but time had gathered a mist across it which was almost like absolute oblivion.   To break through this would be to stand before her in a new, humiliating light — to remind her that the alienation from degrading antecedents had, after all, been but partially effected — to let her see that the mirk and smirch from which her kind hands had plucked me was not wholly washed away.

In the meantime I had inevitably met her other nephew, Foulke Dorian.   He still abode in Paris and still confirmed, by his unceasing attentions to Ada Gramercey, the report that he was her undiscouraged suitor.   I was presented to him by Miss Gramercey herself, while we both chanced to be standing at that young lady's side during an evening entertainment.   It occurred to me that his bow was wholly without cordiality, and indeed a trifle arrogant.   By this time he undoubtedly knew my name, and must have known as well that his aunt was in Paris.   Not to have sought her out was fast taking the hues of intentional rudeness. Few words were then exchanged between us, and none that referred to our brief acquaintance of long ago or to my present position in Mrs. Dorian's home. When we again met he gave me a cold bow, which I answered as coldly. Did he resent my agreeable reception by Miss Gramercey? or did he bear some sort of grudge toward his aunt? or was there any possibility of his not being aware what relations I held to Mrs. Dorian? I consulted with the latter on this subject, and she replied in rather vexed tones:

"If I chance to come across him, Otho, I shall tell him very plainly what I think of his having failed to look me up. Meanwhile, I should advise you to take the first opportunity you have of mentioning me, besides making a pointed reference to yourself."

Such an opportunity soon came. One evening I dined in Miss Gramercey's charming apartments, overlooking the Champs Elysées. It was a dinner of ten or twelve, and composed chiefly of my own countrypeople. Colonel Gramercey, a most urbane and faultless host, conducted the gentlemen into a pleasant little smoking-room after dinner, for coffee and cigars. The weather had been sultry all day, and now a refreshing breeze blew across a little balcony straight into the small chamber where we had gathered. Foulke Dorian lit a cigar, and then moved toward one of the long windows, presently disappearing on the balcony beyond, which commanded a brilliant view of the great thoroughfare glittering with a thousand merry lights. I followed him as he thus disappeared. He turned on hearing my footstep cross the sill of the window. He looked well that evening, in the sense of elegance, composure and skilful tailoring. His dark attire and white necktie became him admirably. He had a pale, calm, inexpressive face, with eyelids that drooped a little languidly and a mouth whose rather sensuous fulness would have been improved by a mustache. When you pronounced him markedly gentlemanlike in appearance you paid him all the praise that was justice, for a supercilious curl nearly always lay at the corners of his lips and an air of lazy importance inseparably marked his manner.

I was determined to act with extreme politeness. When, on turning, he had recognized me, in the soft yet sufficient light, I at once spoke, joining him where he stood beside the filigreed rail of the balcony.

I spoke in English. "You have probably forgotten, Mr. Dorian," I said, "our first meeting many years ago in America, while we were both still boys."

He smiled faintly though civilly, and knocked the film of ash from his cigar with the pointed nail of one finger. "I do remember it," he replied, in a low drawl that certainly betrayed no interest whatever. "We met only for a few minutes, did we not? I believe you were taken suddenly ill, or something of that sort, and Mrs. Dorian led you from the room."

This allusion to what then occurred was not pleasant, as may be imagined. But in another way it gratified me, since I could now make prompt use of his having so soon brought up the name of his aunt.

"Quite right," I assented composedly. "My health at that time was poor. But your aunt's kind nursing soon restored it, and this is only one of the many services which I owe her. By the way, did you know that she is in Paris at present?"

My direct question embarrassed him, as I could see. But he quickly regained his collected look. "I heard of it a short time ago," he said; and he convinced me that the words were false.

"She has more than once spoken of you," I now struck in, "and you must allow me to add that she is hurt at your not having sought her out."

"I—I should have done so," he said, with his neutral drawl, just giving me a glimpse of his chill, dull eyes under their lifted lids. "One has so many engagements here. It is quite a rush, nearly always. Of course I must call. Pray tell my aunt that I will do so."

"I will tell her with pleasure," I replied. "She will be very glad to hear of your intention."

He gave me another sidelong look while he puffed at his cigar. "Shall you be in Paris long?" he asked.

"I am undecided. There may be reasons for my going to New-York. Reasons, I mean, which concern the settlement of Mrs. Dorian's property."

"Ah?" . . He swept his eyes over the dusky yet bright expanse below us. "You are a Belgian by birth, I believe."

"Yes."

I hated the lie heartily enough, but in his cool, indolent way he had dragged it from me.

"You have relatives in Brussels, I suppose?"

"A few distant ones."

"Whom you never see?"

"Rarely."

"Ah . . yes . . and my aunt has formally adopted you. You will become her heir, no doubt.. It would surely be most cruel if she did not make you so, after being so good these many years, would it not? But I fancy all that is thoroughly arranged."

The tinge of sarcasm in his voice was just observable and no more. But it was there beyond question. I felt stung to anger, and yet I masked the sensation under a careless repose.

"Mrs. Dorian's inclinations are her own. It is probable that I will receive a share of her fortune, however, if I should outlive her."

"Outlive her." He took his cigar from his mouth and leaned back his head a little, laughing as at some unexpected joke. "Really, that is very good! It's what they call a happy way of hitting off a thing."

"I had every intention of being serious," I answered, with tones dry and hard. "I am so attached to Mrs. Dorian that the thought of her death brings me pain."

"Of course . . yes . . naturally."

I could have struck him for the latent sneer in this interruption; but I continued, without seeming to notice it.

" And in regard to her provision for my future, I had imagined, Mr. Dorian, that you were already informed on that point nearly as well as myself, since you must have known that from childhood I have been the *protégé* of your aunt."

He straightened himself a little at this. He slightly shrugged his shoulders while doing so. "You will pardon me," he replied, "but I possess very little information on the subject."

I bit my lip. "Your father was made fully aware of the facts in the case," I said.

He smiled now, and there was something in the smile that sent a thrill through my nerves. It was like a light cast on steel. "Ah . . yes . . the facts in the case," he murmured. "They were given, I recollect."

Just then two of our recent companions came

out upon the balcony. Foulke Dorian at once addressed them in a playfully genial manner on some subject with which I had no concern. I retired, soon afterward joining the ladies. Ada Gramercey was unusually gracious that evening. We made an appointment to ride together on the following afternoon. She rode admirably, but as a rule with no one except either her father or a groom as escort. It was held an honor for any male friend to be permitted the chance of accompanying her. But my pleasure at the prospect of to-morrow was diminished by hearing her soon afterward say: " We shall start for Austria next Wednesday. It was decided only a few hours ago. Papa's health is not of the best just now and he needs the change. Besides I have never seen the Tyrol." I felt my heart sink. I believe that I realized my love for her in that one moment more forcibly than ever before. " And shall you be gone till the end of summer?" I inquired.

" Yes."

" And then?" I still asked.

She laughed, calling to a little pet dog, agile and beribboned, that had just scampered into the room. " Oh, then we shall go straight back home to America."

I could not repress the words that now rose to my lips. " And Mr. Dorian will probably go back in the same steamer."

She looked at me with haughty surprise. "He is at liberty to select that one if he chooses."

But I was not rebuffed. "He will select it," I said, very softly, and no doubt reproachfully. "Perhaps he will follow you to the Tyrol as well."

She turned to me a face that was more clement than I had expected ; it seemed to pardon while it disapproved my boldness. "He will not follow me," she answered.

"Then may I?"

"No."

"You do not put it very forbiddingly," I pleaded.

"But it is 'No,' all the same. I shall have papa to look after. And then people are always saying stupid things."

"Well, let them say what they please. They already say that Foulke Dorian is devotedly fond of you. I should not at all object to their making the same disclosures with regard to myself. The truth is not always unpleasant to hear."

She gave a slight demure nod, and touched the petals of some roses which she wore at her breast, and which I had sent her that afternoon. "You are very kind," she said, using the conventionality of phrase because it suited her coy, random whim. "But papa and I have made up our minds to take the Austrian trip alone."

"I wish you would answer me one plain, fair

question," I said, while my heart beat a little at my own audacity.

"What is it?" she asked, amiably low-voiced.

"Do you care for Foulke Dorian?"

She set her lips together somewhat primly, but in a way that was infinitely becoming. In those days of brilliant success, with not a cloud on the sky of her complete happiness, with admirers by scores, with a worshipping father who indulged her least whim, with wealth, beauty, homage, health, flattery as the very air that she breathed, was it strange that even she, possessing an intellect far above that which one finds in the average feminine recipient of ordinary compliment, should employ her arts, her touches of coquetry, her delicate *minauderies?*

"I care for all my fellow-creatures — or try to do so," she said. "Mr. Dorian is one of them."

"I congratulate you on your elastic philanthropy," I returned, with bitterness. "Mine does not extend so far."

Our conversation was now interrupted by one or two departing guests. I took my leave soon afterward, full of disquietude, perplexity, distress. Foulke Dorian was not only my possible enemy but my evident rival as well. Like all men in love, I argued from Miss Gramercey's recent evasive answer that she set his devotion above my own, and that his ultimate conquest was imminent. But apart from this trouble, I was assailed by another. Dorian's ill-hid impertinence rankled in my breast. What had he meant by those drawled questions, those ambiguous references? While I was being driven homeward I scouted as absurd the idea that he could have made any real search after the truth. That I had been born years ago in Brussels of parents whose name was Claud, could not by any possibility of search have resulted in his power of denial. It surpassed rational credence that he should have the shadow of a fact wherewith to equip himself against me. No, I convinced myself, his hatred (if hatred it could be called) was due solely to his fear lest I might win the woman of his choice.

Before retiring that night, I knocked as usual at the door of Mrs. Dorian's sitting-room. My guardian was there alone; Casimir, who kept fairly early hours, had already gone to rest. I seated myself at Mrs. Dorian's side, and narrated just what had passed between her nephew and myself. She slowly nodded while she listened, and at length, when I had finished, she said:

" His father has set him up to it. Depend upon what I tell you, Otho. He has inherited the old grudge. Bah! as if I would swell their millions by leaving them more money! He will probably come to me, now; if he staid away it would look like open warfare, and that is what he wishes to avoid. *Dame*, when he does come I will show him what respect is due us both."

"I beg that you will say nothing of any slight to me," I broke in. "You must indeed promise me that you will keep wholly silent there. I have no wish that Foulke Dorian should exult in having inflicted upon me the least uneasiness. If he is ever really insulting I assure you that I shall resent it."

"As you please, Otho," said my guardian. "I shall doubtless have my hands full, fighting my own battle. If he attempts the *collet monté* style with me, I shall very soon give him a taste of my temper. It is too preposterous! These Dorians were plain weavers a few years ago. New-York doesn't often draw a social line anywhere, but it drew one at them, with their lack of grammar, their primeval manners and their vulgar house in East Broadway. How well I remember that house, with shades at every window, where a swan was floating on a lake at the foot of a marble staircase. Ah, the great Balzac would have loved those shades; he would have told you just how many feathers there were in each swan. And by the way, there were not any; they were mere white daubs. I sent them flying, those swans, when I married Monsieur Steven's brother. All the old French people welcomed me as soon as I went over. There were some very charming French residents in New-York at that time — no doubt they are there still. They knew very well who the De Lilles were; my marriage simply made the whole Dorian family; from that time ever since they have assumed airs."

"How then," I asked, "do you account for Foulke having shown you the disrespect of never having visited you while here?"

Mrs. Dorian tossed upon the lamplit table at her side the French novel which she had been reading when I entered. "All the hard things that are said about one's self manage to reach one somehow," she exclaimed — "by hook or by crook, as the English say. I was talking with that little gossip of an American, the other day, Mrs. Merrimac. You have met her — you told me. Her husband knows Monsieur Steven, the father of Foulke. It turns out that this estimable old gentleman — he is now old and a confirmed invalid, I believe — considers that I have behaved shockingly in having adopted a boy who was no kin to me. He growls about it quite eloquently among a few of his intimates. He thinks it a wrong to his own son, Foulke, as the money which I possess originally belonged to his brother."

"This throws a new light upon Foulke's conduct," I said. "But did you not tell me, madame," I added, "that Mr. Steven Dorian was himself very rich?"

"He has millions. He is now one of the great New-York capitalists. He was always economical, to express it charitably. But of late years he has become notoriously avaricious. To Foulke he allows *carte blanche* in everything, but to him alone. He covets my fortune — every *sou* of it — for his son. Ah, it is not new, this sort of disease; it is one of nature's subtle revenges. The man who fails to do more than just keep body and soul together is often happier than he who crowds his bank-vaults with specie. All that unused gold reaches out a thin yellow hand and clutches him. Before he knows it he is a miser. And there is no more biting kind of poverty than that. Monsieur Steven, they tell me, has the malady in its most raging form. If I go to America with you and Casimir in September it will be something to see in that dreary country. I have never met a real miser; it will be very interesting to watch Steven; it will give me one of my impressions. I think I will say this to Foulke if he visits me and attempts to show any of his condescending grandeur. By the way, I hope he will come; I am bristling for an interview."

"That is very evident," I smiled.

On the following day Foulke Dorian did come. His visit was paid in the afternoon, at the very time when Ada Gramercey and I were taking our ride together. I shall never forget that ride. As we returned homeward through the breezy twilight between the lovely bordering boughs of the Bois de Boulogne, we let our horses slacken their speed to a walk. A delicious turfy smell exhaled from the woodland all about us, balmy residue of a shower which had fallen in torrents that morning and then left the sky richly blue. Seated there at my side on her glossy thoroughbred, clad in her dark, trim habit, with her pure, chiselled face rosily tinged by recent exercise, and the abundant auburn hair peeping in one thick knot below her hat rim, she made a figure irresistibly patrician.

"I should like to ride on like this forever," I said. And then, because the words struck me as commonplace and precisely like what every lover in every novel I had read is sure to say under similar circumstances, I gave a most prosaic little laugh and continued: " But I should like to do more, Miss Gramercey — something equally impossible, too."

" What more?" she asked, stooping down to pat the neck of her beautiful horse, in whose thin skin, moist from his galloping, the large swollen veins were visible.

" Oh, I should like to sweep Austria from the face of the globe."

" How unkind to poor papa! "

" I should dislike being unkind to your father, of all people. All people but one — yourself."

Her hazel eyes were full of a smiling roguery as she turned them on mine. " Then you should not object to my seeing those delightful mountains," she said softly.

I leaned much closer to her; our horses' necks almost grazed one another; I could have touched her hand so easily, where it lay in its drab gauntlet, idly holding the reins !

"I object to losing you — that is all. I want always to have you near me. I love you. You are every thing on earth to me. I wish with all my soul that you would let me one day call you my wife."

She averted her face, but I could see the color fade from it. In the peace of the sweet, damp woods where we rode I heard the hoofs of the horses fall solid on the yielding soil. She kept silent, while my heart beat with hope and with despair equally. It seemed an age until she said :

"I have not thought of marriage . . yet. I have often told myself that I would never marry while papa lives."

"And you will not alter this resolve now?"

She slowly shook her head. "He needs my companionship more than you know."

"If you were my wife he could still possess it."

She quickened her horse's pace a little. "It is growing late," she said. The words sounded almost like a jeer to me. My thoughts had flown to Foulke Dorian.

"Will you give me no answer but that?" I appealed, in a tone more demanding and ungentle than I was perhaps aware of.

Her own pride of manner came back to her in an instant. "You are exacting," she said, letting me see her full face once more, lifted rather haughtily above her slender white throat.

"And you are wilfully cruel," I returned, with unrepressed heat. "Either you wish to play with and torment me, or you care for someone else better. Which is it? I have the right to know."

"I do not perceive your right," she said chillingly. "It exists only in your imagination, Mr. Claud."

"You do care for him," I exclaimed with bitterness. "I mean Foulke Dorian. And you will not tell me so — I think because you are ashamed."

"Ashamed?" she repeated, with a scornful surprise.

"Yes. He is such an empty, arrogant, self-sufficient creature, totally unworthy of you in every way. It is monstrous that you should love him. Ah, he has gone more adroitly to work than I, however! He has deluged you with adoration for months! Flattery is what you prize, and he has given you plenty of it. When I next meet him, have I your permission to congratulate him?"

She looked at me with flashing eyes and a curled lip. Then she smote her horse once, sharply, and made him break into a canter. I did the same with mine. A few minutes later I had repented of my tirade. She kept her face away from mine throughout the rest of the ride, which she managed, with the increasing speed of her horse, to make almost as brief as possible. She reached the inner court of her own dwelling at a swift gallop. A groom came forward and assisted her to alight. But I wheeled my horse so that he barred her progress indoors, and stooping downward I said, looking her straight in the eyes:

"Forgive me — do say that you forgive me! My sole excuse is that I love you. Pity me and be kind!"

She stood there in the early summer twilight, with her skirts gathered about her pliant figure, a picture of enchanting maidenhood.

"You were very rude — unwarrantably so," she said. And then she made a gesture as if to pass within the house. I stretched my hand downward. "But you will pardon me," I whispered. She did not take my hand. A smile of irony crossed her face. "Is this your mode of flattery?" she asked. "Well, you shall see how little I prize it." She at once swerved aside from me and passed hurriedly into the house.

I rode away full of misery and indignation. On reaching home I went up into Casimir's new studio, a large, airy room, hung with some fine old tapestries which we had purchased not many days ago together. I found Casimir seated at his easel, no longer painting but regarding his canvas by the dreamy light which streamed in from a broad adjacent window. He gave me the smile of welcome that so few others could ever win from him, and at once asked me concerning my ride, which he knew I was to take with Ada Gramercy that afternoon.

"Oh, it has made me wretched," I told him, sinking into a chair at his side. Instantly his hand, soft and white as a woman's, stole into mine. "Otho!" he exclaimed, "you love her — I guessed it a week ago.   But she cannot have refused you!"

His admiration of me was so profound and loyal that such an event appeared to him incredible.

"It is almost as bad as a refusal," I said gloomily. "Perhaps it is even worse."   And then I told him just what had occurred, sparing myself in no detail of the narration. "No doubt," I finished, "you will assert that I am dreadfully to blame."

"No," he declared, the affection that he felt for me blinding him with speed to my fault. "You spoke a little hastily toward the last, but you had asked her to be your wife. You had paid her that honor. She should have remembered it and valued it. If she really cared for someone else more than you" (and my friend pronounced these words as though he were touching upon some remote chance) "then she would have made her position plain at once. To tell you that you were exacting because you wanted a simple answer to so grave a question —*peste!* it was atrocious! To you, Otho, it was insolent!"

"Ah, Casimir," I said, "I am afraid you side too warmly with your friend. You treat the case as if I had been a royal prince proposing to some lady of inferior quality."

"She is a queen in her way — be assured of that," said Casimir, with his voice full of sympathy and disapprobation combined. "A queen of coquetry and vanity, who delights in having such men as you are sue to her, that she may afterward boast and exult."

"No, no," I replied. "If I thought that it would not be so hard to forget her. But I must believe otherwise. I must believe that she has treated me thus because of Foulke Dorian only. He is a man of no charm, no intellect, wit, amiability. Even his adherents (and he has a few in Paris whom his great reputed wealth attracts) have more than once admitted this. But months ago he began his suit, and has pushed it with dogged perseverance ever since. It is that determined, unremitting courtship which is nearly always sure of conquest in the end."

"And if she prefers such a man to you," exclaimed Casimir, rising and throwing an arm about my neck, "then she is not worthy of wasting another thought upon."

This truly passionate partisan made by no means the best of counsellors. I do not think that just then I could have had a worse than Casimir. Egotism is such an easy pitfall, and when we are anxious for the doleful comfort of convincing ourselves that we have been wronged, admiring assurances of it carry danger in their delivery. Already Foulke Dorian had become odious to me; his reception of my overtures on the balcony had certainly pushed this result, though it was fated to occur after my unhappy interview with Ada Gramercey.

And yet now, at this very point in my life, I owe to myself the statement that I struggled against nursing and brooding upon my hatred. I recalled the past. How fearful is the significance of those words no one can here dispute. I strove to set before my vision in unflinching lines the fact of my proven fallibility. If the devil were really in my blood, let the devil be cast out. If Dorian did not accompany the Gramerceys to Austria — and I had been assured that he would not do so — why should not Casimir and I take a trip to Holland or northern Germany until the time came for the American voyage? In this way I could avoid all meeting with the man I detested, provided he should remain in Paris throughout that intervening time; and if he should depart for any other portion of Europe I would thus run but slight risk of encountering him. My guardian had a dinner engagement that evening, and Casimir and myself dined together at a favorite café. During our repast I made to him the proposal of this plan, which had been forming in my mind by a half-unconscious process. He accepted it without demur.

The prospect of escape gave me a dismal pleasure. It was torment to think of Ada Gramercey leaving Paris with our quarrel still unhealed, but I had not only the pangs of love to fight against —I must also struggle with those of a darker sort. Foulke Dorian's very name had become an abomination to me. I realized what that meant —or rather I trembled with a sort of dumb horror at what it might mean. Leagues of social and educational difference lay between me and the rough, turbid-souled peasant whom I had seen vilely strike my mother down and stain me with her innocent blood. Still, I was his son. I had already had reasons to recall it. I dared not forget it.

When Mrs. Dorian returned at about eleven o'clock, that evening, I heard her quick step in the corridor outside my own suite of apartments and went to join her at once. I had previously learned from one of the servants that Foulke had visited her during the afternoon.

"Oh, yes, he came," she said, setting a brilliant bouquet of roses that she held upon the mantel and throwing off a gossamer gold-threaded shawl upon the back of a chair. Then she dropped into the chair and began pulling off her long, modish gloves. In her festal dress of bright tints, with her jewels and her corsage of flowers, and her hair, that age had not yet markedly tinted, worn quite elaborately, she looked like one of those gay, fashionable, self-poised, worldly wise and time-defying Frenchwomen out of the pages of her own beloved Balzac. A lamp, in a rosy shade, stood near her on a table draped with a rich embroidered cloth. All the rest of the room was in shadow save that portion where she sat. It was like a picture by some deft *genre*-painter among her own clever countrymen—the artists whom Casimir held in disgust as grossly unspiritual. Mrs. Dorian did not appear at all spiritual; she was clearly the reverse, but by no means grossly. And the crisp, fleet words that she now spoke, broken with little scraps of low, guttural laughter, did not in any degree interfere with the *ensemble*.

"Oh, yes, my dear Otho," she continued, tugging at her gloves, "he came, he saw, but unlike Cæsar, he did not conquer. Oh, I was quite prepared for him, I assure you. He was *bien ganté;* he was *bien chaussé;* he was elegant-looking and aristocratic in the extreme. I could scarcely realize that he was a Dorian; I put up my glasses and began searching for some vague sign of those multitudinous freckles; it seemed impossible that they had all vanished. But like the swans from the windows of his uncle's hideous house in East Broadway, they had positively flown. It is marvellous what one generation will do. Foulke is really a gentleman. I believe that I presently told him so—or something rather like it."

"A somewhat belligerent way of opening the

conversation," I said. "You must have received him with a rattle of musketry."

"He stood fire very well. I began by asking after several branches of the family which I was sure he felt ashamed of. His father and uncle felt ashamed of them years ago, so what might not one expect from him? I inquired concerning the health of Mrs. Judkins and Mr. Bigsbee and Mrs. Crump. Very unaristocratic names, are they not? By no means so graceful and smooth as Dorian. But they belonged to people who are or were the near kindred of Foulke. He knew nothing about them, however. At this I took occasion to be vastly astonished. *Mon Dieu!* not to know one's own relations! It was horrible! Ah, his papa had doubtless brought him up in this way. And poor Mrs. Crump! To forget her — the sister of Monsieur Steven's own mother! She had kept a millinery-shop in Division Street; I had bought one or two bonnets there myself, out of sheer good nature. . . And from this sort, of prickly reminiscence, my dear Otho, it was an easy digression to the reports which I had heard concerning his papa's extraordinary avarice."

"No doubt you found it so, madame," I said, smiling. "How Mr. Dorian must have enjoyed his visit! Pray, did he leave in a fury?"

"No. It was a kind of white heat. I don't believe he will ever come again, and I am sure I don't care. He deserves all that I gave him, for ignoring my presence in Paris. And then to think of their showing any resentment, he and his father, as to how I may leave my own money!"

"You referred to this!" I exclaimed.

"*Assurément.* Why not? I had heard it. If it was false he could refute it. But he did not. He saw very well that I knew how true it was."

"There was nothing said regarding myself?" I inquired.

"I mentioned your name once or twice, quite carelessly. And I noticed that each time I did so his lips tightened and his eyes sent me a slant, odd look from under their drooped lids. He has such extraordinary eyelids, by the way. They gave me quite an impression; they remind me of window shades that have become loose on their rollers. And do you not think his smile remarkably acid and his eyes remarkably dull and cold, Otho?"

"Remarkably," I said.

X.

PARIS had now grown exceedingly hot. There had been a faint rumor of cholera, too, that year, which combined with the heat in sending droves of people out of town. I had hoped against hope for some message from Ada Gramercey before she left with her father. None came, and I at length learned that they had taken their departure. Soon afterward I began my preparations for starting with Casimir. Mrs. Dorian did not at all object to remaining behind. She declared that even when deserted Paris was agreeable to her and that she needed repose in order to collect her energies for the unpalatable American journey.

Once or twice in the club of which I had become a member I saw Foulke Dorian. We exchanged, on these occasions, a cool and distant nod. His presence there brought me some comfort, at least. He had not followed the Gramerceys to Austria, and very possibly he had been forbidden from doing so.

But I was fated soon to meet him in a very different way. It had never occurred to me that Casimir's existence and change of fortune might both have reached his knowledge. I had given no thought to the question of whether these facts, once disclosed, would interest him or not. Mrs. Dorian had openly told her friends that Casimir and I were now her co-heirs; perhaps she may even have mentioned the subject to Foulke when he had visited her. The studio of my friend, although translated to the same house in which we all three dwelt, was frequently the resort of a few fellow-artists, and in a manner separated from our lower apartments. The *concierge* had indeed grown to regard it as a special abode by itself, and those whom its young proprietor received there or those whom he did not had become a matter of entirely his own concern. He was still by no means above selling his pictures, and the altered conditions of his life had attracted purchasers who had never before paid heed to his work, but who now regarded it with new eyes, as gilded by the halo of an assured prosperity. The moment we rid genius of the necessity to strive, it is surprising how swift a turn takes place in the tide of appreciation.

One afternoon, having returned from a ride, I went up into the studio, expecting to find Casimir busy there. But he was absent. I had dismounted hastily in the court below; I still held my riding-whip, and stood carelessly striking it against one limb and gazing out of the great north window, which commanded a fine view of certain buildings and localities, for a longer time than I was perhaps aware. Any *coup d'œil* of Paris always fascinated me; it reminded me of a sleeping tigress; you never know at what moment she may not wake and stretch out a murderous claw.

Suddenly a knock at the door roused me. I quickly crossed the room, opened the door, and found myself face to face with Foulke Dorian.

My surprise was intense. I saw him start, and then control himself. He advanced across the threshold; he held in his hand something that looked like a letter, and which I afterward perceived to be unsealed. His embarrassment was at once evident as he began to address me in confused, almost haphazard words.

"I — I beg pardon. I wished to see — I had been told — I have a note of introduction to — yes, to Monsieur Casimir Laprade."

"This is his studio," I said. "But he is not here at present."

"Ah . . yes . . thanks," was the reply. For a moment he seemed about to retire from the chamber. Then he put up an eye-glass and glanced about him at the quaint, decorative surroundings.

"A very pretty room," he soon proceeded, his customary drawl returning to him with renewed self-possession. He now directed his gaze upon myself, letting the glass drop on its thin silken cord. "Do you think that Monsieur Laprade will be away all the afternoon?"

"Most probably not," I answered. "Do you care to wait until his return?" I wheeled a soft-rolling cushioned chair two or three paces toward him as I spoke. It cost me something to show this courtesy, but I performed it with steeled nerves.

"You're very good," he said. He looked down into the velvety recess of the chair, but he did not seat himself. "I could call again, of course. What are the gentleman's usual hours?"

"He is generally here during the morning," I said. "But he often paints until evening as well."

"Ah . . yes." He had begun to stare about the room again, repeating the operation with the eye-glass and letting it drop when he re-addressed me. "The young man is a decided genius, I hear. Rivière gave me my note of introduction. Do you know Rivière?"

"Not well. He is a friend of Casimir's, I believe." I purposely called my own friend by his first name.

"He speaks with enthusiasm of Monsiur Laprade," said Foulke Dorian. The tone was now just tinged, and no more, with a sarcastic incredulity. "It gave me a curiosity — I mean a . . er . . wish — to see some of his work. It is for sale, I hear?"

The rising inflection on that last word was condescension itself. I bowed quietly. "Monsieur

Laprade sells his pictures now and then," I said, " when the mood pleases him."

Those dull eyes fixed themselves upon my own, now, with a sleepy steadiness. " Ah . . quite so. He is not compelled, then, to paint for . . er . . subsistence?"

" By no means," I replied. " His aunt (who is also yours, Mr. Dorian) has the warmest admiration for his talents."

" Indeed! You mean that she supports him?"

" I mean that she has adopted him as her son," I said, biting my lip.

" Yes? Truly? She is a very benevolent person, that aunt of mine, is she not?"

" She is one of the best and noblest women in the world," I said, with a decision and force of speech that widely differed from the loitering drawl I had just heard.

He walked toward a canvas that hung not far from where he had stood and peered closely at it, as a near-sighted observer will do. After a little pause he said, still scanning the picture: " You speak from experience, of course."

" I do. From a longer and deeper experience in Mrs. Dorian's goodness than Monsieur Laprade's."

He slowly turned and faced me again. There was an indescribable chill, a stealthy, insidious hostility, about this simple movement. It somehow prepared me for some bit of sly, masked assault.

" I am sure it is very good of you not to feel

jealous, Mr. Claud," he said, "at the arrival of this new claimant for my aunt's favor."

He was busying himself with a button of his neat-fitting gloves as I responded: "Casimir Laprade and I are devoted friends, and I could not have more affection for him if he were my own brother."

"Really? That is very fortunate."

"I do not see that it is especially fortunate," I returned, with curt speed, "except in the sense that disinterested friendship is always a precious thing."

He gave a low laugh. "I .. er .. I was not taking so elevated a view. The affection, it occurred to me, might be fortunate in other ways. If Mrs. Dorian were to die, for instance. There would, if I may so term it, be a peaceful division of the spoils."

I felt myself flush as I replied: "Your allusion cannot be misunderstood; it is too uncivilly manifest."

He made a dainty, deprecating gesture. "Uncivilly, Mr. Claud?" he murmured.

"Precisely that."

"But I am never willingly uncivil." He said this with an air of offended *hauteur*, but with a touch of satirical compassion as well.

"If the rudeness were unintentional," I returned, "I find it none the less unpleasant. We usually do so, in these cases."

He lifted both hands, smiling. "Ah, you are not to be appeased." Then he gave his silver-tipped walking-stick a jaunty little ruminative twirl, watching it as he did so. "Frankly, I don't think I will wait for Monsieur Laprade, as I see that you are bent upon being quarrelsome. Are you not a little disposed in that direction? It seems to me that I have heard so." His smile was very bright and keen as he spoke these words; it made his eyes look duller.

"I don't know what you have heard," I said, involuntarily taking a step nearer to him. "I must request you to explain your meaning."

"Ah . . you bring me to account, eh? You are so fond of bringing people to account." The sneer was now perfectly undisguised.

I spoke very calmly. "Innuendoes are objectionable to me," I said. "That is all. And if you choose to call it bringing you to account, I do so."

He moved in his easy, well-bred way toward the door. "I really have no more to say. I must wish you good-day, Mr. Claud."

"Pardon me," I broke in, still tranquil. "But you have referred to reports concerning myself, and you have done this with a contemptuous accent and bearing which I cannot permit to pass unnoticed."

He turned short, facing me again, and throwing back his head a little. His anger was now

evident, though I had as yet shown none whatever.

"Oh, if you want facts," he retorted, with a
harsh note in his decorous, modulated drawl, "I
can remind you of your having been rude to Miss
Gramercey."

"You mention Miss Gramercey's name. Did
she tell you that I was rude to her?"

He twirled his stick again. "Her manner in
referring to you told me so."

I went straight up to his side till we stood
scarcely three inches apart. No doubt I had
grown pale, and I think my next words were
somewhat hoarsely spoken. "I demand to know,"
I said, "whether Miss Gramercey told you what
took place during our last meeting."

He receded from me. "And I refuse to reply," he said, with fastidious disgust and a good
deal of smothered wrath as well. "However,
even if she told me nothing I could draw my
inferences."

"What inferences?"

"That you quarrelled with her. You and she
have not met since you rode out together on
Monday last. You made no adieus to her. The
whole matter is quite apparent. She has been
very *commode* and nice to you. Of course you
would have gone there if the former terms existed. I have no more to say. Good-afternoon."

He bowed slightly and slipped past me. As

his hand touched the knob of the closed door I said, with louder voice than I had yet used:

"Since you are so quick to read the moods and feelings of this lady, it is too bad that you were forbidden from accompanying her. Your services as an interpreter would have been invaluable."

I threw into this speech a scathing irony. Self-control for the moment left me. But instantly afterward I regretted what I had said, so fixed was my purpose not to give anger the least headway.

His hand trembled a little as it grasped the door-knob. Something like a speck of flame seemed to prick through the dulness of each eye. He appeared irresolute whether to hide his rage by an immediate exit or to remain and give some open proof of it. At length, with a flutter of the lips that betrayed agitation more than his high-pitched, querulous voice did, he chose the latter course.

"You are so like my aunt. I am constantly seeing new points of resemblance between yourself and her."

Not the least hint of his true meaning had yet entered my mind. "It is an honor to resemble her," I replied. "You compliment me, Mr. Dorian, against your will."

"An honor!" he exclaimed. He lifted one hand to his mouth as though to repress an explosion of mocking laughter which I could not but hear and see. "Excuse me, but the *honor* of such a resemblance might be held somewhat questionable."

I still did not dream of his true meaning. I thought that he was merely casting a slur upon Mrs. Dorian, whom it was supposable that he should dislike after the reproofs which she had lately administered.

"You may hold your aunt in fine scorn," I said, "but to me she is very dear. I love her devotedly, and I will not permit her to be lightly spoken of."

"Yes . . ah . . yes . . I understand. You regard her as a son. A son . . yes. It is very clear to me, naturally."

For the first time a suspicion of what he meant flashed upon me. And yet even as it did so I sought to drive it back. The thing could not be. His nature was perhaps a mean one, and we were both in love with the same woman. He did not like me — perhaps he detested me. But a jibe that would tip itself with such acrid venom! No, impossible! I was wretchedly in error; I had misinterpreted — misjudged — imagined.

"Mrs. Dorian has been a second mother to me," I said, measuring each word. I do not think there was any threat in my tones, or any sign of what thought had just swept through my brain.

"A second mother?" he repeated. "You forget how much you and she look alike. Is it quite certain, my very lofty and assuming friend, that we are not blood relations? No doubt you were born in Belgium, after all, and were kept there discreetly until that eccentric French lady, my aunt, thought it safe to have you appear in New-York. Eccentric French ladies sometimes commit imprudences, you know, before marriage as well as after. I don't believe my late uncle could ever have been induced to acknowledge you as his son, and after his death Mrs. Dorian would of course have found it awkward to account for you except as she did. I should say, for my part, that the whole affair had been most cleverly managed and that" . . .

Until now I think he had preserved the current of this atrocious insult because my pallor and my look of horror may have seemed like the consternation of discovery and affright. The effect of these stabbing sentences had been to make me for a brief while speechless, even nerveless. But suddenly a great rush of passion dispelled all that. I sprang toward him, and in an instant our separate strengths were pitted against each other to the full. And mine, trained and nurtured by years of healthful exercise, far exceeded his. I whirled him about, and forced him into the chair lately proffered him. My hand, in a tense clutch, was fixed upon his collar. I cannot be sure just how long my own fury seemed to myself uncontrollable. His first gasp for breath calmed it, placing it within the bounds of that resentment

which seeks to chastise rather than destroy. I
released him, but as he feebly tottered to his feet
my eye fell upon the riding-whip which I had cast
only a brief time since on a near table. I seized
it, and darting toward him as he stood dazed and
disarrayed before me, I rained upon his head and
face a series of merciless cutting blows. He tried
to grapple with me while I did this, but I held
him at arm's length with my disengaged hand.
Then, the ignominy of my punishment complete, I
flung him from me with violent force. He fell in a
half supine posture against the tufted chair, but as I
threw away the whip he again struggled to his feet.
His face was livid, and the lash-strokes already
showed their marks upon it in reddish welts.

I folded my arms and looked at him. "Take
your hat and cane and go," I commanded. "Go
at once. You have my answer to your base lie.
If you speak a word I will do worse than I have
done already."

He obeyed me. It did not then seem strange
that he should offer no further resistance. Afterward I wondered at it as a show of singular cowardice. But not then. A sense of power used in
a supremely just cause made his submission the
one necessary sequence. It must have been the
worst kind of physical fear that impelled him.
He looked a most pitiable and abject figure as he
staggered off, crestfallen and certainly tingling
with pain.

I dropped into a chair when he was gone, breathing heavily and feeling the blood still surge through every vein. Composure gradually came to me, and with it that reflective change which is like the blue of sky after the dwindled tempest. But I could not accuse myself. I had punished no personal wrong. The outrage uttered against Mrs. Dorian's good name might have fired many a more sluggish defender. Owing her the inestimable debt which I did owe, could I tamely have borne this monstrous aspersion.

The light had grown dim in the studio when Casimir, with his buoyant step, entered it. I rose and stretched forth both hands toward him as he advanced. He gave an alarmed start. The late, scant sunshine of the chamber revealed to him how pale and perturbed was my face.

"Otho," he said, anxiously, taking my hand, "what has happened?"

"Don't ask me," I exclaimed. . . . It was a mere form of speech. There was inexpressible relief in having him question me, and in the thought that I could unburden to him my swelling heart. I dropped his hands and flung both arms about his neck. And then, leaning my head upon his shoulder, I sobbed like a child.

A little later I dashed away my tears, in shame of them, as men will nearly always do. But Casimir, thrilled and pierced by sympathy no less than astonishment, now clung to one of my hands with both his own, imploring that I would tell him the cause of my grief. His love came forth in those moments with a new beauty and pathos. I doubt if I can call it by its rightful name without declaring it a love as deep as any that man has ever felt for man.

The studio was filled with dusk before our talk ended. I told Casimir everything which concerned Foulke Dorian's conduct and my reception of it. He shuddered and clinched his hands when I came to the deadly insult paid my aunt.

"The viper!" he cried. "If you had killed him, Otho, I would not have blamed you!"

"Hush," I said. The word 'kill' hurt me; I recalled the first blind, mad sensation when I made my attack. "There is more to tell you, Casimir," I slowly went on. "It concerns this resemblance between Mrs. Dorian and myself, which you have no doubt observed."

Casimir's eyes widened. "You are really related?" he asked.

"No." . . I was glad that the studio had become so dim. I did not want him to see my face as I went through the full history of my own life. . . He listened without a word for a long time, while I spoke what it now seemed best that I should no longer hide. The warmth and vigor of his friendship, disclosed anew at so trying an hour, had filled me with confidential longing and robbed my narration of all reluctant shame. I omitted no detail.

Before I had ended he knew my past life in its entirety.   And my final words were these:

"Now, Casimir, I have told you all. But it seems to me that this should be only the beginning."

"The beginning, Otho?" he said, in a voice rich with tenderness and feeling. "I do not understand."

"I mean, Casimir, that others should know the truth.   Yes, the whole world.   Am I wrong? After what I have done, will Foulke Dorian scruple to publish his suspicions, tainting with their foul falsehood the honor of her who has been my priceless friend?   And if his slander gains belief, as slander so often does, how can I curse myself enough for not having forestalled its malice?"

I felt the pressure of my companion's hand in the deepened dusk. "Accept my advice, Otho, if you always reject it hereafter.   That your father died upon the scaffold is no real disgrace to you — God knows it is not! But society, which is always cruel enough to hold it as one, must not be given this easy means of hurling at you an unmerited contempt.   And as for Foulke Dorian's future course, trust me when I assure you that self-interest, if not cowardice, will prompt him to shield his aunt's name. He has no shadow of proof that what he said was true. He does not really hold it true. He tried to sting you with it because he hates you, and he hates you because he is jealous of you."

"Jealous?" I murmured. My thoughts flew to my father, as they always did when I heard that word. And what wonder?

"Yes," pursued Casimir. "How often we say of men's quarrels: '*Il y a une femme là-dessous*'! And we are nearly always right. He will say nothing; he will do nothing — at least, not for the present. He may take some mean revenge in the future. You have, in that case, only to be on your guard. A snake coils and glides, but he dies easily; one stout stroke will kill him."

"This is the land of duels," I said. "I expect a challenge. If I receive one" —

"From him?" broke in Casimir, with a scornful laugh. "From a whipped dog like that? No, indeed!"

"But if a challenge comes," I said, "I will meet him. And you, Casimir" . . .

"Will stand handsomely by you. Never fear. But you are wrong. He will cure the marks of your horsewhip with something safer than new blood letting — rest sure of that."

Casimir was right. We waited several days in Paris, delaying our intended journey, to give Foulke Dorian the opportunity of communicating with me if so disposed. But he made no sign. For my own part, I loathed duelling, and held it as one of the darkest social ills. But I could not help, in the present case, a desire to afford redress where I had dealt such deep humiliation, however wantonly incited it had been.

In the next week Casimir and I left Paris. Mrs. Dorian knew nothing of what had passed. I accepted my friend's counsel; I preserved absolute silence in all ways. Our trip was a delightful one. We spent nearly a month in the old Dutch and Flemish towns, besides catching a farewell glimpse of my beloved Switzerland. In early September we returned and found Mrs. Dorian resigned yet melancholy over the projected American journey.

I made inquiries concerning the Gramerceys in Paris, but could learn nothing. By the middle of September we all three took passage for New-York.

XI.

A QUARTER of a century or so has made striking changes in New-York. Dwellers in the city itself do not recognize how radical these are. It is not only that bold avenues have pushed their way up along the island, lined on either hand with solid and stately buildings, and easily prophesying how Central Park will one day cease to be a suburban contradiction of its name, and lie, like Hyde Park in London, midway of a huge, busy, compact metropolis. The mere growth of the city is evident enough, as also its partial gain in architectural grace after the long undisputed rule of severe ugliness. Houses are frequently reared, at present, without violating every known law of beauty, or sometimes they gleam like happy incidents of true art amid surroundings that accentuate the hard prose of brick-laying and stone-cutting. In this way we all know that New-York has at last waked from her slothful indifference. It has already become commonplace to give her the credit of such reformation. We drive upon her broad boulevards, sweeping miles out into the country, and though they are now lonely enough, fancy

easily borders them with noble structures. We
think what palaces may one day loom above the
glittering Hudson, on that imperial thoroughfare
which is now the Riverside. We mark here and
there in the really grand park a statue exquisite
and perfect as that of Shakespeare at the southern
end of the Mall, and people the whole forest-like
expanse with busts and statues yet unhewn from
their marble or uncast from their bronze. The
sense of promise in all this is overpowering. The
city has grown so mightily in less than three short
decades! — since the days when I watched the
black mass of rock from my bedroom window,
and seemed to hear not far away the hum of that
slowly creeping civilization which would soon
shatter and crush it! We feel on the threshold
of an immense creation, as our eyes roam over the
vast area on which a magnificent city shall one
day stand. But a strange depression waits upon
this contemplation. We shall long ago have been
dust when all is finished and splendid. The wea-
riest of us have a thrill that we cannot at first
explain. Then it resolves itself into this: We
should like to come back and see it in all its
grandeur — when it has had a past, a history, a
record of far-reaching traditions. The field for
speculation is immeasurable; the optimist may
dream of civic ideals made tangible, the pessimist
may see luxury throned on ruined republican-
ism. But there is mortification, almost pain, in

the thought that *we* shall have moved only among crude and feeble beginnings. Perhaps our descendants will wonder that we ever cared for Rome, Paris, Vienna, when this superb Manhattan Island shall contain its lordly repositories of painting and sculpture, its treasure-stored museums, its countless monuments of majesty and dignity!

But the changes now most appreciable to one who looks below the surface of our metropolitan progression are those that possess a purely social import. The modes of living have been altered in more ways than we at first realize. Foreign customs have crept into New York at a stealthy but sure pace. Twenty-five years ago a good many people dined at two o'clock and supped simply at half-past six, who have to-day quite forgotten the indulgence of any such primitive habits. The dining-room was not seldom in the basement portion of the abode, and food was cooked and served with homely skill and in few courses. The upper dining-room, adjacent to the drawing-rooms (then so commonly called " parlors ") had only begun to assert its claim, like the butler and footman who superseded the widely accepted " waitress." Late balls, with a profusion of viands, were rare. Very few people, even of the wealthiest class, kept more than one private carriage, and many kept none at all. Extravagant and sumptuous costumes among women were by no means usual. Neither old nor young gentlemen of any class whatever habitually donned evening attire, and "the dress-coat and white cravat" were as often seen at a morning wedding as at an entertainment prolonged until midnight. The fashions of England and France were already aped by a certain throng, but its number was not large and its influence was little felt. To-day it would be hard to find a boarding-house in the extreme East or West portions of town where a six-o'clock dinner is not held *de rigeur;* and tea, when not drank daintily at five o'clock, is nearly sure to be an accompaniment of breakfast. As for costly equipages, these, like butlers and footmen, are now a legion among us, and too frequently the funds that secure them are squeezed out of meagre incomes, or robbed from the over-trustful grocer and butcher in adjoining streets. The clerk in a Sixth Avenue dry-goods store who anoints his locks and takes his sweet-heart to a dance where the tickets of admission are not more than a dollar each, will hire the con-ventional swallow-tail coat for one night if he be not already fortunate enough to own this gar-ment; and the lady whom he thus escorts will spend her last savings to air a costume of becom-ing richness. New York has not a vestige left of her old provincial moderation. She has gone the way of all great cities, though there was incentive for trust in a wiser and calmer growth. It has been of little avail that the vast Atlantic rolls between her and monarchical cities. From the pretence and vainglory witnessed throughout every various grade of her society to the grossness of her political corruptions, she offers hardly a point of divergence. Not even her worst vices have a touch of originality; they are all imported —smuggled through, as one might say, free of duty, to cheat that revenue of decency which the thrift and honor of her patriots and founders once firmly established.

When Mrs. Dorian, Casimir and myself reached New-York, the transition period had more than passed its primary decisive stage. Of course I now saw the social side of the great city for the first time. Even if I had been brought into contact with it in my childhood I would have been too young for any basis of comparison to aid my present survey. And now it all struck me as very interesting, novel and extraordinary.

"One must be terribly respectable, here, or one is nobody," declared Mrs. Dorian, soon after our arrival. We were then at an elegant and commodious hotel, and were looking about for more permanent and domestic quarters. "My poor old house in Lafayette Place will no longer serve, I fear. It is too far 'down town,' as they say here. How the city grows! It is strange that anything should grow so much and improve so little."

"I think it has improved greatly," I said. "It is not the same city at all." And now I turned to Casimir, who was present. "But Casimir is by far the best judge. He sees it for the first time, with unprejudiced yet artistic eyes."

"You wish to have my frank opinion?" asked Casimir, with a twinkle in the gray eyes to which I had just alluded. Thus far he had been rather oddly reticent concerning his new place of abode. He heaved a great comic sigh, and shrugged his shoulders. "It is ugly . . so ugly!" he murmured. "I have no words to tell how ugly I think it. I see rows and rows of houses without one least little beautifying touch. It is to me like a city built by people whose religion is to worship grimness and awkwardness, and who must ignore all beauty on pain of death."

"Delightful!" cried Mrs. Dorian, clapping her hands. "Casimir, like a true poet, has said just what was waiting to be said. I never walk out into the streets here but I wonder at the folly of people for paying the rents they do pay. It is like putting a premium upon hideousness."

My guardian owned a number of the houses to which she so disdainfully referred, and she at length resolved to take up her residence in one of these. It was situated on Fifth Avenue, and after a speedy but thorough renovation it made for us a most agreeable home. Her other property I soon found in a deplorable state. Her American agents had done their duty in a slovenly way, and with regard to neglect of the offices assigned and accepted by them, her lawyers had shown clear

culpability. I was inexperienced in all the dis-
entanglements which were destined to follow, and
yet as neither my nerve nor my judgment was
lacking, several weeks of close application gave
me the clew of the labyrinth. The task set for
me by the faulty stewardship of others presented
sharp difficulty. More than once my investiga-
tions verged upon a discovery of something worse
than indolent management. Hours of daily labor
were not alone necessary, but the employment of
capable assistance as well. I set up my office,
like any ordinary man of business, and immersed
myself in documents like the busiest of lawyers.
The responsibility of re-arranging affairs which
had become wretchedly confused was by no means
a light one. Mrs. Dorian's perfect trust in my
capacity for the work, however, acted with stimulating effect; it put me on my mettle, and
doubled my self-reliance. Rapid insight and the
habit of precise thought proved an invaluable help.
What it was requisite to learn I acquired with
speed and surety, although months elapsed before
I had attained any thing like complete mastery
over the details connected with this large and
actually imperilled estate.

But the absorption needful for my new occupation was of solid mental value. It kept my mind
from brooding over a love which I now reflected
on with despair. This love was still deeply rooted
in my heart, inalienable from life itself. I would

have given worlds for the old freedom, but I knew that it lay forever beyond reach. My guardian easily obtained for me an *entreé* into what were held as the best circles. I saw many refined, beautiful and attractive women; but I had also seen many while in Paris and elsewhere. None were like her; her gesture, her glance, her voice, her serenity, her delicate wit — no, not even her peculiar alluring coldness. Just as she had been when I last beheld her, she reigned now as my realized and incarnate ideal. I felt only a melancholy pleasure in talking with other women, since those who reminded me of her did so at their own cost, and those who greatly differed from her wasted upon me their brightest smiles.

Still, society here amused me. My old unconscious art of pleasing people made them seek me on all sides, and shower invitations upon me with lavish hands. I sometimes marvelled to myself that I should be so popular. It seemed strange enough that the shallow trick of saying the right thing at the proper moment, of wearing a gay smile or giving a tender look, should achieve such easy conquest. I took no pride in my success, and won it without an effort. All this has so boastful a ring that I hate to record it. And yet what is there to plume one's self upon in the possession of a talent resultant from no virtue or excellence? I was young, strikingly handsome, highly educated, and credited with the heirship to great wealth. But everything was not said in that. My ability to attract and charm was spontaneous, unsought, and as much born in me as the curve of an eyebrow or the tint of a complexion. And its careless exercise often hid a dreary heartache.

"New-York society agreeably disappoints me," I said to Mrs. Dorian one day. "These fashionable persons among whom you have introduced me are very much like those I met abroad. It is true that they are imitative and unoriginal, and that their assumptions have no place in a country like America. Still, I find little vulgarity — or rather much less than the conditions of their existing at all would have prepared one to expect. What in Europe is transmitted hereditary usage here becomes unwarrantably snobbery; and yet it is all manifested with a surprising tact and cleverness. There is a good deal for the philosopher to lament over, but there is also a good deal for the unthinking participant to enjoy."

"You echo my own opinions," exclaimed Mrs. Dorian, who had chosen a new mood, a new receptivity of impressions, and who had long ago, of course, ceased to surprise me by the slightest novelty of enthusiasm. "My dear Otho, I am in sackcloth and ashes. New-York has altered beyond my most sanguine fancy. Of course she has become imitative; but when I last knew her she had not the faintest faculty even of imitation.

Her *beau monde* was a doleful stupidity in every sense. A few of her Dutch families were banded together in a ridiculous little self-admiring clique. Her entertainments were the soul of dulness and insipidity, without the least air, grace, style. Now I find her quite changed. Her Assemblies at Delmonico's are really brilliant and enjoyable, with their cotillon, their bevies of fresh young damsels, their floral adornments, their tables of banquet. And such a multitude of new faces! So many names that one never heard before! What an amazing place it is, when people can absolutely make a solid, distinguished position here in a few short years! My old friend, Mrs. Stuyvesant Trinitysteeple, laughingly confided to me, the other day, that a certain Mrs. Johnston Smithson, was in great doubt concerning myself. She wanted to know whether I had ever really been anybody in New-York; she had met me somewhere, and liked me, and wished to send me a card for her reception, but she was not sure whether it was just safe or no. Mrs. Trinitysteeple, who is very free of speech, declares that she made bold to reply: 'My dear Mrs. Johnston Smithson, about six years ago a great many similar questions were asked concerning yourself. Yet a much longer time ago than that, Mrs. Dorian was not only my intimate friend but received in the most exclusive set; so you need not feel at all anxious on the subject of her right to drink tea with you.' What a crushing reply, was it not? And how the dear dead Balzac would have exulted in describing such *nouveaux riches* as the Smithsons! But I enjoy this modern element of change excessively. Formerly there were so few pushers and strugglers; it was all one prim monotony; scarcely a single person was trying, as now, to buy his or her way past the select limits. Now there is color, vivacity, a rivalry of extravagance, a contest of castes. Presently we shall have a New-York novelist; he will discover something to write about, and consequently he will exist. They tell me that Newport in the summer has become very delightful; the aspirants, with their ambitions and their dollars, are building beautiful villas there and making it a second theatre for their efforts to be received among the old cottagers. It is a charming little city by the sea; I was there years ago, I remember, and liked its delicious air. Shall we go there next summer? Casimir would delight in it, I fancy. He could be as abhorrent of the fashionables as he is now, and yet fit up a studio looking straight out upon the broad ocean."

"I think I should prefer a quieter place, madame," was my answer. "All this whirl and glitter is well enough here in town, but it often fatigues me . . and then a little time for rest and reading and sensible repose would not be amiss in the warmer months. . . Still, let Casimir and you decide."

Not a vestige of news concerning the Gramerceys had yet reached me, and it was now nearly the beginning of March. I had met many to whom Ada Gramercey in her merry-makings of the previous year had been admiringly known. But none of these, as it chanced, could give me tidings of her present whereabouts. She was still abroad with her father; I learned this, and I learned no more. By some unhappy accident none of the friends of her own sex with whom she would have been likely to correspond entered within my own radius of acquaintanceship. This one was in mourning; that one had gone to Washington for the winter; or still another had herself crossed to Europe. But I was certain of a single disturbing and bitter fact: Foulke Dorian also remained abroad. To associate his absence with that of the Gramerceys had of course become inevitable.

Mrs. Dorian had meanwhile paid a visit upon her brother-in-law, which she described to me with repelling realism.

"I am sure, my dear Otho, that I must have audibly shuddered when I saw him. He still lives in the old Washington Square house where his wife died. I was conducted up-stairs to a large front room, quite bare and grim in its appointments. There he lay, on a lounge in one corner. He was wrapped in a faded dressing-gown. His body had apparently shrunk to nothing; his face was bloodless and withered, and the hand which

he extended to me was like the yellow claw of a
bird. The balls of his eyes appeared to float about
in their murky spaces; they were like the eyes of
a blind man, they were so filmed and glassy, and
yet you somehow knew that they saw. He asked
me to sit near him, and with a voice that was
precisely in his old nasal key.

"'Guess you think I look pretty bad,' he said
to me. 'Most people do. They don't tell me so,
but I can see it in their faces. See it in yours,
Louise.'

"'You certainly do not look well, Steven,' I
answered.

"'No more do you look young. S'pose you
think you ain't aged, but you have. Never you
mind me. Good for twenty dead men yet. No
mistake. Lucky you came when you did. Super-
intend all my business. Mornings usually engaged. Plenty o' life in me. Mean to make a
few more dollars before I go.' Here he laughed
a husky laugh that ended in a spasm of coughing,
while he rubbed his skinny hands together as
though they were numb and he wanted to put heat
in them by the friction. It seemed like mockery,
Otho, but I expressed a hope that he would soon
recover, and asked who were his physicians.

"'Doctors?' he cried, with another wheezy
cough. 'Gave 'em up long ago. All humbugs.
Besides, too expensive. Can't afford any. Doctor
myself.'

"We talked on for some time, and I found that nearly everything he said dealt with either one of two questions — avarice or personality. He has always secretly disliked me, and he now made his illness and feebleness an excuse for all sorts of venomous allusions. On the other hand, I perceived that he was living in the most pinched state of economy. Coal was so dear that he would not pay the price of it, and used coke — as a sleepy, crumbled fire, not far off, assured me. The charges for gas had become extortionate, and he burned candles altogether. He talked of the whole outside world as though it were in a huge conspiracy to defraud him. And finally, after having referred to my increased figure, my sallow complexion and my generally deteriorated looks with enough brazen impudence to have convulsed me with anger if anger at so pitiable a mummy had not been quite ridiculous, he suddenly remembered you, Otho, and inquired sneeringly about your health. I told him you were very well, had grown wonderfully handsome, had taken high collegiate honors in Zürich, and were now both a comfort and a pride to your second mother. But I have never seen such malevolence as he then exhibited. It was like the prolonged snarl of a sick animal. He threw aside all the double meanings of sarcasm; he became snappishly insolent, and with a kind of grisly candor. His avarice and his personality had now blended their forces.

I had no business to leave my money off among Tom, Dick and Harry. I ought to be ashamed of myself, and I very well knew it. Foulke had written him from Paris that I had made you one of my heirs, and a French ragamuffin of an artist the other. It was scandalous that my husband's fortune should not be left in the family — or at least a good half of it. Foulke would know how to save it, invest it, put it to good uses. Foulke was not only a Dorian, but a splendid fellow besides. I was doing an outrageous thing, and he felt it to be a shame that the law could not reach me. And while he said all this, Otho, he lifted his shrivelled shape from the lounge and shook at me one of those yellow hands that had already amassed millions."

"Such behavior," I said to Mrs. Dorian, as she paused, "has a flavor of insanity. It can only be condoned on that ground, truly !"

" Ah," exclaimed my guardian, " it was horrible, and yet it was superb. That lean, cadaverous, repulsive old man, in his faded dressing-gown and with one foot in the grave, produced upon me an impression which I positively treasure. He is no longer a man; he is a passion, an appetite, a greed."

" He is still a father," I said.

"Only because his son is a part of him. It is the egotism of paternity; it is in itself a kind of avarice. He believes that Foulke will continue the clutch upon those millions when his own yellow hand is unnerved by death; that is all. He is *farouche, effrayant*, but he is keenly interesting. He should be painted or written about. I should like Casimir to see him. Casimir, I am sure, could make something grand and terrible out of him." . .

The winter had nearly come to a close when I asked Mrs. Dorian if it would be possible for her to obtain some definite tidings regarding the Gramerceys. She looked at me with a surprise that soon gave place to sympathetic pity. She understood me, and promised so readily to use every means in her power that I regretted not having sooner engaged her kindly services. "But, Otho," she presently asked, "have you seen no face while here that could make you forget Colonel Gramercey's daughter? Are you hopelessly committed to that one memory, *mon cher?*"

"Hopelessly," I answered. There was a break in my voice as I spoke the single word. And then I told her as much as a man cares to tell on so delicate a subject, though strangely enough it was one which I now often discussed with Casimir. But in many ways Casimir had become almost my second self. Not even the devoted friend to whom I then appealed could rank her influence and intimacy beside his. I had grown to lean upon his love like a staff, and to expect his loyalty and allegiance as if they were the very warmth and light of the sunshine.

In another fortnight Mrs. Dorian brought me news that was like a sudden grievous blow. She had sought out a relative of Colonel Gramercey's and learned that the recent calamitous failure of an old and widely trusted New-York banking-house had wrought serious disaster to his fortune. It might be absolute ruin; there was no telling as yet. The affairs of D—— & Co. were still in a state of utter turmoil. Their name had stood among the very highest and their credit was deemed unassailable. Others besides Colonel Gramercey were known to have suffered by their unforeseen collapse, but it was believed that he, of all who trusted them, had sustained the severest losses.

"No doubt they will now soon return," I said to Mrs. Dorian. And then I added, with a touch of bitterness hard to restrain: "Perhaps this event will force her marriage with your nephew; we may hear, in a little while, that she is coming back as Mrs. Foulke Dorian."

"Otho," answered my guardian, looking at me very intently, "will such an event break your heart, *mon ami?*"

I laughed. "Hearts do not break so easily," I replied. "What Frenchman was it who said that the heart is a muscle, and consequently tough?"

By the middle of March I learned that they were home again. And then, but a few days afterward, tidings reached me that the Colonel had been stricken down with paralysis, and that his life was despaired of. The story ran that being in unsound health when the failure of D—— & Co. occurred, the effects of this intelligence had finally prostrated him.

I at once found out his dwelling and presented myself there in person. It was a little after eight in the evening. The servant to whom I gave my card civilly assured me that Miss Gramercey could see no one whatever. Her father was pronounced better, but still she rarely quitted his chamber. I left my card and departed.

Another fortnight passed. Early May had now set in, and with some of those raw, rainy gusts which make her praises for mildness most ill-suited to the American calendar. The buds broke forth in Union or Madison Squares below skies of tender color and in breezes of elastic freshness. Spring, that gives its deeper thrill to so many old sorrows, brought to my longing a stronger throb. It was fortunate that no imperative task now claimed me, for the constant recollection that she was near and in sad trouble scarcely ever passed from my thoughts. I had written her a score of letters and destroyed them all without sending. My moods of humility were fitful, and rapidly followed by those of accusation and reproach. I think Casimir's incessant reminders that I had been unfairly dealt with vitalized the latter. Even amid her distress, he argued, she might have seized a moment to acknowledge my visit, if only by a single line. Still, I have no doubt that these counsellings from one who held homage as my rightful due on every side would not have prevailed with me but for the unceasing goad and hurt of what I believed to be Foulke Dorian's continued suit. Not more than a week after the arrival of the French steamer which had brought Colonel Gramercey and his daughter to these shores, I had seen Dorian's name announced in a newspaper as among the passengers of an English steamer just landed. One evening we unexpectedly and most awkwardly met. I went to a certain reception, given at what would here be called the fag end of the season, and reached the house somewhat late. As I entered the dressing-room for gentlemen (with its lounge, bedstead, chairs and floor thickly overspread by bundled coats) I perceived that a male figure stood before one of the mirrors. His full-length view was reflected before me as I crossed the threshold; he was languidly pulling on his gloves; he looked thoroughly the man of fashion, the elegant idler, and it occurred to me while I drew closer that he might be an acquaintance whom I had met during the winter gayeties. Then, in a few seconds after, I discerned his face; the mirror showed it me; it was that of Foulke Dorian.

I had time to repress all signs of discomfort before he turned. He presently did turn, and at this I met his eye with cool apparent indifference, while removing my wraps.   I saw him start, stand as if dismayed for an instant, and then walk away. Soon afterward he passed out into the hall.

Later I saw him again in the thronged drawing-rooms below stairs. 'How he must loathe me,' I thought as I detected his dull gaze more than once slipping covertly from my face. 'It must be the sort of hate that only cowards like him can feel. If she had seen me lay that lash over his smooth, decorous face, I wonder whether she would have no scorn for him to-day.'

Of course a man reared as he had been, with the custom of command among servants, so-called inferiors, with the indulgence and precedence easily secured by liberal wealth, must have writhed in spirit under the disgrace of stripes like those I had given him. It could not be otherwise; and yet did not his non-resistance of the crushing disgrace affirm a temperament unmanly, despicable, with blood that was ichor, and a craven, dastard heart? I might be prepared for some mean revenge from him — a blow in the dark, a stab in the back. Not only the way he had taken my punishment but the insult by which he had called it forth should both forewarn me.

"You spoke of living quietly this summer, Otho," said Mrs. Dorian to me, a few days later. "Shall the affairs of the estate be sufficiently settled for you to leave New-York all through the coming season?"

"I fear not," was my reply. "I shall have to visit town at least once or twice each week."

My guardian appeared to muse. Her face betrayed no sign of the subtle little plan that she was hiding from me, nor did the faintest suspicion of it for a long time afterward enter my brain.

"You said something the other day," she continued, "about having put Rockside in the hands of an agent for rent this summer."

"Yes," I returned, absently.

"My late husband and I spent many months there. It is a charmingly situated place; its lawn slopes directly down to the waters of the Sound; and then it is only an hour by train from town."

"Yes . . . Rockside," I murmured, recollecting. I had had so many matters of rent to concern myself with, latterly, that it required an effort of memory to recall just what were the conditions dependent upon the purchase or lease of this special property. "Ah, true," I went on, brightening. "It is about six miles from New Rochelle; it is fifteen acres in extent; the house is large and roomy, with a splendid water view."

"Admirable!" declared Mrs. Dorian, laughing. "You describe it like a house-agent. Well, go on. How many bedrooms are there, and what is the state of the drainage?"

"I can't say," was my answer, "but I am sure of one thing: Rockside is terribly out of repair. A succession of yearly tenants has not improved it. Money must be spent if we expect to rent it again."

"I've a caprice to go and see it, Otho. If we are pleased, why not spend the money for our own comfort there? From now until June there will almost be time to build another house. I've an idea that we could render it thoroughly charming. Let us make the journey and decide."

I acquiesced, and we made the journey. Casimir went with us. We found an old-fashioned mansion, standing on a slight eminence and overlooking a magnificent sweep of water. Some stately elm trees grew near the huge white Corinthian pillars of the front piazza. Lower down were cedars and hickories in profusion, and then a strand of rugged, jagged rocks, which the recession of the tide showed to be densely hung at their bases with clusters of tawny sea-weed. Nothing could be lovelier than the whole romantic and delightful situation. All this New-York and Connecticut shore of the great Sound is indeed incomparable for beauty. Nature here meets the vast inland sea with a pastoral tenderness of union. For miles and miles the lichened rocks are fringed with foliage, and the waves, sobbing among uncounted coves, reaches and crannies, often glass the foliage that bends above them. On a summer day the immense sweep of waters will gleam blue as turquoise, and hundreds of white sails float by in the dreamy marine distance. Dimly aloof can be sighted the low sand-hills of the Long Island coast, far less fair on a nearer view, but delicate and visionary when the pale, drowsy clouds hang brooding above it.

Casimir was in ecstasies over the place. "Here I shall be inspired to paint as never before!" he exclaimed. "Ah, let us come here by all means. It will be a divine relief after the horrors of that shocking city!"

I shook my head ruefully and pointed toward the house, through whose dingy and uninviting chambers we had lately wandered. "Marvels of alteration and beautifying might be made yonder," I said.

Mrs. Dorian laughed. "We will accomplish the marvels, then," she announced, and with an air of determination which struck me as sudden, but which I afterward too clearly explained. "Aladdin's palace was built in a night, but we have a number of days in which to decorate and adorn ours. Casimir, being an artist, shall choose all the designs and colors. You, Otho, shall attend to the practical improvements. We shall be as extravagant as you please, my friends, so long as we transform with the wands of real enchanters."

Wealth like hers could of course produce nearly everything but the impossible, and May had not ended before Rockside had been converted into a most beautiful home. Mrs. Dorian remained in town until all had been finished, insisting that neither Casimir nor myself should tell her anything of what our repeated absences and consultations had brought about until all was in perfect readiness for her reception. Then, at last, one pleasant day in early summer, she left the city and took up her abode in the newly appointed dwelling. She expressed glowing satisfaction as we led her from room to room. She declared that she had not for months received so exhilarating a series of impressions. Casimir had been in his element with the wall-paperings and tapestries and general upholstery of the prim, grave old house, and I had spared no detail of purely comfortable renovation. Gardeners had been put to work with telling effect upon the lawns, drives and paths; the remodelled stables were stocked with horses and carriages; servants and grooms had been engaged in adéquate number, and past doubt the whole result of labor so amply aided by capital was one full of dignity, ease and elegance.

"Do you know," I said to Mrs. Dorian, as we stood in the soft twilight of the piazza on the first evening after her arrival, "that more than once I have been a little perplexed by your willingness to come here at all?"

She slightly lifted her brows. "And pray why, Otho?" she asked.

"Well," I replied, lowering my voice, "if you will permit me to say so, madame, I should not suppose your association with Rockside had been precisely of the pleasantest, since, as you have often told me, your married life was by no means a contented one."

"Ah, very true," she returned, with that curious sadness of hers which was always promising to flash out into some *bizarre* drollery. "Those rocks down there by the water could tell you how I languished. The late Mr. Dorian made the place a perfect prison. He was so economical that he would not let me have a saddle-horse, and so prosaic that he thought my wanting to have a little summer-house built on the shore and covered over with vines a piece of insane sentimentalism. I was bored to such an unspeakable degree in those days that I used to wonder if fate were not arranging that I should become the heroine of some picturesque infidelity. I seemed to be living through the prologue of an excessively improper novel — a French one of course. But it all ended there. It always did end there."

"I am sure that it always did."

"Yes." She gave one of her low, odd laughs. "My tempter always continued to be imaginary. If he had not, I might have entered upon my widowhood with a surprisingly bad conscience."

"You could never *encanailler* yourself except in fancy," I said. "But I hope we have driven away all dreary memories, Casimir and I. I agree with you that the place is now really very pretty."

"Surpassingly so." She laid one hand on my shoulder and looked at me searchingly in the mellow dusk. "I hope, Otho, that you will be happy here."

"I shall certainly try to be."

"That is a very unsatisfactory answer. We are never happy when we try to be; the trying usually makes us only more miserable."

"I am not miserable," I said.

She walked away from me and paused at the edge of the piazza, looking to right and left across the vague expanses of lawn, where the boughs of dark trees had begun to vibrate with the salty, fluting night-wind. "It was always a rather lonely spot," she said, as though following out some new and silent train of meditation. "We had no neighbors in the old days; have we any now?"

I joined her, and pointed toward a somewhat thick grove of trees perhaps a hundred yards away. "Our domain ends there, as you probably know. One day as Casimir and I were walking along the rocks at low tide we found ourselves in front of a good-sized cottage, built with a broad veranda and having the air of being occupied by refined people. It is no doubt of comparatively recent date."

Mrs. Dorian's face was turned from mine, if I mistake not, as she carelessly said: "Yes, the shore on either side of us used to be quite uninhabited for a mile or more." Then after a slight pause she added: "Did you find out who lived in the cottage?"

"No. I asked one of the men that day. He knew the real owner's name, but said that some tenants had rented it of him for the summer."

The following morning was brilliant and breezy, and we all three felt the effects of its glow and freshness. The tide would not be risen till midday, and Mrs. Dorian, several hours before that time, went with Casimir and myself for a stroll along the rocks. Casimir was in high spirits; he spoke of the sea, the air, the varying tints everywhere.

"I shall paint your portrait here better than I could ever have done it in that disagreeable city," he said to me, with an arm about my neck. "Here is an opportunity, dear Otho. I want it to be a masterpiece, you know, and with so much lovely nature looking over my shoulder while I work, I am nearly sure not to go wrong."

We presently came to that part of the shore directly opposite the neighboring cottage, which was a sort of Queen Anne structure, with one or two marble urns gleaming about its doorway and a general surrounding of culture and nicety. The trees grew so thickly near the shore that we had to look upward through vistas of leafage for a full view of the house and its environment.

"There is a lady walking on the lawn," said Casimir.

"Yes," said Mrs. Dorian. "And she appears young and graceful."

In another instant I had seized Mrs. Dorian's hand. "Good Heavens," I murmured, "she is Ada Gramercey."

My guardian turned her face to mine. Her checks were flushed and her eyes were twinkling. "My dear boy," she exclaimed, "you know now why I wanted to come to Rockside. She is there with her father. Don't stare at me so stupidly. You are as pale as a ghost, and look as if you were going to faint."

I drew a long, tremulous breath. "I never felt more like fainting in my life," I answered, stammeriugly. "You — you should not have done this, madame. You —you should have told me before."

Mrs. Dorian pressed my hand. "Forgive me," she said. "It was my secret — my surprise. I hope you will not be angry."

"I am not angry," I answered slowly. . . "But how strange it all seems! It is like a dream. But still a very happy dream." . . . I could say no more. The tears blinded and choked me.

XII.

WE went back to our own home a little later. As we did so Mrs. Dorian spoke. "Otho," she said, "I learned several weeks ago that they were there — that they had rented the Lamberts' cottage. Old Mr. Lambert told me one day at an afternoon reception. He knew that my own property adjoined his, and made certain inquiries about Rockside. And then my plan was formed. I was a little afraid that if I let you know the truth your pride or your sense of correct usage would forbid the whole affair. So I waited until you should make the discovery for yourself, which you have just done."

"I fear that it will prove a discovery full of torment," I said. "We are near each other and yet still very far apart."

"Perhaps you are wrong, Otho. I mean to pay Ada a visit very soon — no doubt to-morrow. I owe her such a civility, surely; I knew her mother quite well. It may be that she has heard we are here. If so she will be prepared for me, as it were. If not I shall be such a surprise to her that she will probably reveal some pleasant truth which I can impart to you afterward."

I sighed and shook my head. "You speak as if you were certain that she cares for me."

"Certain?" echoed my guardian. "I haven't a shadow of doubt! You can't mean that you really believe she prefers that supercilious, artificial Foulke Dorian to my brilliant Otho?"

Mrs. Dorian paid her intended visit on the morrow. It is needless to state with what anxiety I awaited her return. I met her carriage (she had chosen to drive) at one of the lawn-gates, and on seeing me she alighted from it, walking toward the house at my side.

"Well," she at once began, "I must confess to you that I have had a most unsatisfactory time. Ada received me with a very gracious and amiable manner. She is a little paler and thinner than she used to be. The Colonel was taking his afternoon nap; he is still feeble and requires much rest, but she has strong hopes of his one day becoming almost well. She spoke of him a great deal and described some of the details of his illness; she is certainly a paragon of daughters. She had heard, about a fortnight ago, that we would occupy Rockside this summer."

"We?" I said interrogatively.

"I suppose she must have taken the 'we' for granted. But she did not put it that way, Otho; I am bound to be truthful. Her 'you' was comprehensive, inclusive — at least I so construed it. I behaved with a splendid hypocrisy. I unblushingly told her that we had heard only yesterday who our neighbors were. She never changed color by a shade during all our interview; her self-possession was admirable, but too admirable. When I said: 'Otho and I caught a glimpse of you on the lawn the first morning after our arrival,' she preserved a composure that was delicious; she has not been a belle in the fashionable world for nothing. But I admit she disarmed me. My usual audacity did not stand me in good stead at all; the only pointed remark that I had the courage to risk was an expression of your very kindly wishes and of your intention to offer them in person at some future time."

"That was indeed a stroke of boldness," I said, with melancholy consternation in my tones. "And how did she receive it?"

"With a little non-committal smile and an inclination of the head that was serenity itself. . . . But don't see everything *en noir*, dear Otho, merely because she was so equable and placid. For my part I would simply go there and have it out with her — as the Americans say. Her fault hitherto has been coldness, but the danger to her father has softened her; one could perceive this while she spoke of him. Of course I did not mention their loss of fortune, so I have no proof of how she bears that trouble. With philosophy, I should imagine, however. She has the look, the mien, of one who would bear it that way. . . .

And now let me give you a bit of counsel, *mon ami.* Be calm, persistent and brave. Such a woman as she is requires more than lukewarm wooing. Let her see that your love has mastered your spirit — all women like to see that; but never let your tenderness take the tint of weakness; I am sure that would never please her. Don't be afraid to tell her that you think her an angel or a goddess; the darker she frowns the more she will secretly enjoy it. What she will not enjoy will be professions *à demi-mot* — an unwillingness to show her just how hard she can make your heart beat and just how much happiness it is in her power to bestow upon you." . .

I recoiled from the possible pain which an open visit might bring me, but for several mornings I left Casimir painting in his studio and stole forth, with a half guilty feeling of trespass, to the rocks whence I had recently gained sight of her. But disappointment repeatedly followed these anxious little excursions. Sometimes an hour of watching through the boughs of the mingled cedars and hickories would not even bring me the meagre comfort of a fleeting face at one of the windows. Again, I would have some such transient view, but it might have been that of a servant's face, so quickly the vision passed. One morning, however, fate was suddenly kinder. Dressed in white and holding a book in her hand, Ada appeared on the veranda, pausing there for a moment and then slowly descending to the lawn. In a little while I saw that she was advancing straight toward the water. I felt my heart leap in my breast; then I became quite tranquil again. She came nearer, and I retired into the shade of some branches, where I could observe and yet miss immediate observation. Five or six rough-hewn steps led to the flat surface of a large rock, and just as her foot had cleared the last of these, I moved from my ambush.

She gave a great start on seeing me. I at once raised my hat and came close to her side. I put out my hand then, saying as quietly as I could manage, "Good morning."

She extended her hand in return, repeating my own words. It seemed to me that she had never looked so beautiful as now, with a wave of rosy color flying across her face under the cool white muslin of her sun-hat.

I knew that she would hold any attempted subterfuge as trivial, and I had not the least desire to offer one. "I saw you coming across the lawn," I said, retaining her hand until she gently withdrew it, "and so I waited, in the hope that you might care to meet me."

Her ordinary repose had nearly if not quite come back to her. "It is many months since we have met," she said, somehow avoiding my direct look, though not with actual evidence that she was doing so. "Did you come from the village?"

"From the village?" I asked, grateful for the chance of a temporary topic far away from that tumult of feeling which her voice and presence roused. "Can one reach the village by this route?"

"Oh, yes." She pointed in a direction just opposite to that which I had taken. "The shore curves inward a few yards farther on. There is a little path leading through the trees, by which one can take a short cut to the village. It is very convenient in pleasant weather; it is such a pretty walk."

"Were you going by that way?"

"I? Oh, no. I rarely leave papa for any length of time. And during the past day or two he has not been as well as formerly."

"I see. You merely came down to the rocks for a breath of this delightful air. I am very sorry to hear your father has had a relapse. Mrs. Dorian brought good news of him."

"It is not a relapse," she said, quickly, as though the word jarred upon her. "I am thankful that it need not be called by so serious a name. He has fits of severe weakness; his strength comes and goes — that is all."

"And you have nursed him so devotedly!" I said. My voice betrayed me for an instant, and I saw her glance soften and then droop. But I had no wish to stir any depths to-day; what I longed for was the old familiarity of intercourse,

that normal pulse-beat of talk which has no dis-
concerting pause or flutter. I wanted to push the
past out of sight and keep it thus. I should have
liked to make a new past—a sweet idyllic background for the interchange of future vows—
through the summer days that were still unborn!
And yet all this desire was so futile! That which
we had both been and done and suffered could
not be thrust away. It lived in the very light of
her eyes, in the sound of her speech. More, it
had become part of the rustling leaves and breaking waves; the lips of the wind whispered it to
me and the blue of the heaven confirmed it.

"Your father was always so dear to you," I
went on. "There are few daughters who would
have shown your unfailing tenderness."

"They do not deserve to be called daughters
who would not show it," she answered, with a
shocked surprise. "Poor papa had not only illness to contend with; there was that other trouble.
It came so hard to him. You know what I mean,
of course."

"Yes. His reverses of fortune. . . And did you
mind them much less?"

"I?" She made a sad little gesture with one
uplifted hand. "No doubt I would have cared
a great deal more but for his dreadful seizure.
When the news first came, it was a blow to me.
Why not? One feels at such times as if the
ground were failing under one's feet. I had never

thought about money at all; it was like the air I breathed — our income was thousands more than we needed." She smiled now as she looked at me. "I used to give away in careless charities each year more than I now live upon. But it is a great mercy that something has been saved. They tell us we shall never positively want; there is consolation in that thought."

We spoke together for some time about the failure which had been so disastrous to others besides her father and herself. I found that she had been penetrated by the liveliest sympathy for these others. "Some, I hear," she told me, "have been made quite penniless — people who had but little, and had placed it all with those trusted bankers. I turn bitter when I reflect upon the wrong they must endure."

" And you are not bitter about your own loss? " I asked.

" No; there is always a feeling of gratitude that the very worst did not happen. While papa constantly required me, I should have been called upon to work, as it were, with bound hands. And even if I had been free, this necessity would have distressed me terribly. I can't account for the distaste I have to earn my own living. No doubt I could have got a place as governess in some family; my knowledge of languages and music might not have rendered it difficult. But the demand would have stung, almost crushed me.

I know this repulsion is wrong, wicked. But I can't control it. I begin to think it some deep hereditary fault. Am I not right?"

"Pride does not die easily," I said.

"It is pride," she answered, plucking a bit of green fringe from a cedar at her side, and slowly nodding her head. "I would give so much to conquer it, but I cannot. I have often heard that sorrow humbles; but it has not humbled me. I think it has brought me nearer to the big, struggling world of humanity, and that is all. Nearer, I mean, in spirit but not in real equality of fellowship. I still hold myself aloof, as one not to be counted with the general herd. I'm not afraid to call it by its proper name — arrogance, if you please. But it is there, and it will not perish."

"Do not regard it as arrogance," I said softly. "Learn to look upon it as a wholesome self-esteem, and then it will cease to disturb you."

She smiled, but her eyes were melancholy. "No, I can't deceive myself in that way. I have outgrown the love of flattery which I once had — if I ever really had it, as you told me."

"Oh, forget and forgive those foolish words of mine," I suddenly pleaded. "You don't know how I have repented them since they were spoken."

She met my look unhesitatingly, then. "I have forgiven them long ago," she said, in her sweetest tones. Her face saddened instantly as she continued: "All that sort of pride has quite departed from me."

"And — and you admit then," I stammered, "that I — I had some cause for — for losing control there in Paris that afternoon?"

"There is always a cause for everything," she replied, turning as if to re-ascend the stone steps. "But so many of us will not make allowances; we simply hug our wounds and feel cruel toward those who have given them."

"And were you really wounded?"

"I was not . . flattered."

"And you felt cruel toward me?"

"I did at first . . but afterward I " —

"Ah," I broke in with fervor, "afterward your troubles came, and they softened you! But I have been fearing otherwise for months. I feared so more than ever when you refused to see me in New-York."

"Papa was very ill then. I could see no one." As she thus spoke she had begun to ascend the steps. I had followed her several paces unconsciously, and she was looking at me now across one shoulder.

"You are going?" I faltered.

"Yes. I must go." Her voice was very kindly, but it was nothing more. She put out her hand, which I took. "Good morning. . Mrs. Dorian said, I think, that you meant to come and see papa."

"Yes," I answered. "What time will be the best?"

"At about four in the afternoon he is usually able to go down stairs for a little while. But you must expect to find him greatly changed."

"May I come this afternoon?"

"No. I fear he will not be well enough to receive you."

"To-morrow, then?"

"Yes, to-morrow."

She went lightly up the steps without another word.

I wondered, through the rest of that day, whether Mrs. Dorian or Casimir noticed the joy which filled my heart and seemed, so far as I could tell, to dance in my gaze and ripple through my talk. But if either had made a discovery of it I received from them no sign that this was true. From then till to-morrow at four spread outward like a small tract of eternity itself.

When this appointed hour came I took the path along the rocks and went up to the Gramerceys' lawn by the same steps which she whom I loved had ascended on leaving me. Ada met me on the veranda before I had time to ring the bell.

"Papa is quite bright this afternoon," she said, "and is waiting to see you in the sitting-room." Then, lowering her voice, she proceeded: "Try not to show any surprise. You will hardly recognize him at first."

I needed her warning. The Colonel was seated in an arm-chair as I entered the small, tastefully appointed chamber. He did not attempt to rise when I advanced toward him. His smile, full of a rich, dignified cordiality, was the same as of old; all else had changed with him. His form had shrunken; his face was almost deadly pale; his eyes, ringed with gloom, were dim and faded; all his martial stateliness of the past had vanished, and there was infinite pathos in the tremor of the waxen, transparent hand which he gave me. I was deeply touched; I scarcely knew what to say; and when he himself spoke, his hollow, hesitating tones were the last pitiful proof of his complete physical ruin. And yet his mind seemed clear enough, and with the evidence of its soundness I could also trace the well-remembered courtesy, the infallible signs of gentlemanly high breeding. He made no reference to his own ills; he appeared to prefer that these should not be touched upon. In his wreck and downfall he was still able to perform the part of host, and caused me to feel this by a sort of impalpable emphasis. The grand manner was still preserved in him; you realized that only death could destroy it, and death could surely not be far distant. Now and then his daughter would help him in the shaping or ending of a phrase, but always with that consummate tact which had doubtless been lovingly studied in hours of vigil and ministration. She had taught him to accept the aid of her brisker speech without letting it remind him of his own need; she had become to him like the staff whose handle so perfectly fits our grasp that we lean there forgetful of how much we owe its support. She had in a way placed her youth and her fresh young vigor between himself and too keen a recognition of his shattered state. It was very charming to note this half-conscious dependence and this capable, alert response. She grew if possible dearer to me as I watched how duteously, promptly, unerringly she performed her more than filial part.

"She gets her pride from him," I said to myself. "It is the pride of race, the honor of self because one's ancestry has been held honorable. There is the old *noblesse oblige* about it, telling of all that was best in those motives and claims which brought forth the patrician spirit. They are both true aristocrats, and their pride is not their foible but their right."

Stanch republican as I was, I believed this of both father and daughter, though my creed was doubtless rooted in my ardent love. Ah, how would such pride as hers counsel her if she knew my own origin? Would not repugnance be instinctive, and could I dare to blame her for its betrayal?

My interview with the Colonel was not a long one. Ada soon insisted upon conducting him upstairs, though she made it graciously clear to me that his exit need be no signal for my departure. She presently returned, and we went out upon the veranda, sitting where a breadth of loose-matted vine gave us glimpses of the intensely blue afternoon sea, like the vignettes you sometimes meet in books. It was such delight to be her sole guest, having her unshared heed, marking the flex-ile lines of her shape, the rich tints of her auburn tresses, the manifold shades of expression that came and went on her clear-cut face. She had brought a piece of sewing with her that represented no dainty bit of fancywork such as the most indolent lady will use her hands upon in pretty semblance of toil. It was a genuine seam, binding together two portions of a sleeve, and she plied her needle-strokes with sincere energy, quietly remarking as she began them :

"I hope you will not mind my industry. It has become more or less necessary nowadays, you know."

"I can mind it only to applaud it," I said. "The new attitude fits you astonishingly well — much better than the embroidering of those birds and roses which with many women are an affectation of toil."

She gave a little sigh. "My birds are flown and my roses withered, I fear."

"Some day they will sing and bloom again — I hope."

"Hope is not realization." She bent her head a trifle lower while thus speaking.

" Perhaps it is not, with me," I answered.

She lifted her eyes for a moment. "You have all the world before you. Hope should be your most natural impulse."

"It is. But 'all the world' has nothing to do with it at present. Its object is more limited if not less ambitious."

She chose to leave this reply unnoticed. "You have thought of no career as yet?" she questioned.

"I have thought of only one—politics. I have no aptitude for any other. The law repels me, since I possess just enough imagination to resent its dryness. Trade of all sorts I should dislike, though if my dear guardian had not made it so needless for me to think of a commercial future I should probably now be buying and selling something somewhere. In letters I should make the most pronounced kind of failure, for I should never actually fail. I should always be producing some work full of reflections from others. I know that the majority of books are made in this way. A few real geniuses lead 'the mob of gentlemen who write with ease.' And I don't like the mob in literature. I am an aristocrat there, if nowhere else. Perhaps I have the *maladie de perfection* . . who knows? But it results in apathy, nevertheless."

" And so you prefer politics?"

" I did, but I have lived long enough in this

country to shrink from touching them. A man who would reach to-day the highest offices under our government must wade through slums and cess-pools. I don't see how he can escape the grossest soilure. I maintain that he scarcely ever does escape it. It is horrible to think of the things our most trusted statesmen must have heard and seen! And to hear and see them makes a share in their scurrility almost unavoidable. I came to America with such fine expectations in that way, but now they are all dreary disappointments. . Casimir Laprade is an enviable fellow. He truly has all the world before him. He has the gifts of a great painter, and no wayward inclination to misuse them. I sometimes think that he has all the imagination in painting that Poe had as a writer. But he is a Poe with a *morale*, a wholesome and unerratic method — a splendid though mystical sanity, in short. You have heard me speak of Casimir before. We are devoted friends. He is with us now at Rockside; perhaps Mrs. Dorian told you."

" Yes. She mentioned that he had come with you. I should like to see some of his painting."

" It would give us all great pleasure if you would visit his studio."

" Thanks," she said.

" You will leave your father for an hour or two, some day, will you not? " I continued. " Rockside is so near."

She did not answer, though I waited several moments for her to do so. And then I again said, breaking the silence:

"I shall not feel that you want really to be friends with me unless you consent. That will put the final valued touch upon our reconciliation."

She stopped her needle and looked at me with a faint, arch smile. "You told me that you repented, yesterday."

"I told you the truth."

She shook her head, still smiling. "You forget. Repentance does not exact conditions; it receives them."

"Frankly," I said, changing my tone, "do you not think I had some cause for grievance that afternoon on the Bois? Remember that I constantly witnessed Foulke Dorian's attentions to you. He had followed you from England to France, and " —

"He was privileged to cross the Channel when he chose," she broke in, her color altering. "I did not encourage him to make the voyage."

"People said that you did."

"What will people not say?"

"But he returned to America a little while after you returned."

She gave her head a slight impatient toss. "You must recollect that the Atlantic is a common thoroughfare."

I saw that she was annoyed; the sarcasm had left her lips with no mildness of accent. But I had fanned the spark that was so ready to turn a flame; my reticence had slipped its fetter; in an instant more I felt myself urged to say:

"Of course you cannot prevent him caring about you. But do you let him visit you now? Have you given him to understand that you will not become his wife?"

I leaned forward as I spoke. She must have seen that my eagerness was not only passionate, but that I was trying to keep it within bounds. If the stronger gleam in her eyes came from displeasure, it quickly faded.

"I have given him to understand that," she said, very slowly and meaningly. "And more than once. He does not visit me. There are reasons apart from the refusal I just mentioned."

"Reasons?"

"Papa does not like him — has never liked him. He has not told me why, but I gained some knowledge of the truth from other sources. He thinks that Mr. Dorian behaved in an ungentlemanlike way to a friend of his. Papa is very punctilious; the affair concerned a debt of honor, I believe — a bet made at the Chantilly races. He learned the facts just before we went to Austria. He has requested me not to receive Mr. Dorian hereafter. I do not mean that he has forbidden it — but with me requesting and forbidding are the same. There, that is all. . . Now let us talk of something pleasanter, if you will. Describe to me some of Monsieur Laprade's wonderful pictures. That will be the next best thing to seeing them for myself." . . .

I left her that day in a state of buoyancy and exaltation. And for many days afterward I talked with her father and herself inside the cottage, sat with her on the veranda, strolled with her on the lawn or watched with her the restless water as it lapped and plashed on the jagged rocks. In a hundred ways I must have let her plainly guess my unchanged love, but by degrees I had grown to await her bidding for its full avowal and to find the thrall less irksome because it was so coyly and charmingly imposed. The Colonel's health continued feeble, and he would sometimes pass the whole day in his own apartment. On this account Ada delayed her little expedition to Rockside, short as was the distance between our two homes. At last, however, she came to us. Casimir not only showed her his pictures, but made it plain that her beauty and intelligence had won him as an admirer. She, on her own side, expressed delight in his painting, though now and then she would venture upon a criticism delivered with modesty but firmness.

"Mademoiselle has evidently studied art," he said, as we stood, a group of four, in front of what was perhaps his most ambitious canvas. He spoke with his accustomed suavity, but I could detect behind it that respectful attention which no mere politeness could imply.

"I have studied much less than I have observed," was her answer. "But it seems to me that I am unwarrantably bold in passing any judgment whatever upon your work, Monsieur Laprade. It all strikes me as astonishingly brilliant and novel. Mr. Claud has been preparing me for a disappointment," she added, with a glance in my direction.

"For Heaven's sake let us know the worst!" exclaimed Mrs. Dorian, in her most rattling vein. "Till this moment I had believed that Otho and I were both pledged to an unalterable approval of whatever Casimir did. If Otho has presumed to desert unqualified praise for any kind of criticism, I beg that you will expose his horrible treachery."

"I mean only that he praised Monsieur Laprade without the least reserve," said Ada, laughing, "and in that way he made me tremble for the fulfilment of my own expectations."

"Ah," declared my guardian, "then he has been loyal, after all, and I apologize to him for my base suspicions."

"Do you dread critics?" asked our visitor of Casimir.

He appeared to muse for a moment, and his luminous eyes took that thoughtful look which always gave so magical a charm to his fair, poetic, picturesque face.

"I often think there is only one just critic," he said gravely and slowly. "I mean . . . Death. He is apt to write of us in very black ink on very white paper; but he tells the truth about us in the end."

"How dreadful of you, Casimir!" cried Mrs. Dorian. "And yet how charming! You have given me one of my impressions. *Tiens.* . It will do for a future picture by yourself. I imagine a skeleton, with a notebook in its bony hand, going through the galleries of the Louvre and alternately grinning or scowling."

"Ah, madame," I said, "it is we who represent the skeleton of which you speak. We are posterity and we are forever passing judgments upon the works of the dead. I think that in the main Casimir is right. Every genius or every pretender finally gets his due in just that fashion." . . .

"Do you find my friend's embodied dreams too sombre?" I asked of Ada, as we walked toward the cottage together, about an hour later. "Do you think that like the painter of whom Shelley sang he dips his pencil too deeply in the hues of earthquake and eclipse?"

"He is gloomy, beyond a doubt," she answered, "but it is the gloom of life itself and not a mere morbid craving after what is sinister and repellent. That picture, for example, which he calls simply 'The Choice,' and in which we see the dark angel, with poppies on his brow, repulsing an old grief-stricken woman while he has flung a strong arm about the unwilling shape of a delicate, beautiful young girl — how true that is, and how exempt from the least cynicism! It is a sort of universal allegory." She paused here, and I thought she had finished speaking, when her voice presently resumed: "Still, for such a man as he I should fancy that there might be peril hereafter."

"Peril?" I said, surprisedly.

"In the artistic sense — yes. He loves shadows so much. You likened him to Poe, and with good cause, I think. But he is a sort of Poe touched with sunshine. And yet, if some great grief or disaster came to him, would not the sunshine die out of all that he did? Might not his work turn grim and even malign? I may be wrong, yet this thought struck me as I stood there in his studio, and watched not only his paintings, but his fine, sensitive, mobile face."

"I should not wonder at the result which you half prophesy," I returned; "and yet Casimir will no doubt escape it. The great grief will be spared him, I should say. He loves his art passionately, and will never fall in love with any less ethereal mistress. There lies his safeguard."

"Sorrow has other modes of reaching us."

"I used to think so. Just now I feel as if she had only one."

"You don't mean what you say," she reproved, with a very serious glance up into my face. Still,

I somehow did not believe that my words offended her. After a little silence she said: "He is a Parisian by birth, is he not, this Casimir Laprade?"

"Yes. He is the only child of Mrs. Dorian's sister."

"And you. . . You are a Belgian? You were born in Brussels?"

"Yes."

"It is a charming city, Brussels; it is a little clean, white, brilliant Paris. I spent such a happy autumn there when I was a mere girl. I was never tired of attending service in that stately, drowsy old Sainte Gudule, with its magnificent stained glass windows, and its buried kings and queens in their solemn tombs. I wonder it did not turn me into a Catholic. Poor mamma, I remember, grew frightened lest it would. . . . Ah, you had a most beautiful birthplace! You were left an orphan there, were you not, at quite an early age?"

"Yes."

"I recollect hearing it. Someone in Paris told me, I think. And your mother was a friend of Mrs. Dorian, though not related to her?"

"Not related . . . no."

"It must have been very sad." She spoke tenderly; she had used her gentlest tones throughout all these latter sentences, with not a suggestion of idle inquisitiveness and with much compassionate delicacy.

"Sad?" I questioned.

"I mean having to leave your native land and come all alone across that huge waste of ocean."

"It was very kind of Mrs. Dorian to let me come." I could think of nothing else to say. My own words sounded harsh and curt to me. All this was pure torment. I had dreaded it so long. The lies rang so despicably in my ears as I uttered them! And yet how could I avoid them? Only in one way. Only by telling her that I was the son of a loathed criminal.

But my torture had not ended. "Will you think it strange," she pursued, "if I ask you something about your family? I am fond of old family records, and especially foreign ones. Now, I suppose you came of a long-descended race, which" —

"You forget," I broke in, with a laugh that made her start, it was so chill and hard, "how republican a distaste I have acquired for all pre-rogatives and mementos of that patrician sort. I believe my family were very honest folk, educated, refined, but not noble in the least degree. That is all I know or care to know."

"I have displeased you," she said, raising her brows in surprise.

"Not at all," I hurried, forcing from myself a much more natural laugh. We had by this time reached her gateway. "I must leave you here," I continued, putting out my hand as we both paused. "I promised to give Casimir a sitting for my portrait this afternoon. He complains that it will not be begun till the summer is ended." . . .

But I gave Casimir no sitting that day. I roamed off into country roads and by-paths for hours, and did not return to Rockside until a short time before dinner.

Hypocrisy had always been one of my hatreds. I meant to marry this woman if it were possible, and I had now a secure belief that she would soon plight with me a lasting troth. If I married her under my present name, would not the deception be wholly unjustified? From all points of purely honorable feeling, yes. And yet to the world I was Otho Claud, not Otho Clauss, and had been so for years. I had reason to expect, moreover, that if my true origin were revealed she would turn from me. She might love me, but she would turn from me. Her pride had cast her in that mould; it was a pride that might even alter her love. But for this agonizing consideration I would willingly tell her all; no sense of personal shame would now restrain me. But to tell her and witness the estranging, sundering result! That made a coward of me, and that alone. I dared not risk the hazard of losing her. It would be easier to cut off my right hand, or to hold it in a destroying flame. The worst conceivable suffering or calamity would be preferable. And after all, was the deception in any tangible manner a wrong to her? Would not Casimir counsel it? Would not Mrs. Dorian insist upon and implore its continuance? Thousands of men placed as I was then placed would have regarded what now rose before me in the stern lines of a duty as the mere shadow of one and no more. There was hardly a possibility of my real name ever transpiring. My guardian only waited my word to transfer a large amount of property before her death into my keeping. I would be independent, and in all eyes the possessor of an unblemished name when I stood at the altar with Ada Gramercey. And through the rest of my life discovery was equally certain not to overtake me.

Before re-entering the grounds of Rockside I had made my resolve. I would keep silent. The struggle — and there had been a bitter struggle — was now past. I conceded the imposture to my own conscience, but its commission I had likewise declared to be incited by copious excuse, defended by ample palliative and extenuation.

The lawns of Rockside, trim and velvety, sloped shoreward in sweet, fresh curves as the slant light of early evening struck them. I was not yet wholly calm, and perhaps on this account I sought the rocks before passing into the house. Once among their ledges and crevices, now so familiar both to sight and tread, I moved on for some distance in the direction of the Gramerceys' cottage.

Suddenly I stood quite still. It seemed to me that I was turning to stone like the rocks themselves. Through an opening in some trees that drooped lower than the rest, I had gained a view of that part of the shore where Ada and I had first met after so many mouths of separation.

She was there now. A man was at her side. They were speaking together. I saw him take her hand, bend over it and kiss it. She drew her hand away, but with no sign of anger. Then she went on speaking, though I could not hear what she said; I was too far away for that.

I had clearly recognized the man He was Foulke Dorian.

My heart began to beat with great throbs. My limbs grew so weak that I sank down, and at the same moment my head whirled dizzily. But I soon rose again, peering at once through the branches.

Neither he nor she was there. Both had vanished. Had it been a horrid illusion? Had my senses tricked me? Could it all have been actual?

XIII.

THIS doubt was only a proof of my mental turmoil. To think soberly would have been to scoff it. But I could not think soberly. If the ghost of someone whom I knew to be dead had appeared before me and then melted away, my belief that hallucination had victimized me might have been much less positive than now.

But of course the intense unexpectedness of what I had seen explained this dubious mood, necessarily transient. Opposite conviction ensued, and with but too sharp a haste. I did not need, a little later, to pick from that very spot where I had witnessed Ada Gramercey in converse with Dorian a long white thread glove such as she had worn that very day, for my certainty of the whole proceeding to be verified. As I crushed the soft substance of the glove between my fingers and palm, there must have been a fierceness in that slighter act akin to the force that might go with one dark and violent. I lifted my hand to my forehead and found it beaded with cold drops of sweat. The thought distinctly flashed through my brain that if the man whom I had just seen were then within my reach I would kill him. Murder was in each breath I drew, and I think it made my face white and dilated my eyes. I even sprang up the stone steps, in another moment, and swept with a rapid gaze the tract of lawn about the cottage. It was quite empty, as I stood there among the trees, gasping and clutching the glove. I was mad, as men are nearly always when they slay. The spells and curses that witches were said to cast in old times may have sprung, like so much that is laughed at as fable to-day, from a germ of solid fact. Long ago my mother, with either a strange prescience of what would befall me, or with only the dreading foresight engendered by deep love, had named this frenzy a curse. It was now like a sudden vital change of my whole nature. Every high and sane faculty became a turgid blur. Reason was blotted out, and prudence, humanity, pity, self-esteem, were whirled away as the wind whirls a ring of dust. Manhood sank and faded; the mere gross animal rage that sets a fang in flesh took its place. To live was to thirst for redress of wrong, and burn with a sense of unparalleled outrage. So must my father have felt on that horrible morning. If his frantic spirit had driven mine from its body and entered there instead, I could not have more fatally resembled him than during that distracted interval.

Some dim conception of this likeness must have forced itself into my brain, and with abrupt saving effect. For the revulsion suddenly came, and it afterward seemed that no other influence had wrought it. I remembered that I was his son, and without one wild detail missing, the whole picture of his crime, lit as from infernal fires, loomed ghastly upon my recollection. In an instant the murderous mood ended. I was rational, self-controlled, a being of judgment, intellect, temperance. I shuddered as I descended the steps leading to the shore. A frightful question was thrilling me: What might have happened if that tyranny of blind, headlong trance had lasted instead of ceasing? . . .

It was night when I passed indoors. Dinner had been served several hours ago. Mrs. Dorian met me in the hall with an anxious face. "My dear Otho," she said, "we did not know what had become of you. But of course you dined with the Gramerceys. I really can't think what made me worried about you. It was absurd, of course. Casimir, who would rise with the lark if there were such things as larks in Westchester County, has gone to bed. I have been all alone in the sitting-room for quite an age, and this stupid novel, the last of my lot from town, would not let me read it, so I became nervous, hearing little sounds everywhere. It is wonderful how dull a French novel gets when it is written to *exploiter* the beauties of virtue. I think it must have been the flapping of that great moth in the lamp that made me nervous. What a beautiful moth, by the way! It gives me an impression; it has such an evil, *funeste* look, with its big spotted wings; it might be a bad spirit in disguise. And it has nearly put out the lamp, poor horrid creature. I can scarcely see you in this dimness."

I was glad of that. "I will go up stairs, madame, if you will permit," I said. "I am a little unwell."

"Unwell, Otho? You don't mean that Ada" —

"I mean nothing about Ada," I broke in, with a laugh of so much neatly counterfeited mirth that it half re-assured my hearer. "There is nothing wrong. . . . I am somewhat tired. Pray excuse me. Shall I ring for the servants to close the house?"

"No," she said. "But Otho . . you are sure?"

"Quite sure," I said, repeating my laugh, and with more skill than before.

I passed that night sleeplessly, alone with my sorrow. I did not doubt that Ada Gramercey had been faithless and treacherous to me. Had not her own words proved it? Every sentence that she had spoken with reference to Foulke Dorian was revived keenly in my memory. What had all this been but calculated double-dealing? As for the motive, I could ascribe it to nothing except relentless coquetry. Other women had played pitilessly like this with men before now. That I had ranked her incapable of such hypocrisy was no argument against her having practised it. Other men had been similarly deceived. Besides, she had never accepted my love. It had been urged upon her in Paris, and she had virtually refused it. Here she had permitted and smiled upon my devotions, but no more. If she had spoken untruly with regard to Foulke Dorian it was her own affair. I had received no right to upbraid her for broken faith. There had never been any question of faith or unfaith between us; there had been sentiment, congeniality, intimacy, social relaxation, and nothing more. I had hoped for much, but the span of hope has many airy cubits. In this case had it not towered vastly above fulfilment?

"You do not look yourself," said Casimir to me the next morning, as he and I met. "I hope, dear Otho, that you are not going to be ill. What is this American disease that they call malaria? Owen, the head gardener, tells me that it rages. hereabouts, aad that his poor wife is in an ague with it at least twice every week."

"I suppose Owen is entitled to credence," I replied, "and I have heard that malaria is as wide an evil in this remarkable country as legislative bribery or municipal theft. But I don't think it has yet claimed me, Casimir. . I slept rather ill and awoke with a slight headache . . that is all. I will try a walk in the morning air. I have no doubt that you were abroad hours ago, so I will not ask you to go with me."

I should indeed have been nonplussed if he had

proposed to go. For I did not mean that my walk should be a long one. It would terminate at the Gramerceys' cottage. The glove which I had found yesterday was on my person. I intended to return it to its owner. Not in silence, yet not in stormy accusation. I was prepared to be thoroughly calm. My turbulence was all laid at rest, and only a dull, steadfast, persistent heartache held its place.

I took the inland course to the cottage; it may have been that I had some lurking dread lest I should see, if I went by the shore, a repetition of last evening's occurrence. The very quiet and serenity' of the little simple domain mocked me with my own wretchedness as I passed round to the seaward-fronting veranda. A few short hours ago I had been so happy here, and now I had come for a farewell meeting with her whom to distrust and despise was, alas, not to cease from loving! I had already thought of a speedy departure for Europe, whither in the course of a little time my guardian and my sole dear friend might both join me.

A minute or two after I had rung the bell at the open entrance I saw her emerge from the little sitting-room that adjoined the hall. She slowly advanced to where I waited. She was clad in her customary white dress, and she had a few garden-flowers in her bosom. Her beauty pierced me with pain. I took her hand because she offered it to me, but I did so with a strange thrill of despair, as though realizing it was for the last time on this side of the grave !

She appeared to notice nothing unusual in my face or bearing. She spoke of the fine weather, going forward almost to the edge of the veranda, and then returning in my direction with a smile and a slight shiver.

"It is a little cool here, is it not?" she said. "Shall we go into the sitting-room?"

As we passed thither I asked about her father, tranquilly enough. She told me that he was sleeping when she had last left him. "He spends so much time in sleep," she continued, with a faint sigh, while sinking into a chair, "that if one judges of how much better or worse he is only by his wakeful hours, one is often in doubt. I hope your portrait has progressed favorably, since yesterday?"

I had seated myself before I answered: "How did it strike you yesterday?"

"Oh, as a mere sketch."

"But a true one?"

"A little ideal, if you will pardon me. Not that I do not like a portrait which shows us at our very best. That is the prerogative of portrait-painting. It is charming to have a friend transmit our image to canvas, as Monsieur Laprade is doing in your case."

"Why?"

"Because the friend becomes a gentle eulogist, and if he be gifted, and faithful to the requirements of his art, he may surprise those who know us well by showing them how careless has been their everyday estimate."

"Then you think that people who like us are apt to deal in these unjust opinions?"

"Yes," she returned thoughtfully. "Monsieur Laprade said that death was a critic. Is he not also in a certain way a portrait-painter? We die, and we are at once recollected in a new light, as it were. Traits and qualities are remembered and appreciated that were forgotten or neglected in us before."

I saw my opportunity then, and quietly took it. "But while we live we are so apt to afford sad proofs of mastering and fruitful faults."

She looked at me with some surprise for a moment. "You say that very dejectedly. Are you *distrait* this morning?"

"I am unhappy."

Her face grew serious. "Something has happened at home?" she murmured.

"No; not at home."

"You have had bad news from abroad?"

"Not from so far away." I drew out the glove as I spoke. "You dropped this on the rocks yesterday — in the afternoon, I think. It is yours, is it not?"

She took the glove. "Yes; it is mine. Thanks."

There was not a sign of embarrassment in her reply.

"Very possibly you lost it while you were there with Foulke Dorian," I went on.

She gave a start then, and looked at me fixedly. But her color did not alter in the least. "You saw me?"

"Yes. I saw you — and him." My voice must have trembled now. "I saw him take your hand and kiss it. I — I was not spying upon you — please be sure of that."

"I did not imagine that you were," she answered, with immediate haughtiness. "You are surely above any such action."

"Ah, don't take that for granted!" I said, with a rush of bitterness, as I rose. "To anyone who had deceived me as you had done I might have paid guile for guile."

Her brow clouded, and she bit her lip. I felt her anger to be unwarrantable, shameless; I could have born the most artful feigning of innocence better.

"You were never once deceived by me!" she exclaimed, with indignation. And then, abruptly, while her eyes dwelt upon my face, an entire change swept over her. She rose and regarded me with a sorrowful amazement. "If you saw that man kiss my hand," she said, "you must also have seen that I gave him no incentive to do so. His coming to this place has been a source of distress to me. He had learned of that path leading from the village to the rocks; probably the boy who had brought me his urgent note but a short time before, begging that I should meet him, had told him of it. He has possessed himself of several large mortgages once owned by my father; he wished to return these for a merely nominal sum; he wanted me to arrange a deception by means of which my father would believe himself almost re-enriched through a stroke of pure good fortune. Papa was to be made greatly his debtor, yet never to know this. The proposal was one which he begged me earnestly to accept, and which I could not but heed with gracious consideration, although I promptly refused it. I meant to keep the whole affair a secret, and not even to tell my father of its occurrence. If this be guile, then I have employed it."

Perhaps she would have spoken further; I cannot say. My own contrition broke all bounds, here, and I hurried to her side, in a passion of joy and self-reproach.

"Can you ever forgive me?" I cried. "I have been the maddest of fools! You are truth and honor itself, and yet I seized the first little chance to wrong, to distrust you! But it is the fault of my love — that only! Oh, Ada, if you had let me really believe in your love, all might have been different! But you have kept me forever at a distance. You see, I leap over that distance now — I can't help it.   I must never look on your face again if you do not love me enough to be my wife!"

Her eyes were shining in tears as she said: "I do love you." . . .

Late that same afternoon I told both Casimir and Mrs. Dorian that Ada Gramercey had promised to marry me.   Both faces brightened as they heard the tidings.   My guardian kissed me; Casimir warmly grasped and pressed my hand.   It was several hours afterward, and while we were alone together, that Mrs. Dorian said:

"There is no reason that this should be a long engagement, Otho."

"Naturally," I answered, "she wishes to protract it on her father's account."

"But he may linger like this for years."

"Not years, I think.   He will either partially recover or die.   All the physicians have told her that."

"Did you speak of . . pardon me . . anything so terrestrial as *la question d'argent?*"

"My dear madame," I cried, with a laugh and a blush, "we have spoken of nothing but our mutual love."

"Delightful," she approved, with a droll nod of mock grimness.   "Just as I imagined.   The rest will come soon enough; it always does.   And when it does I want you to feel that you can talk with perfect security of giving her all that she once had. On the day before your marriage, *mon fils*, I want to make over to you a comfortable sum." She then named the sum, and its size caused me to utter a surprised exclamation.

"That is too large," I protested. "It will dig a decided hole in your own fortune."

"And leave a solid wall to surround the hole," she said gayly. "No, Otho, I insist. I can't marry you off more than once, I suppose, and if done it shall be done handsomely."

The poor invalid Colonel gave me his congratulations on the next day. Ada had rendered my own course an easy one; it seemed to me that I had no *rôle* except that of profuse smiling and cordial hand-shaking. Her father was plainly pleased at our engagement; from the first he had liked me, and knowing as he did of my heirship to Mrs. Dorian's wealth it would be idle to imagine that satisfaction of a worldly sort did not concern his present feelings. In the days of his health and prosperity he might have welcomed a son-in-law with slight concern for mercenary endowments; but now, with the shadow of the end creeping slowly across his few residual days, there was little wonder that his enfeebled mind, conscious of its own half-shattered state, should rejoice in the thought of leaving the child whom he loved re-installed among her old soft surroundings.

I said something of this sort not long afterward to Ada herself, and then added (since the occasion had an aptness which it might hereafter lack) the precise words of Mrs. Dorian's generous proposition.

"How devoted that woman has been to you!" she answered. "She must have had the most tender regard for your mother, in the first place."

"She had," I replied, believing that I spoke the truth.

The next three or four weeks were loaded with happiness for me. Our lives are like those of certain trees; they have their periods of bleak, nude dearth when the wind and sleet strike them; their rich-clad hours of summer; their terms of autumnal blight and omen; but they have also their spring of dewy blossoms and silvery song. It was the springtime of the soul with me. No future period, however benign fate might prove, would be just like this. I told Ada so, in our many walks and talks. "I feel like a miser," I said, "whose precious gold is slipping through his fingers. In all the years of love that I hope God keeps for us we shall never be quite as we are now. Our sunshine will never be just of the same quality. It may turn mellower, and even in a way warmer; but now it has a fine airy excellence that we shall somehow miss hereafter. Let us make merry in it while we may."

She looked at me with a rueful little smile. "How can I make merry," she asked, "in the face of such a chilling prophecy?"

"I did not mean it to be chilling," I declared, sorry for my bit of sentimentalizing.

"But to enjoy perfectly is not to deal in such reflection."

"True enough. And yet it seems to be the doom of all perfect joy that it casts this shadow. Don't you remember reading of the two lovers who came to the edge of the great cliff at Sorrento? One of them proposed that they should both leap over it, hand in hand, since the future could hold nothing more charming than the present was, and the chances of a regretted change were almost certain."

"But they did not take the leap," said Ada, with a smile.

"Oh, no. They preferred to accept the other chances. We all do."

Her smile deepened to one of mischievous meaning. 'I am glad I did not let you go with papa and me to the Tyrol," she said. "You might have proved a dangerous companion in a mountainous country."

"Oh, if I had suggested the leap, it would have been the merest poetic posing. You'd have seen through it in half a minute. I could never consent to lose you in that way."

"But if we had both leaped together?"

"My plight would have been a pretty one! Angels go straight to Heaven, and so I should have been left without you." . .

Once a real gloom crossed the brightness of those blissful weeks, and a darker gloom than she guessed. We had been speaking of old acquaintances in Paris, of their weaknesses, foibles, follies and general characteristics.

"Mademoiselle X—— made a wholly heartless match," I said. "She married the Count's name only."

"It was a very distinguished name."

"Ah, I remember . . you believe in all that."

"I believe in an unsullied name — yes."

"Unsullied?" . . The word pricked me. "His was hardly that."

"I know; it was historic."

I laughed a little drearily. "He traced back among mediæval ruffians."

"But a good many of his ancestors had been gentlemen."

"Tell me," I said, looking at her intently and feeling the growth of a restless annoyance; "if I had a name like his, would you prefer it — or are you indifferent on such a subject?"

She answered my look, and I saw a shade of pique cross her face. "Why ask me this question, Otho?" she returned.

Her voice had a faintly harsh ring.

"You need not answer it," I said. "You have already done so."

She grew nettled at this. . "Really, you take a great deal for granted!"

"Certain signs are conclusive." . . I kept silent for some time while she watched me. Then I slowly continued: "You know that I am right. If I were a duke, an earl, a prince, you would love me more than you do now."

She threw back her head and regarded me with angry astonishment. "How can you speak like this, Otho!" she exclaimed. "It is trivial!"

I took both her hands in mine, an instant later, and gazed steadily into her face. "Yes, Ada," I said, "it was trivial — boyish — absurd. I admit that it was!" Then, as suddenly, I dropped her hands. "But . . something made me speak as I did . . I scarcely know what."

"Your own want of reason," she replied, her resentment by no means cooled.

"No," I affirmed, with a touch of excitement; "it was not that. It was something else. . . Stay: if I were still Otho Claud, just as you know me now, and yet, if" —

I abruptly paused. A sense of whither my own thoughts were carrying me had produced this hesitation.

"If," she repeated, echoing my last word. "If what, pray?"

I gave a brief, curt laugh, and finished my sentence. "If I bore some stigma, through . . through the misdeeds of my parents — if I were branded, not by my own shame but theirs — would you still care for me, hold me dear, be willing to join your fate with mine?"

"Stigma? . . shame?" she again repeated. Her face grew full of pain. "Oh, Otho," she burst forth, "why do you even think of any thing so . . so unwelcome and distressing?"

She may not have noticed how much paler I had grown; but I am sure that my color had faded. "You abhor the idea," I said, accusingly. "But if such a stigma, such a shame, rested upon you, I should hold it as less than nothing!"

"Ah, you say that!"

"I am certain of it. Your father—he might be a thief, a murderer"—

"Otho!"

"It is true!" I hurried on eagerly. "No matter for the source you had sprung from; provided you still remained who and what you are, I should count all former circumstances as paltry. You would be yourself—your origin would not in the least concern me."

She made a dissatisfied, rebuking gesture. "Why have you brought up this question?" she appealed. "I am sure that I said nothing to provoke it."

"I have brought it up that I might confirm my belief. You know what that belief is; I have told you."

"If you possess it, you should not inform me of it. To do so, Otho, is the merest idle borrowing of trouble."

I shook my head stubbornly. "You do not

deny the charge. You do not assure me that it is baseless."

"But no such conditions as these exist. You imagine them."

"Without doubt. . . . Yet they might have existed."

I thought she was about to give me an indignant answer. But in another instant her eyes filled with tears and her lip trembled. "Obstinate, fanciful Otho!" she murmured. "Well, then, it would make no difference — none whatever. I should deplore, regret, even sorrow that such a thing were true, but the love I bear you could not alter because of it. . . There! are you satisfied? or will you still cruelly persist in tormenting me?"

"No!" I answered eagerly, taking her in my arms. "Oh, Ada, I am foolish and cruel! Forgive me! I will never annoy you with these aimless suppositions again!"

Still, for a long time afterward, the remembrance of her perplexity and hesitation staid with me. I hated to recall these, just as I hated my own rashness in having touched upon so perilous and suggestive a point. Hereafter, I concluded, greater self-control and discretion must assuredly be used. I must school myself into guarding against any outburst of this futile, profitless kind.

September had now begun, bringing us days of hazy mildness, with long, cool nights full of sweet, augmenting moonlight. Possibly by contrast with the dark events that were soon fated to follow it, this mellow autumnal interval holds a sweeter worth. I seem to hear the crickets and katydids now, calling plaintively and multitudinously through the still, breezeless air of those lovely nights. But their strange song, which carries for so many ears a dirge over the fading year and the falling leaf, bore to me no such mournful note. All my life was in one flush of promise and expectancy. I might easily have thought dreary thoughts, if love had not laid her tender veto upon their indulgence. I might have shuddered at the knowledge — now so vivid and indisputable — that I had been marked among all humanity as they are marked to whom a dread disease has come as a bitter birthright. I might have reproached myself for the commission of a deceit which argument and analysis, however acute and searching, could not wholly justify, and which they who were aware of it authorized and approved simply because of their fondly blind affection. But I had become exempt from dismal visitations. The perennial sorcery of the world had me well in its golden meshes. Painful introspection and solemn self-reproach were both under the ban of exile. They stood like proscribed guests beyond my lintel. My chamber, merry with lights and garlands, was no place for their grave shapes and hollow footfalls. At some future hour, when the feast glowed less gayly, they might steal in — unwelcome and unbidden. But now they must remain without, where the sound of my viols could float to them but in festal echoes.

A certain morning at last came when I happened to enter the hall of the cottage and discover Ada at some distance away in the act of reading a letter. On perceiving me in the doorway she made a hasty movement as if to conceal this letter. Then, seeming to think the better of such an action, she quietly folded it and was placing it in the envelope as I advanced toward her. We met, but I did not kiss her as usual. Instantly the old unrest had me in its keeping; an irrepressible suspicion had broken forth. Still, I strove to give no direct sign of my discomfort, but talked on with assumed carelessness. She answered me in the same vein, and meanwhile held the letter in one hand, tapping it unconsciously against the back of the other. Then, suddenly, she receded several steps and looked at me with a smile full of melancholy amusement.

" Oh, Otho," she exclaimed, " how easy it is to read your moods! "

" What do you mean? " I asked, biting my lip.

" Mean? " she echoed. " Why, that you are secretly in a fume of displeasure. And why? Because, when you appeared yonder a few minutes ago, you imagined that I wished to conceal from you this letter."

" Did I merely imagine it, Ada? " I said.

She shrugged her shoulders impatiently and lifted both hands. "And if you did not!" she replied. "What then? Grant that I did wish to conceal the letter." She shook her head very sadly, and half turned away from me. "Ah, jealousy like this, so ready to spring up at a moment's warning — what name shall I give to it? What name but one can I give to it, Otho? — insult!"

"Insult!" I repeated, with a pang of conscience as I spoke the word.

"Yes. You see me impelled to hide from you a piece of writing. That is enough. You forthwith give full rein to injustice. You accuse me without a moment of hesitation." She faced me again and held out the letter. "There — read if you desire. Satisfy yourself whether I am wronging you by any deceitful correspondence with some unknown lover — for that is the shape which I am sure your fancies have taken. There is the letter, I say; read it!"

"No," I answered; "I will not read it." These words I pronounced in a low, resolute tone, but at once I hurried on, with remorse in my eager sentences. "You are right, Ada. To doubt you is to insult you! I shall not even ask you what the letter contains. Keep it. Keep it and pardon me." I was trembling with excitement as I put my arm about her waist and drew her to my breast, kissing the pure breadth of her uplifted forehead.

"The letter is from Foulke Dorian," she presently said. "You must let me tell you about it, Otho, even if you will not read it. My sole motive in not wanting you to know of the letter at all was a wish to spare you pain."

"I am certain of it!" I murmured, from the depths of my new contrition. "And he has written you again, Ada?"

"Yes. He wishes me to hold another meeting with him, as before. He has some new proposition to make; he wishes my consent to a new plan of making papa accept his assistance. At least that is what I have gathered from his writing, though here and there its exact meaning struck me as vague. . . . You will not see the letter, Otho? You are sure?"

"Sure," I said, meeting her look with a smile of penitence. "Let it all pass. Tell me no more. As for meeting him" —

"I can do so if I choose?" she broke in, with a soft laugh, finishing my response. "Ah, that is the way with you fiercely jealous people; you go from one extreme to another; you blow hot and cold. . . . He does not mention that he knows of our engagement. His ignorance of it may be counted as a sort of excuse for his writing at all. But I shall not meet him again. He has no right to ask me — not a vestige of right. I shall not even notice his letter. There; are you satisfied?"

"No, I am dissatisfied," I returned. "With myself. Bitterly so."

This reply held a deeper significance than she guessed. But she spoke almost blithely now as she said:

"Such storms as yours only leave the sky clearer. At least they claim so who are skilled in the psychology of lovers' quarrels. We are not so skilled; are we, Otho? We have had too little experience in them as yet. . . . But you are quite certain you will not see the letter now?"

"Quite certain," I said.

"' *Assez,*' as your dear guardian would put it. Then I shall burn the letter. There is a fire in the sitting-room; it was made to take the chill off the air if poor papa found any when he came down-stairs. I think that it must also have been made," she added, with one of her smiles, "for the destruction of this horrid letter. I will go and drop it, envelope and all, among the hottest embers. So perish all causes of disturbance between you and me. . . Wait a moment, and then I will join you for a little walk about the grounds. We will find that vine on which you saw the red berries; I want to gather some for the sitting-room mantel." . . .

I had never known her more exquisitely kind and winsome than on that special morning. It stands out clearly in my memory, like the frost-touched sprays of leafage which we met, sanguine-tinted against the brilliant September air. I made a passionate inward vow, as we walked together then, that I would never let the faintest shade of disbelief mar my love hereafter. She had been merciful to call my doubt merely insult; it had been blasphemy, sacrilege!

Three or four days of perfect serenity went by. Mrs. Dorian read her French novels, exchanged visits with her neighbors, declared herself the most contented woman in the world, but now and then yawned a furtive yawn at being what she called *dépaysée.* Casimir painted industriously, made a few airy jokes at my lovesick expense, and complained more than once that I could not find for him a spare hour or two in which he might finish my portrait. "If it were Rome during the carnival season, my dear Otho," he lamented one evening while we sat at dessert, "you could not be more perpetually engaged."

"It is Rockside during the carnival season," I told him, smiling.

"That is very pretty," declared Mrs. Dorian, with an applausive tinkle of her coffee spoon. "It must be imparted to Ada."

"She will not thank you for it," said Casimir, with a sly look at me. "She has already a surfeit of that kind of sweets."

"A really picturesque compliment is always a variety," said Mrs. Dorian. "Nothing gives one a keener impression. The man who invents one is almost as great as he who invents a new omelette or sauce; the acquired reputation should differ only in degree."

It was on this same evening, an hour or so later, that I strolled along the rocks toward the cottage. The tide was at its full, but I could see my way with perfect clearness, for the moon was also at her full, making the Sound one sheet of quiet splendor and bringing forth in dark, intense outline against a cloudless heaven the masses of shoreland foliage. The air, like the trees and the water, slept in complete calm. The majesty and tranquillity of the night had an ideal meaning. I remember that as I moved onward beside the still, rich flood of those autumn waters, and let my gaze sweep the scant-starred, glorious, lucid sky, this thought passed through my mind:

"It would be better for us all if night were always as fair and serene as this. Such grandeur would exalt us; such composure would restrain and pacify us; such purity and sanctity would cleanse and ennoble us. Yet these nights are like our better selves; they beam out in the entirety of their beauty but rarely, and between their episodes of radiance lie intervals of gloom, cloud and even tempest."

I had nearly reached the stone steps leading up to the lawn of the cottage. I have known early twilights that were less bright; it was almost as if I walked in full day, except that no day would

have been so dreamy and ethereal.   The very lich-
ens on the rocks were discernible, in their crum-
pled, lace-like delicacy.   The least object in my
path or beside it could promptly have been noted.
It was not strange, then, that as a man's figure
suddenly came round past the clump of trees con-
cealing the path by which you could reach or quit
the village, I immediately perceived his presence
and faced him in surprise.

On both our parts recognition was instantaneous.
I saw him very plainly, as he likewise must have
seen me.   He was Foulke Dorian.

I stood quite still, regarding him.   He, too, had
paused.   Perhaps the moonlight made him look
paler than he had really turned.   I waited for
several minutes, thinking that he would break the
silence.   He remained speechless, however, looking
at me with the old languid droop wholly gone from
his eyelids.   At length, with no thought of wrong
toward Ada, and indeed confidently believing in her
innocence while I remembered the letter she had
recently received from this man, I spoke myself.

"You have no right to be here," I said, with my
voice not raised above its ordinary tones.

As a God may be my judge while I now write
these words, I had no anger against him at this
moment.   I had no feeling except a contemptuous
pity.

I had waited for him to speak; I now waited
for him to reply.

XIV.

He presently did reply, and with a sullen unwillingness, as though the words were literally dragged from his lips.

"My right to be here or not to be does not come from you."

"Nevertheless," I said, "since Miss Gramercey is my promised wife I shall hold myself bound to respect her known prejudices."

I saw his hands, as they hung at his sides, clinch themselves. "I had intended never to hold the slightest intercourse with you, sir," he said huskily. "I think you must know why."

"By all means persevere in your resolve," I retorted. "It is not yet too late to reconsider it."

A certain effect of moonlight brought to his dull eyes a greenish flicker as he now scanned my face. His lip was half curled, not in scorn, but as if from the prompting of deep spite and malice.

"You put upon me in Paris," he said, with the same dogged mutter he had at first used, "a vile outrage. It was the action of a coward; your superior strength made it so. Perhaps you wish to repeat the act."

"Only," I answered, "in case you wish to repeat the unparalleled insult that called it forth. And I think that I can afford, Mr. Dorian, to be called a coward by you, who have proven yourself a conspicuous one. I waited a whole week in Paris to hear from you, and I realized with astonishment, at last, that you meant to pass unnoticed what you now term a vile outrage."

The vicious sneer on his face deepened. He slowly nodded his head once or twice. A touch of the old drawling, insolent tone had come back to him—the tone I had heard him employ with such villanous result in Casimir's Parisian studio.

"Yes. Quite so. You thought, no doubt, that I would drag the name of a lady whom I cared for as I did for Ada Gramercey into a public duel."

"I thought nothing of this kind," I protested, inwardly tingling under the meanness of his implication, though many another than I would have tossed it aside in spirit as wholly despicable. "Miss Gramercey's name would never have entered into the affair, and by no means concerned it. Much as I disapprove and detest duelling, I would still have allowed you the chance of satisfaction for the pitiful beating I gave you. No, do not try to lie out of your own poltroonery. And quit this spot at once, or I may repeat the warning that I administered in Paris."

I pointed as I spoke toward the little grove

of trees whence he had lately emerged; but he did not stir.

"Go," I commanded, moving quickly nearer to him. As I did so a tremor passed through his frame, whether of fear or hate. But still he did not stir.

"The law may make you sorry for this," he said, meeting my look.

"Use it against me if you wish," I responded, "But first you must prove that you are not an intruder."

"It is not for you to say that I am one."

"I happen to have heard Miss Gramercey state that your visits here were disagreeable to her."

He almost closed his eyes for a moment, and a sort of spasm passed over his face. I suddenly felt all hardness leave me; it was like the dropping away of some coarse, bristly garment; my feeling of repulsion, of irritation, became a compassionate one only. I do not aver that any respect had part in it, or that I should not still have shrunk from taking his hand. But in a voice full of mild and even conciliatory change I now said:

"Believe me, it will be quite useless for you either to remain here or to appear at the cottage. If you have any thought of meeting Miss Gramercey on these rocks you will be disappointed; nor will the young lady consent to hold further conversation with you, anywhere or at any time, regarding a certain monetary question. Let me

beg you therefore to depart peaceably at once."
Here I took out my watch; the face was clear
enough, in that wonderful moonlight, for one to
tell the time upon it without an effort. "It is
now slightly after nine o'clock," I continued.
"You can still catch a train to town very easily,
but I advise you not to delay." He had dropped
his head a little while I thus addressed him. As
I ended he raised it, and the sneer on his lips had
deepened. I recoiled from him. "You refuse to
go?" I said involuntarily.

He did not answer me, but he was looking at
me with an expression malignant, almost satanic.
I thought that he was about to speak, and repelled
as I was, I awaited his answer. But for several
seconds he did not make it; his lips quivered, and
seemed to be so dry from some agitation that he
more than once noticeably moistened them with his
tongue. And then, at last, as if with difficulty,
he spoke two words. They were these:

"*Otho Clauss.*"

I stepped backward many paces. If a knife had
been plunged into me I could not have been more
stricken in all nervous power. I must have grown
ghastly in the moonlight. Doubtless no least detail of my dismay escaped him, for he now sprang
unhesitatingly toward me.

"*Otho Clauss,*" he said again.

I tried to be calm. I knotted my hands; I shut
my teeth together; I felt as if waves of fire were

given me instead of the wonted pulsations of my blood. He was close at my side, but I had not strength enough either to motion or to push him away.

I could only do one thing. I could simply ask him, with gasps between the few words I spoke —

"What do you know?"

"What do I know?" he echoed, with a laugh whose jeer seemed to take the whole mute, sweet night under its spell and render it a wild, dancing chaos. "What do I know, Otho Clauss?" he continued. His voice was close to my ear. I wanted to beat it off, as I would the vans of a bat, but I could not. "I know that you are not Claud but Clauss. I know that you are sprung from the very lowest — the scum — the rabble! Your father died on the scaffold for murdering his wife."

I could not speak; I listened; I could only listen. It was somehow as if I listened with a thousand ears. A flash went through my mind, in which I saw, keen as if it had been but yesterday, my father kill my mother in that populous street, on that far-gone Sunday morning. What this man now said to me was an actuality, and yet it seemed to have been led up to before by an immense anticipation. Here was I, who heard it; here was another who hurled it at me. It had been fated to come like this; it had been ordained; I was to hear it again; I had waited for it; my dreams had told me it would some day sound in my ears just as it sounded now.

He had put his hand on my shoulder. I did not shake the hand off. I cannot tell in what tone I questioned of him:

"How have you heard?"

"How?" he said. He laughed, and his hand, which had rested on my shoulder, seized it. His face was close to mine. I had a sense of his patrician gear; an odor beset me from the violets bunched in his coat. (How terrible these trifles were at this moment! How they assaulted me and caught my attention, from no earthly cause!) He realized that he had flung me down, so to speak — that he could say what he chose to me. And he said this:

"Do you deny? No, you do not; you cannot. I have found it all out. 'How,' you ask me? Well, I will tell you how. You thought everything secure, did you not? But one suspected you always. My father suspected you years before — that day when I, like yourself, was a boy, and you almost fainted on hearing that Leopold Clauss, your father, still lived. He was your father. You are the son of that wretch. I don't care if I tell you that my father, Steven Dorian, set me to tracing it all out. He knew that there had been a nurse for you when you were so ill in his sister-in-law's house, after you first appeared there. He had been told so by one of his own servants — a

shrewd woman, who had known Florine. Florine
—that was her name. Mrs. Dorian, your friend
and protectress, had given her a large sum of money
not to speak. My father told me his suspicions
only lately, when I returned from abroad. At
first I scoffed at them; then I reflected; then I
wondered if I could find Florine. I did find her
at last. She was a miserable old hag of a woman,
but her memory was far from feeble—do you
understand? She had had a son, a scamp, who
had dissipated all her savings. She was a devout
Catholic, was Florine; I soothed her last hours;
I got her to confess to me; I was better than a
priest. A priest, if he helps us in our last hours,
is not above taking pay; but I gave pay. I gave
enough pay to make Florine tell me it all. She
had gone with Mrs. Dorian to that hovel in the
Bowery; they took you away together in a carriage; the whole neighborhood had been infested
with small-pox; some people with whom you lived
let you go, though they were loath to give you up
at first till convinced that it was for your good.
My aunt was doing one of her absurdly eccentric
things; she succeeded in keeping the matter a
profound secret. Afterward you lay ill for days.
You raved in your fever; Florine, who had guessed
much, guessed more. Besides, my aunt made her
aware, from time to time, of the complete truth.
. . . This is what I bought of Florine, your old
nurse, Otho Clauss. . . And now I am armed with

what I know. . . You will not let me cross over to the cottage, eh? You will persist in having me go back to town. . . Are you quite sensible? . . Ada Gramercey used to be proud — a *mondaine* of pride — when I last knew her. Perhaps she is changed. But I doubt it. Would she marry a man descended as you are from the basest of *canaille?* Florine is still alive; she can be brought into a court to testify; she is not too old for that!"

He paused. I felt no longer weak, then. I shook his hand from my shoulder.

"You will tell her this?" I said.

"Yes."

"What will it profit you?"

"I love her. You know that."

"She does not love you." I spoke with effort. He saw this, and counted upon my woful disarray.

"You are rich," he said, with his face close to mine, "and her father has lost nearly everything. But I am still richer than you and can make her marry me if you withdraw. I love her, and I am determined to have her. After to-night — after what I have said to you, Otho Clauss, you will, you must, break with her. You will find some excuse. If you do not " . . .

"Well," I said, straightening my form and meeting his look full, "what will you do?"

"I will tell her," he said.

There must have been some startling change in my face, now, as I confronted him.

"You will tell her?" I repeated.

"Yes," he answered.

It seemed to me then as if I were not a man, but a demon. And yet I believe that I spoke with something like repose — the repose of slumbering tempest. "Tell me," I continued, "what you will do after you have told her?"

"I will" (he laughed for an instant harshly) "marry her."

"Fool," I said, still calmly; "she despises you."

He laughed again. "Before she met you she liked me. When you sink back into the place where you belong she will turn again to me. She always hated low descent and bad blood. . . You need not look at me with that haughty air, Otho Clauss! — not Claud but Clauss! You sent me away cowed from that room in Paris. But I know what is behind your bravery now; — nothing but bravado is behind it. You think to" —

I caught him by the throat then. The motive that swayed me was one of absolute jealousy. I believed for the moment that he could win Ada if I withdrew my suit. I cared for no previous taunt; I was conscious solely of one fact — that if the woman I loved should know the truth about me she might — though even years hence — prefer him to me.

That had become my one swaying and dominant

impulse. He reeled as I set my grasp where I knew it might kill. I wanted it to kill. All sense of mercy had left me.

A low, desperate sound of struggle came from him. He twisted wildly to and fro. A thirst for his life possessed me. His hands struck at me while I pushed him down; his strength was nothing to mine; he tottered and fell; my grip was still at his throat; as his head reached earth it struck with a dull noise; I remember that this noise gave me a frightful gladness. I clinched my fingers closer in his throat; I wanted him to die; I withdrew for an instant, watching him, and then I seized a stone, a loose bit of rock, and dashed it once, twice, with awful force downward . . .

It was with me as though I had ceased to be myself and had become my father! The man who had done that hideous thing years ago seemed to do it now again in my body, my spirit. It was the curse of heredity. I wrought the horror, as he had wrought it years ago. I repeated his act. With my brain mad, with my blood fire, I did what Leopold Clauss, who begot me, had done that day in the far past.

I had killed him. I knew it before I looked down upon him and saw that this was true past all mistake.

They who live sleek lives and count their small daily spites, greeds, revenges, as matter of import, can have no concern with what I thought and felt at this time. Scarcely was the act perpetrated than I became once more myself.

Can you fathom the infinite meaning of that anguish?

No. The voices of all the damned, if damned they be and if human sin expiates itself as poem, picture and story describe, could not phrase the horror of my remorse.

I had killed him. I bent over him with dilated gaze and saw that I had killed him. It was I who was his murderer. My years of culture, thought, refinement, self-exaltation, had come to this terrifying end. All the knowledge that I had gained in past years — all the emotions that I had sounded — all the philosophy that I had probed and pondered, rushed upon me now in one jeering swirl and tumult. The exquisite, opaline night flouted me and poured dreadful sarcasms upon me. I, Otho Claud, with high hopes, with fine aims, with culture, with a mind of telling force, with theories of what mankind would become in some nobler epoch, with my poetry, my ideals, my love for art, for letters, for the disenslaving of humanity from false or foolish creeds — I, Otho Claud, so called, was a mere gross, brutish murderer.

A murderer — I? It must be some nightmare. I staggered backward, as Cain might have done, with both hands before my eyes to shut out the intruding moonlight. A murderer? I? Impossible! The delusion must end soon. It could not last. My imagination swept back to domestic scenes, to trivial incidents of bowing before ladies in ball-rooms, to genial moments when I had kissed a hand, buttoned a glove, been suave, amorous, human, inside this bloody and ghastly limit which now set me so inexorably, for all future time, beyond my fellows. I thought of men and women whom I had not remembered for years; their very features were accurately limned in my memory; old echoes of favorite music floated through my brain. . . . No, no! I must be in a dream; I was still a part of humanity; I could not thus have leapt its bounds. I would presently wake. . . . Why did I not wake? Not to wake would be madness. That body lay there. But I had not killed it. I? The thought was folly. I heard Mrs. Dorian laugh her gruff French laugh, and I felt her tap me on the shoulder. "Otho, *mon cher*," she seemed to say, "you are dreaming." *Was* I dreaming? Was that the smile of Casimir, with his paint-brush in hand and his tossed blond locks, and his desire that I should sit to him for my portrait? Surely, yes. No such horrible gulf as this yawned between me and the bright, gracious truth of actual living!

I drooped my eyes. I looked upon the man I had killed. Shakespeare—famed as the master in telling us what human agony can do with the visible universe that engirds it—has made his men and women speak of the sky being drowned in tears, the whole earth being draped in liveries of woe. It was thus with me at this crucial and piercing moment.

"What had I done?" cried my conscience. The blurred and reeling moonlight seemed to answer. I had murdered a fellow-creature — I, Otho Claud!

There he lay, bleeding and dead. It had come to this.

As my brain cleared I thought of the one thing that a being jeopardized as I was must perforce think of.   A sinking sensation came upon me then. I must hide the body that I had slain. I fell into the ranks of the uncounted murderers who had existed since the world began. It was just as if some strong, dark, superhuman emissary of earthly justice had drawn close to me, let me feel the awe that clung about his presence, regarded me with shut lips and implacable eyes, and then coldly set upon my brow the stamp of a frightful fate.

There he lay. I looked down upon him. . . Soon afterward I drew quickly backward. In the lovely night a boat, rowed no doubt by careless villagers, was passing somewhere near the rocks on which I stood. They were singing. What was their song? Something that meant life, serenity, nature, freedom from sin. The boat stole nearer and then glided on. The song it gave me had been happy, and its recession was a new torture. So everything henceforth that had in it the worth, peace and hope of my kind would pass me by. Hereafter I must be isolated among my fellow-beings. Horror would hedge me in; loathing would stand as my sentinel.

What should I do? Could I escape the charge of this crime? Would it be discovered soon? When would it be discovered? Ought I to stand here and wait for those who would come to account me guilty of it?

Regaining a certain nerve, I felt the after-impulse of all assassins rise within me. I grew calm as I grew sensible of my peril. I bethought me of Casimir. He must be told — he must aid me.

I passed from the scene of my guilt. A sudden yearning for Casimir thrilled and ruled me. I must find him. . . I brought forth my watch and tried to see the hour; the white disk that I looked at seemed to spin about. My steps, as I went homeward, must have been random, zigzag. I do not recall how I ascended the piazza of Rockside; I only remember that having gained it I stood before one of the low French windows and saw Casimir poring over a book, seated near a lamp. The window was closed, and I rapped on it.

Casimir started. I rapped again. He rose. Once more I rapped. He perceived whence the sound came, and approached the window near which I stood.

Soon, with his face against the pane, he recognized me.

"Casimir," I said, in a whisper. The house

had been closed for the night. He could open the window only by making an undue noise. His rapid gesture indicated this. "I will join you on the piazza," it seemed to say.

I waited. Presently I saw the doors of the front window unclose. Casimir, in his velvet artist's-coat, with his pure, fine face, with his lightsome, jaunty, foreign manner now appeared.

"Casimir," I said, grasping both his hands as we met. Then I suddenly dropped his hands. It seemed an infamy that I should touch them.

" I was waiting for you, Otho," he said, scanning my face in the dim light, dimmer to him, no doubt, because of the illumination he had just left. "Madame has gone to bed," he continued, "and " . . . There he paused. He had seen. A shaft of lamplight from the broad window must have made him see.

He grasped my arm. "You are white as a ghost, Otho," he exclaimed. "What has happened?"

I did not answer him. As his hand presently touched my own, he shot at me a glance full of alarm.

"You are cold as ice, Otho!" he exclaimed. "What does it mean?"

I made him no answer. By this time he could see me plainly enough. He stared at me, in that quick, searching way which makes the brow of the observer incline itself. And now he spoke swiftly in his own language, putting a hand against either of my temples.

"Otho, I am certain that something horrible has happened. Tell me what it is."

I suddenly drew back from him. This movement was instinctive. How would he regard me when he knew the truth? And until he knew the truth I was a monster of uncleanness beside his unsoiled manhood. His pity might come afterward; but I had no right even to hope for that.

"Casimir," I faltered, "there is something horrible. I — I must tell it you."

He caught me again in his arms. "What is it, Otho?" he demanded. There was love in his embrace. I leaned my head on his shoulder, and spoke.

XV.

Casimir listened.   I felt his form tremble while I told him what I had to tell.

I had bowed my head.   His face was colorless when I raised my eyes to it.   But still it was doubtful, perplexed.   "You . . you have killed Foulke Dorian?" he gasped, at length.

"Yes."

"You are not mad, Otho?   You seem mad."

"I have killed Foulke Dorian."

"Hush!"

With that word, delivered in a wholly new tone, I perceived all distrust of my sanity vanish from his face.

"Where, . . where is he, Otho?   Tell me."

"On the shore opposite the cottage."

"Come."

He took my arm.   We left the house together. He did not speak until we had almost reached the spot.   Then he paused.

"Where?" he said.

I made a gesture.   He went forward, leaving me alone.   Suddenly the same boat to whose voices I had hearkened before, was heard with its high, sweet choric song. I listened, standing alone. It seemed like the song of angels to a soul eternally lost!

A little later Casimir returned. His face, plain in the moonlight, had the hues of death.

" You did this, Otho, — you ! " he murmured.

" Yes."

The look that he gave me was an agony. He suddenly flung his arms about me. What he did was like what a woman might do, but it had none of a woman's weakness.

" You, Otho ! You, so high and noble ! Tell me that it was not your act ! Tell me ! . . . Ah, I see ! Otho, you did do it. My God ! You ! "

" Casimir," I said, disengaging myself from his embrace, " the crime has been committed. . What is to follow ? "

He swept his look over my face in a way impetuously questioning. " Can you ask that ? " he moaned. . . " Otho, we — we must act ! "

" Act ? " I said.

" Yes — you and I — for God's sake don't lose your strength now — now, of all times ! "

" Is it not best to give myself up ? " I asked. " Perhaps it is best. I will do as you say."

" Give yourself up ? " He laughed as he spoke. It was a laugh made of fearful falsettos. " Otho, you must save yourself. You cannot mean that you will attempt anything else ? . . Ah, what would I not do to save you ? It is horrible ; it is a calamity I never dreamed of. But you must be saved. This man came here to-night?"

"Yes."

"Do you know by what train he came?"

"No . . I know nothing."

"Wait," he said, and left me. I sank down on the rocks, with my head on my breast. I do not know how long it was before he returned, but he may have been absent a full hour. As his touch at last fell on my shoulder I started to my feet.

"Well?" I questioned.

"Come," he said, drawing my arm within his. We were presently standing near a sort of chasm in the rocks — a fissure filled with gloom, and somewhat narrowed at its opening. This whole portion of the shore was unusually wild and rugged. It lay several yards beyond the curve where the cluster of trees grew, and at the base of the little promontory thus formed. A path — the continuation of that leading from the village — wound in among the trees a short distance farther inland. That was the path which Foulke Dorian had taken.

Casimir pointed to the long, dark crevice. "I have thrown the body there," he whispered. "It has fallen six or seven feet at the very least. You see the tides do not reach to here. And even if they ever should, they could not dislodge the body, for I have fastened to it a great piece of stone. I have made no mistake. Unless there is a very close search, he can never be found. That blood on the rocks — I have had to wash it away as best I could. I think there will be no trace of it in the morning, but I must return early and see. . . As soon as we can, Otho, we must leave this place. I will invent some excuse; we must go to-morrow, if possible — to New-York first, and then elsewhere. We will be gone two or three weeks; remaining here would put too fearful a strain on both of us. We can come back afterward."

"Afterward" . . . I murmured. "What does that word mean for me? Oh, if I could die to-night! My father tried to kill himself 'afterward.' I should make the same attempt — and without failure. It is the only thing left me."

Casimir, who still held my arm, tightened his grasp upon it. "Let us go back to Rockside now," he said. "There is danger in our continuing here too long. We may already have been observed. . . Come."

He led me away. We re-entered the house as softly as we could. Till dawn we sat together, talking. I had never dreamed till now of the magnitude of this man's love for me. Of course his suffering differed from mine, yet in its way it was just as keen. He had wholly ceased to reproach me. It was broad daylight and the birds had begun their chirping outside in the chill autumn air, when he said to me:

"If you could get a little sleep now — only a

few hours of it, Otho — you might gain strength and composure."

"Sleep," I repeated, with a low groan. "I wonder if I shall ever sleep again."

Not long after this Casimir quitted the chamber. I knew, without asking, whither he had gone. To the shore, that he might search for some tell-tale signs of the murder. He had already destroyed those garments belonging to each of us which bore a single blood-stain; he had cut them into strips first and then burned them to ashes, afterward scattering these forth to the night-wind. No precaution had been forgotten by him; the very water with which we cleansed our hands he had feared to place in the ordinary utensils.

"Will all his alertness profit any thing?" I remember asking myself. "Will it keep me from the scaffold where my father perished? And what if it does not? Such an end will make so slight a difference now! I shall die a thousand deaths from remorse, even if I do not die that one death by justice."

A sort of devil-may-care torpor was over me. If Casimir had re-appeared to tell me that my crime had been discovered and that my arrest was imminent, I should have scarcely made an attempt to fly. While we had talked together my speech had been but a series of despairing replies, and now I sat stunned and apathetic during the absence of my friend.

I had the sense of lying maimed at the bottom of some huge abyss, and of gazing upward to see the light of heaven far and dim, a mere speck of hopeless blue. It was not strange that imagination wrought this graphic allegory within my brain, for the feeling of having fallen or been hurled downward from a lofty height was perpetually active. So many other men pass by slow degrees toward the mental degradation which makes them murderers. I had slipped into mine with hardly an instant's warning. There had been, with me, no previous alienation from moral standards, no crumbling away of principle, no subtle erosion of manhood and honor. My life had suddenly crashed about me, so to speak, in appalling ruin; but the fragments were still fair and sound; they told of the shattering lightning-bolt rather than the slow decay. If my sin had been that of some known monster I could not have regarded it with greater antipathy. And my capacity to do this—to reach a plain, frigid estimate of just how deep and black was the sin itself—to witness it with eyes that were not those of any common criminal but of a being educated and enlightened beyond thousands of his kind—in such capacity could be found all the pathos of my terrible situation. And yet now I despised self-pity as much as I did self-excuse. In those other moments of frenzy it had been easy to shift the blame of my guilt upon fate, circumstance, heredity.

But I did so no longer. The very extent of my repentance had become the measure and index of my responsibility. I had been burdened from childhood with a curse, but no palliative was included in this fact. Untold advantages had been given me as weapons wherewith to fight against and conquer it. That I had struggled was no plea in my favor; I should have struggled with victory. Once previously on that same shore a solemn monition had come to me. If I had seen an ulcer bedded in my flesh I would have sought drugs to lessen and cure it. It was idle to assert that I could not have been the physician of my own soul. The means were within my reach; no vigilance, no fast, no scourge should have been spared. The facile power with which I made others yield to me, love me, grant me precedence and leadership, should have been like a sword of warning waved above that subtle egotism hardening and spreading through all my nature. Humility would have proved my safeguard, as egotism had proved my defeat; for on the latter quality a jealousy like mine feeds, like a ghastly offspring on poisonous diet. In my father it had been barbaric; in me it should have been civilized. No; either my offence was rank and smelled to Heaven, or else all progress and reform, all evolution from beast to man, all rise from savage to humanitarian, all the mighty lesson taught by science, all the imperishable wisdom dug out of ignorance by dead and living thinkers — all was futility, sham, shadow!

Provocation? Yes, I had had it. So much the greater reason for sobriety. Temptation? True, I might have felt it. So much the greater reason for tolerance. Whatever I may elsewhere have recorded in these pages regarding my belief that some limit is set to our human means of escaping a foreordained destiny, I seemed now to behold the denial of this theory seared as with letters of fire on my own conscience. The amplest means of escape had been placed within my control. I could have shaped my destiny as I chose. Ah! may these words, that teem with a conviction bought at so fatal a price, be read hereafter with precious profit by some fellow-creature in peril of a downfall like mine! Not to all are given the shield and spear when the foe threatens. But to me they were given, and how ill had I used them! Over so gigantic a failure as that which I had made of my life the tears of angels might well have flowed and the laughter of devils have sounded!

As I heard the step of Casimir recross the threshold I raised my head and looked at him. Just then I became conscious of a gusty, beating noise against the window-panes, and a moment afterward he said:

" A severe storm has set in. It is the equinox, no doubt. The rain is rushing down in torrents.

No one will visit that spot to-day. The storm began a little while after I had reached it." He was removing his drenched coat as he spoke. "There were a few faint traces on the rocks," he continued, "where I had dashed water, brimming my hat with it again and again last night. But now this drenching rain will wash away everything."

"Satan takes care of his own, perhaps," I said, with a shudder.

He came nearer to me. "Oh, for God's sake, Otho," he appealed, "do not look and speak like that! If you are reckless about discovery, think of us! You have called me your brother more than once. You have often referred to my aunt as your mother."

"Yes," I said, gazing up at him from where I crouched, and slowly shaking my head.

"Then there is she whom you love — Ada! Think of her."

"Do not speak of her, Casimir," I faltered, covering my face.

He came still nearer to me. Presently he had put his arm about my neck and drawn my head forward till it rested on his breast. "Otho," he murmured, "everything is not lost. You did it in a mad moment. No one need ever know the truth save yourself and me. Of course you will suffer. But we will bear the suffering together. Lean upon me as if you were hurt and I were helping you to walk somewhere toward shelter and relief. Think of me as strong whenever you think of yourself as weak. Cling to me, trust me. By and by a change will come. I love you better than I ever loved you before. Oh, brother, more than brother, listen and be comforted. A little comfort will come to you — not much as yet, perhaps, but at least a little — if only you will let it come. You told me to-night that you wanted them to find you and charge you with the deed. Oh, Otho, is love like mine, like your second mother's, like Ada's, to be flung carelessly away? You see I put myself first; I must do that, for I cannot yield to anyone. And you have us all — all three. I alone shall know. The two others will still love you just as before. We will guard our secret so well, unless — Ah! you guess what I mean! But it has not been discovered yet. There is a great chance that it never will be discovered. True, he may have been seen to leave the train at the station. And yet the hour was after dark, and no doubt he went straight from the station to the by-road, which is but a step. Once among the trees it is more than probable that he was not observed. . . And Otho, think! Think, and clearly, with that large, strong brain of yours. It was not such a dreadful thing to have done after all. I might have done it myself" —

"You, Casimir!" I broke in, lifting my head

and looking at him. His gray eyes — those beautiful, dreamy gray eyes — were glistening in tears. Ah, how he loved me! Surely he was right. To this man, so delicate and yet so gallant and virile of nature, I was indeed 'more than brother'! "You, Casimir!" I repeated. "Never!"

"Do not be so sure of that," he went on, forcing my head caressingly downward upon his breast as he spoke. I knew that he was deceiving me, and yet his words, infinitely tender and spurred by a friendship richly unselfish, were not without their faint, gentle encouragement. "Yes, Otho, I might have done it. . . But whether I might or no, remember how he provoked you. What he said to you there in my studio in Paris was infamous. It made me hate and despise him. If you had not punished him then I would have done so, and with as much right as you, for she is of my blood, and the aspersion was vile. Then, there on the shore, he threatened to tell Ada Gramercey the whole truth about your birth. That was the basest kind of meanness. He taunted you as cruelly as one man ever taunted another."

My hand had stolen into Casimir's. I looked up. My eyes directly met his for the first time since I had confessed my guilt to him. He had pierced something sluggish and paralyzed in my spirit; he had given me a sort of reason to believe that I still bore the right of calling myself a man.

I do not claim that I was justified in thus believing. These confessions of mine are never to be taken as an extenuation of crime; they are immeasurably the opposite; they are, if anything, a self-abasement, a humiliation, an effort to express the possibility of human regeneration, human excellence, in spite of all hurtful and destructive hereditary conditions. That I failed momentously is no reason why others, far less finely equipped for success, should not conquer and triumph.

Still, a new set of emotions now assailed me. I bgan to breathe, as it were, with a freer breath. Perhaps Casimir was right. It shot through my mind that in the life of this atom which we call our world, men had existed who were held honorable yet had slain a fellow-man for far less than what had goaded and inflamed me.

"He did taunt me horribly, Casimir," I said. "Ah, be careful," I went on, with a touch of wildness in my tones and the struggle of a sob in my throat. "You may make me hold this crime more lightly than I hold it now. And I know its abomination! I know — I shall always know, even if I one day gain the courage of wanting to live — of wishing to evade the doom that I deserve."

"It is that feeling, Otho," he hurriedly answered, "which I desire you to have. Let me dissolve your torpor, and I shall be content. You called yourself to-night a vulgar murderer — you called yourself your own father, whose deed I know you execrate — again and again. You are not like him. You have been outraged, spit upon, trampled upon, by a coward. Suppose you had fought a duel with him and killed him. It would have been fair; we French think that fair. But he was beneath fighting you; he did not dare meet you. You recall how we waited in Paris for him to give us a sign " . . .

And so he continued, this Casimir, this peerless friend, who reminded me with a frightful sarcasm of the love I had been able to awaken in my own kind, and of what untold benefit a man endowed with this power might have wrought on earth!

But he gained his point. I rose, a little later, with kindling hopes, with a sense that I should strive against discovery, arrest and death, with a longing to have my guilt buried as was the body of him whom I had slain — yes, almost with an impulse to place my act outside the inevitable murderous pale.

Casimir quickly saw the change. He grasped both my hands. The rain was beating furiously against the window panes. Its sound was a sort of doleful encouragement.

"You will act with me!" said Casimir. A sombre joy lit his eyes. "You will not let your despair crush you, Otho! . . Thank God!"

He burst into passionate tears a moment afterward. But the paroxysm did not last long. I saw him make a great effort to master it, and he soon did so. . . . .

At breakfast time we met Mrs. Dorian. We were both thoroughly composed. Casimir played his part, and played it well. He declared the rain to be something intolerable. It was undoubtedly the equinox, and Rockside during the equinox would be *gênant* beyond endurance. Besides, he was quite out of two very important colors. He could not paint without them. He had been so stupid not to send to town for them; they were vitally necessary for the picture he was now painting. What should he do? He must go to town, and he doubted whether he would return till this horrid storm was over. As for myself, Otho, I should have gone days ago. Why did I not accompany him? I knew very well that there were a hundred new matters concerning the estate which I had not yet looked into. Perhaps when I got to town I should find that I would be kept so fearfully busy for a week that I could not think of returning to Rockside till all the *mélange* of business had been settled.

"My dear Casimir," exclaimed Mrs. Dorian petulantly, "I never saw you really selfish till now. You wish to leave me alone in this great house, with this deluge of rain for society. It is merciless in you."

"Ah, *ma tante*," said Casimir gayly, "you will not think it so merciless when Otho telegraphs you that you were in danger of losing thousands by his neglect of your affairs. As for society, we will send you all the new novels we can find, French, German or English."

"Casimir is right, madame," I now said. "It is really imperative that I should look in at the office. Perhaps I can return in a day or two; perhaps even to-night."

Mrs. Dorian yielded reluctantly enough. Casimir and I made some hasty preparations, and by noon announced that our departure would take place at one o'clock.

"In an hour!" exclaimed Mrs. Dorian. "Otho," she went on, "you look pale, worried, *désolé*. . You are like a man who nerves himself to be cheerful. I hope no bad news has reached you in those letters you got this morning. If I guess rightly, *mon cher*, pray do not continue to deceive your best of friends."

"I?" was my uneasy murmur. "If any bad news had come you should be the first to learn it. . . I fear that the storm depresses me, as it does Casimir."

Mrs. Dorian glanced toward one of the jarred and rain-whipped windows. "It is truly another flood," she said, "and I am to be left alone in my ark." She suddenly turned and gave me a keen look. "But you will surely not go without saying good-by to Ada?"

I was prepared for this. But before I could

answer Casimir struck merrily in: "Oh, aunt, do you not see that the prospect of bidding Mademoiselle Ada farewell is what torments our poor Romeo here? But we will order the carriage a half hour earlier than is necessary, and stop at the cottage on our way to the station."

We did order the carriage a half-hour too early, but without afterward stopping at the cottage. I was to write Ada from New-York—if I could. To meet her and to enact this hypocrisy before her as I had done in the presence of Mrs. Dorian, would have been a sheer foolhardy trial of my own endurance. And Casimir, if I had proposed such a plan, would eagerly have discountenanced it.

That night we rested at a New-York hotel. The rain still fell in torrents here as it had done at Rockside. Before retiring, Casimir mailed to his aunt a letter which was a masterpiece of naturalistic deception. New-York, he declared, had impressed him, during this furious storm, as more appallingly ugly than he had ever yet found it. He had conceived an idea of running on to Washington, which he had never seen, and which might prove, now of all other times, a refreshing change. He had induced me to become his companion. I, Otho, was able to send the pleasant news that matters at my office were in less of a turmoil than we had both anticipated. Of course I had written the usual amorous lament to Miss Gramercey, whom at the last moment I had been ridiculously unable to bid farewell.

"But I have written nothing," I said, with a heavy sigh. "My pen has refused to shape a single word."

Casimir lifted a sheet of paper from a table near him. It was covered with characters. "I feared as much," he said. "You have only to copy that." . . .

The next day we went to Washington. Travel and the complete change of scene helped to restore me both in mind and body. With every day the desire to live and to elude punishment became stronger. I felt both craft and antagonism assert themselves within me. My remorse must be deathless, but life with its incessant sting was now vastly preferable to exposure, obloquy, and a shameful end. Life, too, with Ada! That would temper every guilty dream, every secret throe, every ordeal of suspense, every qualm of disquietude, with a new lenitive element. The sun would never shine again for me as of old, but it would shine on her, and therefore I craved not to be shut from its beams. Then, too, there were other reasons for living, even fighting to live. Years might yet be spared to me. What enormity of expiation might I not attain in them! Men had existed before now with skeletons in their closets as bony and grim as mine. They had died at last with the world's respect and honor. I had rare talents, the art of winning esteem and affection with ease. Why should I not some day pass from earth with the consciousness that I had offset against one great crime a thousand acts of goodness to my fellow-men?

The political atmosphere of Washington helped to kindle my new hope. Of course I saw nothing of its purely social side, but this one could easily imagine as being vivacious, interesting and unique. I forgot my former prejudice against mixing in the politics of my native land. The magnificent marble Capitol, whose faults have been so unjustly exaggerated and whose majesty is beyond dispute — the Houses of Congress — the stately squares, parks and avenues of this noble city, all won and invited me. What should prevent my shining here as a true statesman at some future time? If corruption reigned in this stronghold of our republic, so much the better reason why a man of fearless virtue and reformatory purpose should bend his best energies toward ameliorating measures. And why should not I be such a man?

All this time I was training and steadying myself to meet what I knew must sooner or later arrive, — in case detection should not plunge me into open odium and retribution. I watched the daily journals for some news regarding him. Casimir watched them too. Meanwhile I wrote repeatedly to Ada, and received from her the most loving replies. I had grown capable of playing the rôle which henceforth, at any hazard, I must play with firmness and courage. In a fortnight something like the old relations were re-established between Casimir and myself. He ceased to uphold and to fortify me. He saw that I had rallied and meant no surrender. Then, as he thus perceived, he retired once again into his former place of dependence and submission. It was I who now meditated, decided and kept myself in readiness to execute. The feminine part of his nature became re-ascendant; he looked to me for counsel, not I to him. But for the first time I now discovered the effects of what he had been called upon to undergo. The wear and tear upon his sensitive soul had been frightful. He was given to nervous seizures which he tried in vain to conceal from me; he lost flesh and appetite; he dropped into brooding, dismal, silent moods, from which a word of mine would startle him with a smile that was forced and painful. I observed all this with keen solicitude.

"You are yourself at last!" he said to me, one day. "I am so glad, Otho, so glad!"

"And you," I answered, "are losing all the force that once sustained me."

"Oh, never mind that," he said. "As long as I served you with it while it lasted, what matter if it leaves me now?"

I think it was on the following day that I showed him a paragraph in a certain Washington journal, copied from a New-York one.

He read the lines with intent care. "Well?" he asked.

"You see," I said. "He is merely reported to be missing. No one seems to know of the truth. There is not the slightest suggestion of it. The date of his final appearance in New-York is given, and nothing more."

"Yes," said Casimir.

"We must go back," I said, after a long pause. "To remain away longer would be worse than idle. Mrs. Dorian is still at Rockside. We will join her there."

"Join her there?" repeated Casimir, with a start.

"Yes. Are you unwilling?"

"Unwilling? I?" he returned, hastily. "Oh, no; far from it. What made you imagine that I was?"

"Then we will leave Washington to-night," I said.

XVI.

WE reached Rockside on the following evening. Mrs. Dorian was in an ecstasy of welcome at our return. She at once noticed Casimir's altered looks, and expressed fears that his trip had been the reverse of beneficial. We were both prepared for some reference to her missing nephew, and before we had been twenty minutes in her company the reference came.

"My dear boys," she suddenly exclaimed, "have you heard this odd story about Foulke Dorian?"

"We read of it in the newspapers," I said.

"Is it not mysterious?" she pursued. "Nearly. three weeks have passed since he was seen."

"Who last saw him?" I heard Casimir say, but I did not turn my eyes upon his face. The voice with which he put the question seemed even and tranquil.

"A gentleman at his club in New-York," replied Mrs. Dorian. "That was about five o'clock on the afternoon of September tenth. This gentleman exchanged a few words with him before he left the club. He appeared in his usual frame of mind, and said nothing about any contemplated journey."

"Was he on good terms with his father?" I inquired.

"Excellent. The papers declared so, at least. I wrote yesterday to my brother-in-law."

"You wrote?" I quickly broke in.

"Yes. It was only decent, you know. I expressed my warm sympathy, and my hopes that the unhappy affair would speedily be cleared up. It was a mere bit of ceremony, of course. And yet it was performed in all sincerity. How can one help being sincere on such a subject? Foulke, whatever were his faults, was not a dissipated fellow, and I should not be surprised if it were a case of secret assassination. These horrors are occurring every year in all great cities."

I wanted to test my own *aplomb* and self-command. "His known wealth and his regularity of habits would certainly point to some such ugly explanation," I said. And then I looked full at Casimir. "Do you not agree with me?" I continued.

"Yes," was the reply. "Still, many men have disappeared, like this, from wholly opposite causes. *Nous verrons.*"

"Detectives are at work," resumed Mrs. Dorian, "and it is possible that some clew may be found at any hour. Pray Heaven that if there *has* been foul play the *misérable*, whoever he is, may be brought to justice!"

Did my heart sink or my pulse leap at this?

No; I was so thoroughly equipped for it; I had already heard it so often in imagination. Worse would be needed to discompose me, to strike me with the least thrill of real panic. . . And how long must I wait before this "worst" might actually occur? Would it occur at all? There lay the most poignant torment of my position. I might bear severe shocks with coolness. But this waiting for the shocks to come — would there not be a slow, inexorable strain in that which no sharp jeopardy or menace could equal? The battle is so slight a thing, with its heat and hurry, beside the silence and uncertainty that precede it! . . .

I did not see Ada that night. Casimir and I talked in whispers long after Mrs. Dorian had retired. He promised me then that he would go to a certain spot on the shore early to-morrow. I did not like his look, his voice, his eye, his paleness, as we separated. This return to Rockside was evidently telling upon him. We must leave the place within a few days at the farthest. Mrs. Dorian was anxious to go; and as for the Gramerceys, she had told me that evening that Ada had formed plans to live modestly in New-York with her father during the remainder of autumn and the coming winter. The Colonel's condition was far from promising, and he had taken a dislike to the cottage, which he declared damp and full of draughts. I am sure that Mrs. Dorian wondered at my not going to Ada before the next day. Her suspicion that some quarrel had occurred between us became manifest as the evening grew late. But a suspicion of this sort was rather desirable than otherwise. To-morrow would dispel it, when she saw my former devotion perpetuated. As it was, I could not go forth into the darkness, even if I took the inland way toward the cottage. At least for one night I must yield to the horror of thus going, and remain indoors. Hereafter I would conquer it if it still continued. But for this one night — the first I had experienced since the commission of my crime — I dared not, I could not, I would not go!

On the next day, in the morning, I saw Ada. She threw her arms about my neck and gave way to a burst of tears as we met. But they were happy tears. Her love, shown with so sweet an abandonment, was a surpassing joy to me. It gave me fresh vigor of hope, fresh vitality of defiance against all that the future might hold in store. How could I be really vile when such a love paid me such a greeting? . . .

The brief autumn afternoon was nearly spent when I returned to Rockside. Never, since that woful night, had I felt so brave and calm as now. I longed for some stirring development to try me and prove the mettle of my resistance. The love of this pure and adorable woman was something not only to live for, but to breast immense adversity for as well. It should be talismanic with me in the exercise of whatever transcendent tact and cunning events might demand. For if the truth ever transpired, it would drag her down with myself, in one common calamity. By saving my own life, therefore, I would be saving her happiness. Joy was in that thought, and immeasurable incentive also.

"The days without you dragged so drearily, Otho," she had told me as we sat together. "I think I needed your absence to make me completely conscious of how dear you had become."

Of course we spoke of Foulke Dorian. I myself first referred to him. There seemed a brutal daring in this voluntary mention of the man I had killed, but until I did thus mention him a doubt of my own equipoise had perforce to haunt and dispirit me.

On reaching the house I went straightway in search of Casimir. I found him in his studio; seated before one of his canvases, brush in hand.

"You have been painting, Casimir?" I said.

He gave me a smile that compared almost spectrally with his smile of the past.

"I have been trying to paint," he said. "But somehow I cannot seize this subject with the old power. It evades me. You remember what I wanted to make of it *before?*" (That pregnant little word, as softly pronounced by him, had a volume of meaning for me.) "See — this Magdalen .. she was to have wakened from her first dream of Christ. There was to have been sorrow on her face, but a heavenly comfort, too. And now I have put only despair there. Look, Otho, the lips will not curve aright; they are bitter in spite of me. And the eyes — I wanted them to melt in unshed tears, but they are still so hard, so hopeless!"

He tossed his brush away and rose. As he did so the words of Ada were re-uttered within my memory:

"He is a sort of Poe touched with sunshine. And yet, if some great grief or disaster came to him, *would not the sunshine die out of all that he did? Might not his work turn grim and even malign?* " . .

"Casimir," I exclaimed, going up to him and grasping his arm, "you must paint no more at present. It will be torture for me to see a genius like yours fail and seem almost to perish, because I (God help me!) have " —

" Hush ! " he broke in, with an affrighted start. " What are you saying, Otho? And so loudly, too! Some servant might be passing. And do not imagine it is *that!* You are wrong, wholly wrong, *mon ami.*"

" I am right," I answered him.

He started again, and looked at me fixedly. Then he took both of my hands in his, slowly pressing them. "I will do as you advise," he said, in measured tones, as though convinced by me. "I will paint no more for the present. I promise you. . . Yes, it is surely best." . .

A little later I asked him: "Did you go to the shore, Casimir?"

He had seated himself again; he was staring down at the carpet; he seemed not to have heard my question, for he neither lifted his eyes nor answered it. I repeated it, and then he met my gaze. His voice, as he now addressed me, was nearly inaudible, and combined with his manner to betray a vacillation, a nerveless, forceless insecurity, which I had never till this moment witnessed in him.

"Otho," he faltered, "I—I went as far as that dead tree. You know where it stands—just midway between our stretch of shore and that which fronts the cottage. . I—I went as far as that, and then I—I could go no farther. A weight came upon my limbs, a freezing sensation filled my blood—I was a coward, no doubt, but I—I *could* not walk one step farther!" . .

"No matter," I said soothingly. I was standing at his side, and I put my hand on his beautiful, silky blond hair, smoothing it. How strange that I should speak to him in the placid voice I then used! What a complete reversing of our previous acts and words! You would have thought that he, not I, had been the wearer of this deadly and baleful yoke. "Never make the effort again," I continued, in the same consoling tones, "if it affects you like this. There is, after all, no need of going to the hateful spot . . no need whatever."

Five days passed — crisp, brilliant, October days. On the shore in front of Rockside there was a cluster of sumacs. I could see them from the piazza, from the windows, from whatever place on the lawns I happened to glance seaward. They seemed to intrude themselves on my vision, to follow me, to whisper "Look." They were a vivid red; they had the hue of blood. I never went near the shore.

I saw Ada constantly. She noticed nothing novel or different from of old in my demeanor. On seeing Casimir she was almost shocked by the change in him. For myself, so relentless was the pressure upon nerves and brain that I often *felt* as if I were haggard of cheek and hollow of voice. I knew well enough what suspense would do with both visage and conduct if I continued many days longer in this accursed place. But we had already planned an early departure. The Gramerceys were to leave when we did. Mrs. Dorian had begun her preparations for departure.

" Poor Casimir," she said to me pityingly. " He has contracted some malarial trouble here. It must be that."

" Perhaps," I answered.

My dreams, when I now slept at night, were terrific. . . I would wake from them dripping with clammy sweat. Sometimes I lay listening for the sound of footsteps at the door of my bed-chamber after I had thus waked. It seemed to me that I must have shrieked wildly in this mockery of slumber, and that all the inmates of the house had been roused. But worse than such dreams were those of rapture and exquisite peace with Ada as my wife. I would wake from these to the anguish of the actual! And then my dim room, with its familiar appointments, became an abode of misery beyond all that the most antic fantasies of nightmare could make it! Calm, still, shadowy, it racked and tortured me with what really *was!*

It was marvellous that I held out physically as I did during these five days, each one divided from the other by a night of horror. Again and again I saw Casimir furtively watch me, and read in his altered, dimmed, lustreless eyes astonishment at my serenity and control.

I saw the newspapers regularly. Each day there would be some notice in them of the missing man. But no clew had yet been found. The detectives were still at work, but entirely without avail.

On one of these momentous days — the third of the series — a distressing and horrible thing occurred. Though I did not even fancy so then, it was the beginning of the end — like the first stroke of a knell to the being whom it vitally and wretchedly concerned.

Ada had come to Rockside, and after holding a little talk with Casimir she requested to be shown once more the contents of his studio.

"But I have done nothing, Mademoiselle," he answered sadly, "since you last saw my pictures. You are welcome to look upon the old work again, however, if you so desire."

Ada did desire, and signified her wish. "He is miserably unwell, I should say," she whispered to me, as we passed up stairs behind Casimir. "See how he has lost that old springing step of his! Does he ever complain to you, Otho, of feeling ill?"

"Never," I said.

"You have fairly won your leisure," she said a little later to the young artist, while moving about his studio. "You have made yourself a handsome pile of laurels to rest on; you can now afford to be idle."

"It is very good of you to call them laurels," said Casimir, with one of his graceful bows.

"And Otho's portrait?" Ada continued. "Does that remain unfinished still?"

"Yes, Mademoiselle."

"Casimir will finish it when he is better — more *en veine*," I said.

"Perhaps you are too much alone when you paint," said Ada, looking at my friend in her frank, sweet, interested way. "There would be something delightfully social, I should think, in your giving Otho a sitting, for example, while Mrs. Dorian or myself also occupied the studio."

Casimir seemed to muse for a moment. Then he walked rapidly toward a portion of the room in which my portrait was placed. A decisive change now became apparent in his manner; his native gayety seemed to break from repression.

" We will do as you say, Mademoiselle," he exclaimed. " We will do it now."

" Now ! " I swiftly retorted.

" Yes," said Casimir. In a trice he had placed the canvas upon his easel, which stood near a bright window. " I will see what I can do," he went on. " I will see whether I cannot give Otho a sitting to-day."

His demeanor had the buoyancy of former times. He motioned for me to seat myself, and I did so. Rapidly he mixed a few colors on his palette. Ada sank into a chair at my side.

Casimir went to work with apparent zest. The features of the portrait were perfectly limned; the resemblance was already striking. He painted with vigorous strokes for several minutes, after looking at me, and in a way that presently impressed me as wild and unnatural.

Suddenly his look changed to one of extreme dismay and agitation. Before I could anticipate the action, he had dashed his brush upon the floor and sunk into a seat, covering his face with both hands.

Ada rose flurriedly. "He is ill," she cried.

I also rose and went toward him. But as I reached his side he uncovered his face.

"I cannot paint you!" rang his voice, in shrill, plaintive tones. Then it dropped so that I alone heard it. "You are not the same to me as you were! I see you as I saw you *then!* I"—

The next instant I had placed my hand over his mouth. "Casimir!" I said.

Ada was observing intently. As his eyes met mine a shiver convulsed him, and he pointed toward the portrait. Then his gaze drooped, and his head also. In another moment, however, he made a quick, violent gesture, such as a man might make who struggles against a swoon, and staggered to his feet.

"Pardon me, Mademoiselle," he stammered to Ada in French. "I—I am truly unwell. I—I tried to paint Otho, and see what I have done!"

He was motioning toward the portrait. But Ada's eyes did not follow the waving of his hand. She was regarding me in evident consternation.

"Why did you try to stop him from speaking, Otho?" she questioned. "Why did you put your hand against his mouth?"

I hurried toward her. "Ada, can you ask this?" I said. "Foolish hysteria in a man is not as it is with you women . . I did not wish Casimir to make himself absurd, ridiculous."

She inclined her head; an expression of sympathy crossed her features. She turned toward the portrait, clearly visible from where she stood.

"Ah!" broke from her lips. "He has made it so different, Otho! It is not you. It is " —

She paused abruptly, for just then Casimir seized a brush, dipped it hastily in some dark paint, and literally slashed it across the canvas. A laugh sounded from him immediately afterward.

"It is a failure!" he cried — "a horrible failure! I will do it again when I — I am in better mood." Then he flung this brush away, as he had done the other, and re-seated himself.

"Did you see it?" murmured Ada, catching my hand.

"Yes," I answered.

"He — he made it so unlike you," she continued. "He gave the face a horrible expression . . What does it mean, Otho?"

"It means that Casimir is ill — not himself," I responded. "Come."

I at once led her from the studio. . . It may have been an hour later when I returned thither. Casimir sat in the same chair, with a dejected attitude. I went up to him and shook him roughly by the shoulder.

"What wretched folly is this?" I asked of him.

He burst into tears. I stood beside him as he wept. Presently he said, looking up at me:

"Forgive me, Otho! I — I thought I could

paint you as you *are*. But the shadows gather so thickly, now, whenever I touch brush to canvas. I — I saw you, in spite of myself, as *you were that night!*"

I leaned over him and spoke with my lips close at his ear. "Casimir," I said, " you must go from this place. You must go at once."

" I — I cannot go without you," he murmured, weakly. " I cannot be alone. I — I will go when you go — not before."

" Be it so," I answered, after a pause. " On Monday we will all leave. But until then be guarded. I implore you, Casimir — do you understand ?"

" Yes ! "

He sprang to his feet as he spoke the word. His eyes flashed, and he gave sign of being his old self.

" I trust you," I said, grasping his hand. " But beware ! Your nerves are unstrung — you are ill — reckless fits like these carry peril — if you think another of them may seize you " —

He interrupted me with an almost scoffing toss of his disengaged hand. " Nothing more will occur," he said. " It was merely the painting. I should have kept my promise to you. I broke it, and you saw the result. I will not paint again till you bid me."

" Do not," I said.

On the fifth day of this series, while I sat alone

in the breakfast room before an untasted meal, having appeared later there than either Casimir or my guardian, a stern shock came to me.

Mrs. Dorian entered and at once laid her hand on my shoulder. " Otho," she said, " who is here, do you think ? "

" Who ? " I asked, steadying myself instantly.

" Steven Dorian."

I rose. " He comes to speak of his son ? "

" Yes."

" Why does he come here ? "

" He has an idea about coming."

" An idea ? "

" Yes."

" What is it ? "

" He thinks that Foulke was last seen in this place."

I gave a slow, amazed smile. My brain was ice, my nerves were iron. " In this place ? " I repeated. " How absurd ! Where is he ? "

" In the sitting-room. Will you come and see him ? "

" Did he ask to see me ? "

" Yes. He has demanded to see you."

" Is he alone ? "

" No. A man is with him — a detective. And a boy — a lad from the village."

" Really ? And pray what do they all want ? "

" I have no conception. It is insulting for Monsieur Steven to come here like this. But he is so wretched in appearance — so evidently an invalid — that one can forgive him almost when one looks at him."

I looked at him soon afterward. He was seated as Mrs. Dorian and I presently entered the sitting-room, but a man and a boy stood on either side of him. The man was a slender, beardless person, quietly and darkly dressed. I do not know that it would be possible for any member of humanity to make himself more inconspicuous, more ordinary, than this man had somehow succeeded in doing. Nature had certainly aided the effort, if effort it was. A sallow, mottled complexion and a dull, sleepy eye seemed to include every characteristic of his visage. Even to mention these traits of it was to pass undue comment. Everything about his figure bespoke modesty, retirement, a tendency to escape observation. The very lines of his coat and trousers indicated personal sequestration; they drooped and sagged as if chary of contact with more social broadcloth. 'What a man to slip through a crowd unnoticed,' I thought, on seeing him. 'What a man to watch without being watched!'

The boy was a ruddy little fellow of about ten. He looked somewhat confused, and was plainly stupid.

Mr. Steven Dorian sat between the two, as I have stated. He bore every sign of having risen from a bed of illness. Mrs. Dorian's past description had not been exaggerated. He was cadaverous, hollow-eyed, chalky in his pallor, and so pitifully bowed down as to seem almost the size of a dwarf. I should never have dreamed of recognizing him. He grasped a stout stick with a big wooden handle, and his hand was so outlined upon its ponderous hilt that its claw-like effect had a grotesque saliency. He rapped the stick upon the floor as he saw me, and his rheumy eyes gave forth a faint, somnolent twinkle. His face was so lined and wan that it might well have been a ghost's. While I paused before him he said in a jerky, asthmatic voice:

"You're Otho Claud?"

"Yes, sir."

"Your name isn't Claud a bit. I know. My son Foulke knew it, too. Both knew it. Been a fraud. Son of that man Clauss who was hanged for murdering his wife years ago."

I did not flinch. "Otho!" cried Mrs. Dorian, coming close to me. "He said this before. I cannot think how he found it out. I"—

"Let it pass, madame," I broke in, with a voice as cold and regular as human lips ever used. I fixed my eyes calmly upon Mr. Steven Dorian. "Did you come here to tell me this?" I inquired.

"No," he said. "Didn't come here to tell you that. Came here for a different reason."

"Ah? I should have supposed otherwise from your greeting."

"Would you, indeed?" He was suddenly seized with a fit of coughing that lasted for some time and seemed to rack and half shatter his feeble frame. The detective bent over him and took him by both shoulders while the paroxysm lasted. When it had lessened, he continued, still gasping and clearing his throat. "Came, Mr. Clauss — for Clauss *is* your real name — to ask you about my son. He never liked you. Enemies, you and he. Told me so. Yes, sir, told me so. You know better 'n I do 'bout Colonel Gramercey's daughter. That business brought me here. Thought he *might* have come up to this place that night. Find he did. . . . Speak up, sonny."

This last sentence was addressed to the boy at his side. He gave the boy a sharp, abrupt poke with one of his emaciated hands.

The boy seemed to understand. But he was very embarrassed.

"I — I can't speak up much, sir," he murmured.

Steven Dorian rapped his cane irascibly upon the carpet. "Speak up," he cried huskily. "Tell what you saw on the tenth of September last."

"I — I think I seen the gent'man leave the cars at 'bout eight o'clock that night," stammered the boy. "I — I guess it was him."

Suddenly the detective slipped round to the boy's side. His neutral face for an instant became assertive and intelligent.

"You guess?" he growled. "You says a little time ago you was sure."

"Well," admitted the boy, "I'm sure."

"Go on," said the detective.

"The gent'man left the cars," continued the boy. "I seen him at the deepow. I'd seen him afore. He come here by the train a good spell ago—I guess 'twas some time in August. He asked me the short cut to the shore an' I give him the pints 'bout th' ole Harrison road. I went with 'm 's far as Nickleses' ole pull-down shanty. Then I stopped an' was goin' to leave him. But he give me fifty cents then, an' a letter to take, to the small cottage, nigh this house—the one as Mr. Lambert's folks used to live in. I took the letter, an' give it to a young lady as come to the door. That was afternoon. But 'twas dark the next time I see the gent'man, gettin' off the cars. I guess it was him, but I ain't certain sure. 'T looked wonderful like him if 't wasn't."

"Otho," now struck in Mrs. Dorian, turning to me with much smothered indignation, "do you quite see why we should be subjected to this sort of nonsense?"

"Frankly, madame," I said, "no."

"Excuse me, ma'am and sir," here said the detective civilly, "but the boy was recommended to me in the village almost as soon as we got here and made inquiries. He said then he *did* see the missing man—that is, the one that give him the

letter and he showed the road to. I don't mean
to say," continued the detective self-correctingly,
"that he ever saw Mr. Foulke Dorian. But his
parents thought, from the description in the newspapers, and from the description this boy had
given of the gentleman who paid him the money,
and from the boy's conviction he'd seen the same
gentleman afterward, on September tenth, that
matters pointed one way."

"And you have merely this boy's evidence for
thinking that Mr. Dorian left the cars here on the
evening of September tenth?" I asked.

The detective nodded dubiously. "Yes, sir,"
he said. "That's all."

"And you come here," I pursued, "to tell us
that Mr. Dorian did visit this part of the country
on that special night?"

"Ridiculous!" here cried Mrs. Dorian, addressing her brother-in-law. "Steven, what is the
meaning of this visit? You bring your *gend'arme*
with you — it is preposterous! Do you think we
have murdered your son, and hidden him somewhere?"

Steven Dorian answered with his eyes upon my
face, "I think," he said, "that there is something
in this boy's story."

Mrs. Dorian gave an exasperated sigh. "Who
cares about this boy's story? What he says is
the merest absurdity. You come here to my
house with a disguised policeman, and you ask

questions in the village before you arrive here. You pick up a boy who thinks he saw a gentleman whom he showed the Harrison road to weeks before at the station, once again on the tenth of September. Pray who was the gentleman whom the boy first saw? Was it your son?"

"Yes!" exclaimed Steven Dorian, with another rap of his cane, but with his eyes still fixed upon me, although he answered his sister-in-law. "It *was* my son. Know he came to these parts weeks ago. Told me so. Saw Miss Gramercey, too. Met her on the shore. The old Colonel didn't like him, for some reason — something that happened in Paris. Yes, Foulke *did* come here once. Why not twice?"

"You look at me, sir, all the time that you address Mrs. Dorian," I now said. "Why do you do this?"

Steven Dorian rose, totteringly. My placid audacity seemed to have had its weight. "I look at you, Mr. *Clauss*," he said, while accepting on either side the assistance of the detective and the boy, "because I came here to — to" (another briefer fit of coughing seized him) — "well, to remind you that you — you hated Foulke — always. Yes, always."

"Steven!" cried Mrs. Dorian, "what are you saying? Do you dare to assert that my Otho — you may call him Claud or Clauss as you see fit — had anything to do with your son's disappearance?"

"Didn't say *that*," answered Steven Dorian. "Came here to look 'round. Came here to — to " . . . He was again seized with so violent a fit of coughing that he had to put both arms about the detective's neck until it had ceased.

"Guess we better go now," I heard the detective whisper in his ear.

The boy nervously and covertly plucked the detective by the coat sleeve. "Yes, let's go," the boy said.

I now spoke again, fixing my eyes upon Steven Dorian's ghostly, drooped face. I exulted in the masterpiece of hypocrisy that I might here achieve. "If you have any desire to search the house or the premises, sir, I am quite at your command."

"Otho!" exclaimed Mrs. Dorian, now almost in a passion, "this insult — for it is nothing else — has already gone too far! . . . Steven Dorian," she went on, addressing her brother-in-law, "your visit here has had an insulting motive only. You and I were never friends, as you well know. But I pitied your ill health; I was sorry for your suffering. Still, I can't help regretting all the sympathy I ever gave you, when I find you searching in my house for signs of your missing son!"

Those dim, detestable eyes were yet upon my face. "Will you take some refreshment, sir," I asked, "before you leave us?"

"No," he said gruffly. The man and the boy

had to support each step which he now made toward the door. As he passed over its threshold, taking his eyes from me, I felt an immense relief. A little later he had passed into the outer hall. Mrs. Dorian followed the trio. Not long afterward she returned, hurrying to my side.

" Otho ! " she exclaimed.

" Well, madame."

" What — what do you think ? They are taking the shore way. They are walking along the shore to the Harrison road. They are scanning every bit of rock as if they expected to find something. . . Is it not too abominable ? "

My blood froze then. I darted from the room. I gained the shore. The blood-red sumachs seemed to gibe at me. I saw them while moving slowly toward that part of the shore which skirted the cottage grounds. Steven Dorian walked very insecurely. But he was peering downward, and so were the boy and the man who still supported him. I followed them. I knew that there was only one place — the great dark crevice — where they could possibly pause with any positive intent of search.

They presently reached it. I saw the detective disengage his arm from Mr. Dorian's and stoop downward. He was peering into the slim, dusky chasm.

The world stood still with me while I waited, watching.

XVII.

PRESENTLY the detective raised his head. He took Mr. Dorian's arm again. The three disappeared round the bend of the shore. It was their homeward road. They were going back to the village — and thence, of course, to the train.

I took out my watch. It was half-past eleven o'clock. I knew that no train went to New-York till fifteen minutes past twelve. They must wait at the station. But what mattered that? They had come; they had confronted me; they had searched the shore; they had chatted and questioned in the village. But nothing had come of it. Foulke Dorian had taken an evening train hither, and had alighted from it unnoticed, as hundreds of people do in the dusk at railway stations like ours. The boy's evidence weighed nothing. My demeanor had been perfect. A suspicion had brought Steven Dorian to this spot, and that suspicion had ended in vapor. No real clew existed. The body lay far down between the stone lips of that crevice, where Casimir had dropped it. I was safe.

Safe at last!

It had all passed more quickly than I had expected. The aching uncertainty was at an end. A huge gap in the evidence existed. Steven Dorian had come here with a forlorn hope. Detective science had exhausted itself; he had remembered his son's discovery of my real birth : he had connected that discovery with some possible fierce feud. But my magnificent tranquillity had crushed his last doubt. I was safe.

Safe!

I drew a long breath of infinite relief. I sank down upon a flat, jutting rock, and smiled to my own thoughts as they fell like balm upon my wearied, over-taxed brain. To be safe — wholly safe ! how exquisitely comforting ! Casimir had done his work well — my Casimir, my stanch, devoted friend !

Nothing could harm me now. I had erred terribly, but there was escape, delivery. Men would never know. Only Casimir would know, and his fidelity was more loyal in its permanence than the heaven I looked at, the earth I rested on. Ada would never know ! We would marry ; children would be born to us; I would use every talent to win distinction ; the grace of being loved by my kind should be added to the grace of being respected, honored, revered by them. All would be well — all except that one black blot on my conscience. But the years would help to cleanse and even whiten that. Why not? In time I might sleep lightly, dream pleasurably.

I was safe!

It was a lost clew. He had come here, but no one had really seen him come. Was it God's work? I had been wont, in the old Zürich days, to think and speak of God with a certain scientific coldness. Ought I to do so hereafter? What combination of circumstances had saved me except some merciful intelligence apart from mere blind fate? And I *was* saved. It was all ended now.

What could discover and convict me? No power of man. The detectives had tried every method, every resource. The coming of Steven Dorian, in his wretchedly feeble condition, was of itself convincing proof. The father of the missing man had used his last chance, and this had failed. Let him tell the world that I was the son of Leopold Clauss! What did I care? How slight the publicity of this fact seemed, now that I had evaded the darker publicity of arrest and arraignment? Let him tell it if he chose. Ada would still cling to me and marry me. Her affection had been shown me by a new lurid light, but with force that made its deepest springs of impulse plain! . . .

I must have bowed my head while sitting there on the shore, thinking these happy thoughts — supremely happy by contrast with the Gethsemane of pain that I recently endured — when something seemed to touch my shoulder. I was too overjoyed to do more than just notice the contact. The touch was light as a leaf, and if a leaf, then Nature and I were reconciled again, for escape at this golden moment meant pardon, and pardon meant a revivified sense in all that was beautiful on earth!

But the touch grew heavier. I raised my head. Casimir stood beside me. I sprang to my feet. I flung my arms about my friend's neck.

"Casimir," I exclaimed, "it is all over! I am saved!"

He had not returned my embrace. I now observed that his face was deathly white and that his eyes were glittering strangely.

"Saved?" he repeated. "How?"

I spoke many swift words to him; I told him all that had lately passed. He listened, or seemed to listen, with intentness.

"You see," I finished, "this misery of suspense is over. To-day ends it; you know why; I have told you."

"Yes, you have told me," he repeated.

His voice was cold, his tones slow. In a flash it came to me that he bore every semblance of a man distraught. "You have told me," he continued, "that those people have come and gone. They know nothing — they have seen nothing."

I withdrew my arms from his neck. "No, Casimir," I said, wonderingly.

"But I?" he said, with a strange, peering, hostile look straight into my eyes.

"You, Casimir?" I faltered.

"Yes, *I.*" He grasped my shoulder. A sort

of blaze leapt from his eyes and died. "Do you think that I can bear this awful secret as you bear it? If you think that, you are wrong — frightfully wrong! *I* heard every word that Steven Dorian — *his father* — spoke to you. I was listening and I heard. You did it all well. You are a man of such accomplishment, such *savoir dire* — you always were, Otho, and you were then. . But what of *me ?*"

"You, Casimir?"

"Yes — what of *me ?*" His face became distorted with fury. He receded a step or two from me, and then, looking upon him, I saw that change which is so infinitely worse in those we love than the white change of death itself. I saw that he was mad. And I realized that my own crime had made him so.

"Shall *I* carry this horrid secret to the grave?" He pointed at me, with tremulous yet accusing forefinger, as madmen point. "Shall I divulge nothing because you are without conscience, without remorse? I loved you once, Otho, but I hate and damn you now! And I will tell everything! I can wash my soul from sin by no other means!"

He shot past me, and then paused. One of his hands, as he faced me, gropingly reached backward. "The body lies *there* in that place where I dropped it," he went on. "But it shall not lie there much longer. I" —

At this I flung myself upon him. "Casimir," I cried, wildly, "in God's name do not tell! You loved me — you shielded me — you helped me, at that other time! Be merciful now! It is not you I have heard! It is some devil of madness! . . Oh, in pity's name . . think of her — of Ada whom I love! . . Casimir!" . .

He had wrested himself away from me. I staggered backward, and saw him dash round the clump of trees. I understood, then. Vengeance, justice was to fall upon me through this man. This man who had been my safeguard, my protective angel, my absolute and infallible source of trust! Through his madness I was to meet my doom. Not Casimir would betray me — not my old unswerving, faithful Casimir, but some genius of divine wrath, usurping his brain, body and soul. *By this ingress — the one of all others least imagined or imaginable — the penalty of my crime would reach me!*

I moved inland, and waited there behind some trees. I had no thought of stopping Casimir. It would be like trying to stop fate itself; for he had indeed become fate. I waited, gazing through the trees at that part of the shore where the gloomy fissure could plainly be seen. I knew quite well what would happen, now; I knew as well as if I had already viewed it. And presently it did happen, just as it had been pictured in my mind.

Four people soon turned the bend in the shore.

Casimir came first; he gesticulated excitedly as he spoke, though I was too far off to hear his words. In a little while he had paused beside the crevice in the rocks, and pointed downward. As he did so Steven Dorian and the detective seemed to watch his face with the keenest eagerness. . . .

My thoughts flew to Ada, then. All was over, now. She must be told. I wanted to tell her before others could. It was best that way. I think my steps never once hesitated as I walked toward the cottage. I ascended the veranda; the front door was kept closed in this chilly weather. I rang the bell. A moment afterward Ada appeared in the hall. I saw her through the glass panes of the door. My heart gave a great leap. I forgot my own sorrow, so thrilled was I with pity at what she must soon be called upon to hear.

We passed together into the sitting-room, with its well-remembered appointments. A separate farewell seemed to breathe to me from each one. I had taken her hand, and as I moved along the hall with her, still holding it, I heard, her say that my own hand was icy-cold. But I did not answer her until we were seated side by side. Then I said:

"Oh, Ada, better if it were the coldness of death!"

She grew pale. "Otho," she murmured, "what do you mean? Tell me. Tell me at once!"

"You will loathe me when I have told you. And yet it must be told."

"Nothing would ever make me loathe you!" she broke forth, passionately, searching my face with her alarmed eyes.

"Nothing?" I repeated. "Oh, Ada, think! If it only *were* so! But when you have heard, you — you will feel all the love die in your breast, and contempt, if not hate, will take its place!"

"When I have heard, Otho?"

"Yes. Listen." . . . I dropped my face, then, and told her. I no longer held her hand. I was composed enough, at first, but gradually voice and frame began alike to tremble. Yet I did not suppress a single wretched incident. The narration more than once cost me a fearful effort; but I persevered until all had been spoken. Then, amid the new silence, I raised my head and looked at her.

She sat quite rigid and colorless, staring at me. Except for the horror in her eyes there was no evidence that she lived at all. I seized one of her hands and pressed it to my lips, while my tears fell upon it.

"Oh, my love," I moaned, "my lost love! Give me one word — just one, Ada, if it is only 'good-by'!"

Her lips suddenly tightened, then relaxed, and a deep sob broke from them. In another instant she had thrown both arms about my neck.

"Whatever you have done," she cried, "you are still my Otho!" And then, while she yet clung to me, her tears, for a little time, rushed in torrents.

"Bless you, my darling," I said. "I *did* doubt you. You were once so proud, you know, Ada. And even now I should not blame you if you changed. Many a woman's heart *would* change. The crime had no excuse — none. Such crimes never can have. . . And it is so bitter a thought to me now that I shall drag you down with myself into disgrace and infamy! But if you repulsed me from this hour — if you declared yourself alienated, disgusted, outraged by the deed I have done — if you cast me off and snapped with one wrench the ties that love and time have wrought between us, then the world, while it could have no reproach for this desertion, would acquit you of all sympathy with a man so degraded as I. In that way you would escape all odium, and " —

"I do not wish to escape it!" she interrupted, struggling with her tears and clinging yet closer to my neck. "I wish that I could only take it *all* upon myself! I love you, I love you — that is enough! Do not speak of snapping the ties between us! Your misfortune, your misery, your guilt, strengthens those ties, Otho! It makes them like iron!"

She withdrew her arms from me. I perceived

in another moment that she was striving to be more composed. I read her thoughts, now, as well as if her quivering voice had not immediately revealed them.

"But Casimir, as you say, has gone mad. Even if they find the body there, his testimony will not be believed against you. And — and there were no other real witnesses, Otho. You can deny it all. You must! In that way it will not be — you know what I mean — *the very worst!*"

"It will be death for me, I think," was my answer. "Death on the scaffold."

"No, no!" She caught both my hands. "It *shall* not be! So much will depend upon yourself. You must be calm — and I must be calm as well. We — we must laugh at them when the accusation comes. Your previous record is so fine, so spotless. They can suspect what they will, but they cannot prove."

I shook my head drearily. "I am beyond this hope," I said. "The ignominy of such suspicion would be worse than that of death. Death is an end . . . but the other would be a long, doleful continuance!"

"You think so *now!*" she cried, with a sort of wail in her voice. "But will my undying love, my ceaseless companionship, not soften and mitigate your future pain? Remember that I shall always be near you, unswerving, untiring in my offices of comfort. Oh, Otho, for my sake if not for your own, fight, fight to the very last!"

I looked at her with surprise. Every trace of her recent tearfulness had vanished. A color had come to her cheek, a sparkle to her eye. She was so strong, now, and so beautiful in her strength!

I caught her in my arms. "Be it as you say," I responded. "I *will* fight—for your sake, and for the priceless reward you offer! But it will be a terrible battle, and if I come forth from it with my life, the wounds will have maimed and crippled me for all time."

She kissed me on the lips. There was a wild gladness in her look. "No!" she cried, "for I will heal your wounds! I can and I will!"

I answered her kiss. "God has not been unkind to me, after all," I whispered. "He lets this moment measure and unveil your love, in its glory, its courage, its sweetness, its nobility, its power!"

Just then we heard a sound of steps on the veranda outside. I knew what the sound meant.

"They have come," I said. "They have come to take me."

We both rose, as if by one impulse. We were locked in one another's arms. The next instant we heard the bell of the front entrance sharply ring; then a heavy knock on the panels of the door followed it.

"Remember!" said Ada. Her voice was firm and tranquil. "They come with a madman as your accuser. . . Remember — and promise!"

My voice, as I responded, was no less firm than hers.

"I do remember — and I do promise!"

The knock was repeated, heavier, louder than before. Ada still clung to me. We heard voices on the veranda as of people speaking together.

"You — you will fight to live," she persisted, "for my sake. You swear it, Otho?"

"For your sake," I answered, "I will do all that lies in human power. I swear it."

.   .   .   .

CONCLUSION.

WHAT more now remains for me to tell? Did not the whole country ring for weeks with the tale of my agonizing trial as the suspected murderer of Foulke Dorian? But I kept my word to Ada; I fought for my life. At times during the trial, as so many know, the noose seemed tightening about my neck. Ada, brave and almost preternaturally calm, was at my side throughout, and Mrs. Dorian, passionately believing in my innocence, remained there as well. Ada's support was approved by her dying father, whose deep pity her own anguish had aroused. Steven Dorian, aided by the most brilliant and capable lawyers whom money could command, was fierce in his efforts for my condemnation. But Casimir had been my accuser, and Casimir's malady, at the time when the trial took place, had assumed so violent a form that he could not appear in court. Even if he had appeared there, his evidence would have gone for nothing.

There was that one great gap in the testimony. Nothing could bridge it except suspicion, and suspicion, however strong, is not proof. At last the misery ended, and I was acquitted.

But what need even to glance at these details, so familiar to thousands?

Immediately after the trial ended, Ada and I were married with the utmost privacy. Colonel Gramercey breathed his last two days after our marriage. And then my wife, myself and Mrs. Dorian went abroad.

. I have remained in my beloved Switzerland ever since. My life has been one of the most absolute retirement from the world. Mrs. Dorian has often left me, travelling about Europe. Ada has never left me. I have always known that men and women at large scarcely hold a doubt of my guilt. But between me and their scorn has ever risen the angelic devotion of my wife. I will touch no further upon that subject; its sanctity seems to forbid any save this briefly reverent mention. . .

No children have been born to us. This was far best. I am thankful for it.

I have written these confessions carefully, slowly, amid the long leisure of my seclusion. Perhaps when I am dead, my wife, if she still lives, will give them to the world. In any case, I shall shortly place them within her keeping, to preserve or destroy hereafter, as she thinks best.

That is all. My story has been told. Many will judge me, should these memoirs ever be made public. But of all who read them who shall dare to say (whether his verdict prove harsh or merciful) that he has judged aright?

And now only one word more. My wife has never for an instant caused me to regret the promise I gave her of striving to live. Each new day that dawns for us, in our quiet home, her tender and patient look seems to whisper: "Thank God that you are spared me, Otho — no matter at what cost!"